FAKE IT FOR ME

WESTON PARKER

BRIXBAXTER PUBLISHING

Fake It For Me

First Edition.

Editor: Eric Martinez
Cover Designer: Ryn Katryn Digital Art

FIND WESTON PARKER

www.westonparkerbooks.com

CHAPTER 1

ADRIAN

I grabbed a gob of wax and plopped it on my surfboard, slowly rubbing it in. My eyes drifted over the waves rolling onto the shore of Arina Beach in Heraklion, Crete in my home country of Greece. I loved the beach. I loved the smell and the feel of the sand between my toes. I couldn't imagine living anywhere else. When my business had started to take off, advisors told me I needed to be in New York City, London, or Los Angeles, but I wasn't going to leave home.

I didn't have to leave home. I owned a social media firm, which meant I could work from anywhere. I telecommuted all over the world. Companies that wanted my services came to me—that was how good I was—and my company was going to overtake every other social media platform in the world. I was twenty-eight and already making some serious headway in the industry. I was one of the wealthiest under thirty, and I didn't mind accepting all the perks that went along with that title.

I looked over at my best friend, Rand Mattas, who had his eyes on something other than the clear water. A group of women wearing bikinis that resembled dental floss were frolicking on the beach. It was hard for him not to look at the surgically enhanced bodies, but it wasn't my thing. I liked the real deal. The women had on heavy makeup and were more about picking up men than actually having fun in the water. I doubted they would dare get their face or hair wet. Their hair would fall flat, and their faces would wash away. Definitely not my thing, but it was pretty clear it was Rand's thing.

"Keep staring, and maybe they'll talk to you," I teased.

He turned to look at me, grinning like an idiot. "I could go over and introduce myself as Adrian Gabris. Then, they'd be falling all over me."

I rolled my eyes. "I will kick your ass if you try to use my name to get them into your bed. The last thing I need is a scandal. We look enough alike that it *would* cause a scandal. It would take forever for me to clear my name. The press isn't the worst of the problem. It's my mother. My mother would kill me. Slowly."

"Ah, but I have the dark brown eyes of a true Greek man," he replied. "Anyone would be able to tell us apart. I'm also a lot better looking."

"I have the blue eyes that make me look like a real Greek *god*," I shot back. "You know the tales. The gods had blue eyes."

"Tales, fairy tales," he grumbled. "Myths and legends."

We both had the same jet-black hair, olive skin tone, and were both tall with dark scruff that seemed to be a constant on our jaws, no matter how many times a day we shaved. I was about an inch taller than his six-two frame, and I felt a little more muscular, but I knew he would argue with that fact. It was something we'd argued about since we'd hit puberty and I finally managed to grow taller than him. In my large family, I had been one of the smallest. It was greatly satisfying to be taller and bigger than at least one person in my life.

"Can we get in the water?" he asked, a hand on his hip as he stared down at me. "You're stalling. No board needs that much attention."

"My board needed waxing," I told him, ignoring his frustration at my delay.

"You were spacing out, thinking about work," he complained.

I shrugged a shoulder, getting to my feet and dusting the sand from my knees. "I was thinking about the new interns coming in. I'm hoping they will bring fresh insight to the company. We could use new life in that place. It's important we always stay ahead of the game, and we can only do that with fresh eyes and new ideas."

"The Americans?" he asked. "That's who you are counting on to keep us at the top?"

"Yes."

He didn't look convinced. "We're doing fine. There's nothing to think about right now."

I shrugged. "You never know when things might change. We could miss something and get left behind. Trends are always changing. Our clients depend on us to be the trendsetters—not the followers."

He groaned, running a hand through his short black hair. "Stop. Why? Why are you always thinking about work and social media and shit that I don't give two shits about?"

I grinned, knowing he was complaining for the sake of complaining. "Because you *do* give two shits about work. You're the one who is always on your phone, checking Twitter and every other social media platform, trying to find the next thing."

"I have to do that because you don't know how to," he grumbled.

I laughed. "I believe I do, but why would I waste my time when I have you to do it? And now, we'll have interns to do all of that for both of us."

He grimaced. "Are we really going to put the future of the business we built into the hands of some young Americans looking for a little vacation to the Greek isles?" he asked.

I shrugged. "I reviewed the resumes very thoroughly. I'm confident they are exactly what we need, and they work for cheap." I laughed.

"I'm sure they will be fantastic, but can we worry about that Monday?" he asked. "Today is our day off. We're not supposed to think about work. We're supposed to be enjoying the water and relaxing. You work too much."

"I work just enough to keep us both very rich," I reminded him. "You know shit never stops moving. The entire world is on twenty-four-seven. I have to make sure we're staying on top of things. Not all of us can lounge about on a beach, working on our tans all day."

He scoffed. "Without me, the company would sink like the Titanic. You're lucky I like you, or I would have let you go down a long time ago."

I raised my eyebrows. "You sure about that?"

"Yes."

"I just remembered," I said, already making a note of it in my mental calendar. "We need to get a meeting with that new start-up that moved in above us—the shoe company."

"Stop talking about work," he pouted. "We spend five, sometimes six days a week, all day long working. I want to relax and play. We can deal with all of that on Monday. Nothing is going to change in the next thirty-six hours. All work and no play makes Adrian a very dull boy. When Adrian is a dull boy, Rand gets bored."

"You sound like a child," I said with a grin. "You're almost thirty. We have to think about work all the time because it's what keeps a roof over our heads and the heads of our employees. I'm at the beach. I'm having a good time. It's just conversation. Can't you do two things at once?"

"Oh, I can do two things at once all right," he said, his eyes on a particularly voluptuous blonde strolling down the beach in a bright red bikini that showed off all of her assets.

I shook my head. "She's way out of your league."

He scoffed. "I don't think so."

"Look at her," I said. "She's probably not even twenty yet. She's a baby."

"I'm a man in my prime, and there are a lot of beautiful women on this beach who need my attention. I cannot talk or think about work anymore. I need to focus."

I chuckled, noticing his eyes were still on the young woman. "I think you are plenty focused. But she didn't look twice at you."

"That's because I didn't try," he said with a grin on his face, showing off his perfect white smile. "The ladies love me and would be thrilled to have me flirt with them. They would probably settle with some attention from you, I suppose. I am only one man, and there is only so much of me to go around."

"Settle for me?" I scoffed. "They all want me."

I grabbed a sleeve of the torso of my wetsuit and tugged it on, zipping it up the front and hiding the tattoos I had on my chest, shoulder, and upper arms. I worked in business, and I needed to be taken seriously. It was hard enough for big corporate executives old enough to be my grandfather to take me seriously. My image was just as important as my reputation. That was something my mom had instilled in me from a young age. We'd grown up poor, but she always made sure we dressed well and were clean. A boy knew better than to disobey a Greek mother.

"Come on," he urged. "Let's get in the water."

I could hear the women who'd drawn closer to us talking about why they couldn't get in the water. The real reason was pretty obvious —their war paint would melt. Instead, they claimed there were sharks in the water and they didn't want to get eaten. It was pretty clear they were American tourists, judging by their accents.

I tucked my board under my arm and started toward the water. I couldn't resist teasing the young women when I heard one of them rattle off a statistic about shark attacks. It sounded ridiculous.

"You know, the chance of you being attacked by a shark this close to the shore is pretty slim," I said with a smile. "In fact, your chances of dying in an elevator are greater than being attacked by a shark."

"Hell, you're more likely to be murdered on the beach than to be attacked by a shark." Rand laughed before racing past me into the water.

The women gasped. I turned to see the looks of horror on their faces as they stared at Rand's back. I caught up to him just a few feet into the water. "Do you actually think that line will work? You complain about not having any fun on your time off and that you have no social life. Don't blame work for that. Blame your inept flirting skills."

He burst into laughter, dropping his board and paddling out. "They weren't my type anyway."

I rolled my eyes, shaking my head, and I followed him out into the surf. Rand was my best friend and my right-hand man. It was difficult to make any real friends in my position. Rand had been with me from the very beginning. He'd shared the tiny one-bedroom apartment with me while we worked to get the business off the ground. He was the one guy I could trust to have my back. I wasn't worried he was friends with me just for my money or connections.

We surfed for a while, enjoying the refreshing water on what had to be one of the most beautiful beaches in the world. I felt lucky to be alive whenever I got the chance to kick back and relax in my hometown.

I was straddling my board, staring out at the vast sea, catching the sight of some sails on the horizon. It was a beautiful day. Rand was about ten feet away, his board pointed in the opposite direction as he stared at the beach. That was typical. He was scanning the many bikini-clad women, trying to find his mark.

Something nudged my board, causing my body to jerk to the side. I looked behind me and saw a fin slide under the water. "Oh shit," I muttered.

"What the hell?" Rand called. "Was that a fin?"

"Yeah, it was," I said, pulling my feet up and on my board as I used my hands to paddle toward the shore.

"I think we should stay out of elevators for the next little while," Rand said dryly.

I smirked. "I think that's a good idea."

CHAPTER 2

BELLA

My dad walked me into the airport, both of us nervous and scared, but neither of us letting the other one see the anxiousness. I felt jittery, and it had nothing to do with the coffee I had drunk earlier. I was extremely anxious to leave home. It would be the first time I had ever left, and I wasn't just leaving home. I was leaving the country on an airplane. I'd never flown before either, which was only adding to my nervousness.

"You're going to be fine," my dad said in that familiar voice that always made me feel safe and loved.

I looked up into his dark blue eyes that had a kindness about them that reflected his soul. "I'm going to be fine," I repeated.

"You've worked hard for this Bella Kamp, and I'm so very proud of you," he said with a smile, his eyes wrinkling with the action.

I looked at his balding head and thought about how much I was going to miss seeing it every day. He reached for my hand, his hands rough and callused from years of hard work in the mines of northern Idaho. He'd worked two jobs, taking extra shifts every chance he got to give me the best life possible. We'd never been comfortable, but we had food on the table, and our tiny two-bedroom house in a very rural town along the Washington and Idaho border was enough for us.

"I'm going to miss you like crazy," I told him, fighting back the tears that threatened to fall.

"I'm going to miss *you*. You've been working your butt off for this internship. You deserve it. We'll see each other when you get back. This is an opportunity too good to pass up. You got me that fancy phone, and we'll be able to talk all the time. Hell, I'll even be able to see your face." He gave a deep laugh.

"I hate that I'm missing your big Fourth of July show this year," I pouted. "I've never missed it."

"Hey, you'll be here next year," he assured me. "It's the same thing every time."

"No, it's not. It's exciting and big, and there's always something new. It's why the town put you in charge of it all those years ago. You blow things up really well." I grinned.

"We all have to be good at something," he said with a soft smile, never one to accept compliments well.

"You better take care of yourself," I warned him.

He grinned. "I will. Believe it or not, I was taking care of myself long before you came along."

"Yes, but you weren't doing a very good job of it."

He laughed again. "I suppose not. I cannot wait to tell all the guys at the mine that you're working abroad. Not many guys in my position can say that. You got your mama's brains. Your old dad doesn't have shit for brains."

"Dad, stop. You're the smartest, most hardworking man I have ever met."

He shook his head. "I never had a brain for school. It's why I dropped out after ninth grade. I could do more for my family going to work on the farm and bringing in a paycheck than I could by going to school."

I winced, hating that he had to work at the age of fourteen to help out his family. His mom and dad had been dirt poor, and his little sister was too sick for my grandmother to work. The medical bills kept them in the poorhouse. They were all gone now, and it was just my dad, still working his ass off, doing what he could to support a kid without even a high school education.

From the moment I could talk, he told me I was going to go places. He insisted I study hard and go to college. He worked that much harder to make sure I graduated with a bachelor's in marketing. I had applied for the internship, not really expecting to get it. The competition would be fierce. My degree came from a no-name school, and most of it had been online. When I got the letter in the mail, I had nearly fainted.

"I better get in line," I told him.

He nodded his head. "I will talk to you soon. You keep your head up, and don't let those Greek boys tell you that you aren't good enough. You are the best. They are lucky to have you."

I smiled. "Thanks, Dad."

"You're going to be okay," he said, sensing my nervousness.

I grimaced. "I'm a little freaked out that my first time in a plane involves going over the ocean."

He grinned. "If the plane is going down, tuck your head between your legs, pray, and then kiss your ass goodbye while you're down there."

I burst into laughter. "Thanks. That is just what I needed to hear."

"Hey, the death will be quick," he said in an attempt to reassure me.

I frowned at him. "You're not helping."

I gave him another hug, picked up my backpack, and slung it over my shoulder before grabbing my laptop case. My dad had told me I should take a carry-on with the essentials in case my luggage was lost. It seemed like a good idea to me. I did not want to find myself stranded in a foreign country with no clothes, toiletries, and very little money.

I walked to the end of the line, taking off my shoes and getting ready to go through the security check. Just like the first day of school, my dad stood and watched me line up with a proud smile on his face. I was glad I could make him proud. I was going to work my ass off and prove I was worth hiring permanently. I wasn't ready to move to Greece on a permanent basis, but maybe they'd give me my own office to run in Seattle. That wouldn't be too far from home, and I could still visit my dad often.

With one person in front of me, I turned and waved to my dad. Going through the metal detectors was the point of no return. I was leaving home, and it terrified me—in a good way. I made my way into the main part of the airport. I bought myself a water and a bag of chips, knowing it was going to be a long flight.

When it was time to board, I once again found myself freaking out a little. I took my seat next to the window, not sure if I wanted to see the clouds or the plane crashing to the earth.

"Good morning," an older woman said. "It looks like we're going to be seat partners for the next few hours."

I smiled at her, tucking my laptop between the wall of the plane and my leg. I was planning on doing a little work, or rather, a little light stalking about the company I was going to be working for. I would save it for later.

"Are you going to Greece?" I asked.

She nodded and smiled. "I am. Greece is home for me."

"Really?" I asked with surprise.

"I bounce back and forth," she said. "My husband and I moved to America when we were young. Our children are here. He passed away about five years ago, and I went home to Greece to be with my family. I've been here the last month, visiting my children and grandchildren. What about you? You're American."

I nodded. "I am. I'm going to work over there. It's an internship."

"How exciting," she said. "Your first time?"

I grimaced. "My first time *everything*. I've never flown before. To say I'm a little nervous is an understatement."

She patted my knee. "I'll be right here. It will be just fine."

"I hope so."

The captain's voice filled the cabin, announcing we were going to be taking off. Butterflies rumbled in my stomach as the plane began to taxi down the runway. I couldn't focus on what the pretty flight attendant was saying. I was gripping the armrest, trying not to panic. There were about a million excuses running through my head about why I couldn't go to Greece. None of them would make my dad proud. I wanted him to be proud.

"Here we go," the woman to my left said in a soft voice.

I nodded, unable to turn my head or do anything except hold on as if that would do anything to save me should something go horribly wrong. Once the plane finally leveled out and we were in the air cruising along, I relaxed a little.

"That was intense," I muttered.

"I'm Elena," she said, extending her wrinkled hand.

I gently shook it. "I'm Bella. It's nice to meet you. Maybe you can give me some inside tips for living in Greece."

"What part are you going to be living in?" she asked.

"Heraklion," I answered, hoping I was saying it right.

Her eyes lit up. "It is a beautiful city. It isn't like the cities in the United States. There is so much history there. Granted, time is swallowing it up, but there are plenty of museums and other attractions for you to visit. You will stay very busy, I predict."

"I hope I have time to see all the sites before I have to come home," I told her. "I'm expecting to be very busy with the internship."

"What kind of job will you be doing?"

"I'll be working in the marketing department of a social media company," I answered.

She giggled softly. "I have no idea what that is, but it sounds exciting."

"It will be. Of that, I'm sure."

"Do you leave a special young man behind?" she inquired.

I shook my head. "Nope. Just one old guy."

She raised an eyebrow. "Oh," she said, snapping her mouth closed.

"My dad," I said with a laugh. "I'm leaving my dad behind."

"Oh, I see. Are you and your father close?"

I nodded. "We are. My mom died a few days after I was born, some complications from the birth. It's been just my dad and me for twenty-three years."

Her face softened. "I see. Is this your first time away from home?"

"Yes."

"I bet your father is very proud of you."

I nodded. "He is. He tells me all the time."

"Do you resemble your mom or your dad?" she asked.

"My mother," I answered quickly. "At least, that's what my dad always tells me. I'm the same age she was when she died. I cannot imagine dying tomorrow. I feel like I haven't lived. Anyway, my mom had blonde hair and green eyes. I get my height from my dad, though. My mom was a petite woman."

"How tall are you?"

"Five-six," I answered.

She nodded as if I had given the right answer. "Greek men are tall. Maybe you'll find yourself a handsome Greek."

"I have no time for that kind of thing. I plan on doing my time at the company and either getting a permanent job offer or going back home to find another job. I have to start making some money. I don't want my dad to work until he's seventy. I want to get a job and make enough to support him."

She smiled. "That is very kind. Your father must have done a very good job raising you. You sound like a very good person."

"Thank you. He did his best, and I like to think I'm a good person."

I leaned my head back on the headrest, thinking about my dad. He'd be getting ready to go to work at the part-time janitor job he did on the weekends. I told him to quit the second job. I was out of school, and he didn't need to support me. He claimed he was saving up for a rainy day. I was convinced he didn't know how to relax. I was going to make him figure it out.

A violent jerk of the plane had me sitting up straight, my eyes wide as I looked over at Elena. "What's that?" I squeaked.

"Just a little turbulence, hon," she said. "It will be just fine."

My dad's words kept running through my head. Kiss my ass good-bye. That was what he'd told me. He'd been joking, but it was hard to laugh when the tin can I was flying in was rattling and shaking like I was tossed in a washing machine.

CHAPTER 3

ADRIAN

I carried the cold soda into the living room and sat on the couch, glancing out the huge picture windows that ran from the floor to the ceiling and overlooked the expansive backyard of my property. I loved being outside. My job kept me inside most days. I had bought my home and had it completely renovated to give the illusion of being outdoors, with tons of windows that allowed plenty of natural light. My property was very private, meaning I didn't have to worry about anyone peeking. When I wanted privacy, it was easy enough to close the electric shades with the touch of a button.

I put down my drink and reached for my iPad, wanting to do a little internet surfing and see what was happening in the world. It was important I knew the latest trends and kept up on Hollywood. They tended to set the trends. Sometimes, they didn't even realize they were setting a trend. It took someone like me to find something unique and creative and make it cool.

The buzzer at the front gate sounded, the video screen popping up in the corner of my screen. It was Rand. He had the code and was already driving through the gate. I put the tablet down and walked to the front door to greet him.

"What's up?" I asked, surprised to see him on a Sunday evening.

"Let's go out."

I moved out of the way as he walked into the foyer. "It's a Sunday night."

"Wow, that sounded a lot like your mother," he quipped.

"I'm only pointing out tomorrow is a busy day at work and neither of us can afford to go in, dragging ass and feeling like shit because we are hungover. It's called adulting. I would think you've heard of this concept before. You are almost thirty," I reminded him, something I did as often as I could. He was a year older than I was and was going to be hitting the big milestone birthday before me. I wanted to give him as much shit for as long as I could.

"Come on," he said. "One drink. I promise you'll be home by ten at the very latest."

I groaned. "You say one drink, but what you really mean is four and a late night."

"I'm serious," he said, holding up a finger. "One drink."

"We have those interns coming in the morning," I argued. "I don't want to be grumpy and off my game."

He nodded. "Let's go. I'll drive."

I shook my head. "No way," I muttered, caving in to his request for a single drink. "I'll call my driver."

My driver lived in a small house on the property. I never knew when I was going to have to go to a business meeting or when I was going to need to dash to the airport. I had several cars, but I liked having a driver on staff—two actually—but the main driver lived on the premises. He was an older man, a friend of the family who had been out of work and nearly out on the streets. I offered him the guest cottage if he would be willing to be on-call for me. He eagerly accepted, and it had been working out well for the two of us.

Rand grinned, satisfied he'd won again. "Peer pressure is a marvelous thing."

"You suck," I grumbled, sending a quick text to Malachi and requesting his services.

I walked down the long hallway that led to my suite. The home was a single story. I didn't want a staircase, and I didn't necessarily need twenty bedrooms. The house had six rooms, plenty for me and a few family members if they decided to crash at my place. The outdoor pool and the grounds were what had sold me on the place.

I quickly changed into something other than my lounge pants. When I returned a few minutes later, Malachi and Rand were talking about the mild weather we were having.

"Ready?" Rand asked.

"Yes, let's do this," I said. "The sooner I have *one* drink with you, the sooner I can get back."

He ignored my comment. We left the house, Malachi driving us to a local bar that Rand and I often went to after a long day at work. It was fairly mellow on the weekdays, but with summer upon us and the tourists around, the local singles flocked to the bar in search of a tourist looking for a good time. We found a table and each ordered a beer.

"Have you been home lately?" he asked.

I shook my head. "No. I've been busy."

He grimaced. "Your mom is going to drag you home by your ear if you don't go soon," he warned.

I nodded. "I know. I haven't gone home because every time I do, she has a friend who has a daughter who would be perfect for me. The woman must have at least a hundred friends. They seem to crawl out of the woodwork whenever I'm around."

Rand laughed. "Rich, eligible bachelor tends to do that."

"My mother thinks I'm too old to be single," I complained. "She wants me settled down and married with a flock of children to call her grandmother. I don't know why she doesn't go after one of my brothers. They could just as easily get married."

"Because you are her baby, and she knows your brothers are lost causes," he replied easily.

I chuckled. "That's probably true. Although Miles will probably be the first to marry. He's the type."

"You're the type," he said. "You already act like you're an old man, wanting to stay in on a Sunday because you have work in the morning. That's old."

I shook my head. "Not old—responsible. One of us has to be."

He grinned unapologetically. "Thanks for taking one for the team."

"You can pay me back by going out on the next date my mother sets me up with," I told him.

He wrinkled his nose. "I don't know about that. Honestly, how bad can it be? Your mother has good taste."

"It's not my mother's taste that's the problem. It is her so-called friends that seem to be blind to their daughter's looks. The last date I went out with had more facial hair than I did. I couldn't imagine myself kissing her." I shuddered at the memory.

He burst into laughter. "You'd have to hide your razors."

My lip curled with disgust. "No thanks. I like my women feminine in every way."

"What are you looking for?" he asked. "Maybe I can help you out."

I shrugged a shoulder. "I don't know, pretty, but not just on the outside. I want someone who is kind, smart, and funny. I want a woman I can talk to, and she will have something to say worth listening to."

He raised an eyebrow. "Gee, anything else? Big boobs? Big ass?"

I scowled at him. "They are women, not cattle. I don't have a preference. I like legs. Long, shapely legs and a body that is in shape. I don't much care how big the rest of her parts are."

He nodded his head, his eyes scanning the bar as if he was going to find a woman for me. I wanted to remind him we weren't at Girls R' Us and I wasn't shopping for a wife, but I didn't. I knew he would only lecture me about needing to date more and blah, blah, blah.

I worked. I dated on occasion, but in my position, I struggled to believe the gorgeous women who threw themselves at me were interested in the man I was. I was probably jaded, but I had been burned a time or two already.

"What about—"

"No, don't even," I said, holding up my hand.

He sighed, taking a drink from his beer. "You're right. I don't see what you need here. We need to go to the club." He was referring to the night club we would usually visit once or twice a month. We used to go far more often, but it felt like the people were getting younger and younger. I felt old in the club.

"I'm not going out to a club," I said. "I've already told you that."

"Come on. One hour isn't going to kill you."

"No way," I said firmly. "You keep saying one drink, one hour, but I know you. I know that will turn into me getting into bed at three and the room will be spinning. I don't want to get drunk."

"You're no fun."

I shrugged a shoulder. "I suppose I'm not."

"We'll have a drink, we'll dance and mingle, and then we will both go home and go to bed like good little boys," he promised.

"Bullshit," I said. "You know that's bullshit. You never have one drink or dance one time. I can't do it. Not tonight. I have to be sharp tomorrow."

He growled. "I'm going out. I need to get as much living in before I turn thirty. A thirty-year-old man going to the club is weird. I'm still technically in my twenties, and I'm going to take advantage of that."

"Have fun and be safe," I told him. "I'm going to head out."

He held up his beer and toasted me away. I weaved around people, trying not to bump into anyone. Directly in my path was a beautiful young woman, blonde hair, stunning green eyes, and a look of innocence. She offered me a small smile as she stepped to the side to let me pass.

I turned back, wanting one last look. She had a gorgeous body. She was tallish, but not overly so. Her skin was tanned—a real tan, not a spray-on one—and she looked like she might be a runner with her long, lean limbs. She turned, catching me staring at her. I smiled and turned back around.

Any other night, I would have gone after her. I really *did* have to go to work tomorrow. I had a busy day, and I wanted to make sure I made a good impression on the new interns. I wanted to use what I thought was damn good intuition when I first met a person. I almost always knew right away whether a person was right for the job and would fit well with the rest of my team.

I couldn't have my senses dulled by a hangover. When I reached the door, I took one last look back, scanning the crowd and looking for the pretty blonde. I spotted her at the bar, ordering a drink. She looked nervous and a little scared. I pegged her for a tourist and immediately felt like I needed to warn her about coming to a bar alone. It was only then I realized there was a good chance she had a boyfriend and he was likely nearby. A woman like that wouldn't be single for long.

CHAPTER 4

BELLA

If I were someone like my best friend back home, Cara, I would have thought I had died and gone to heaven. There were gorgeous Greek men everywhere. Everywhere I looked, there was a hunk of a man. It was like being inside the pages of a Playgirl magazine. So much testosterone, muscles, and tall, dark, and handsome. I had to remind myself not to stare.

"Can I get a rum and Coke please?" I asked the bartender.

He winked at me before spinning around to make the drink. I turned my head, scanning the crowd. I was a little surprised to see it was so busy on a Sunday night. I was hoping to get a drink, unwind, and do a little people watching. The guy at the hotel's front desk told me this was a nice bar without a lot of *crazies*—his word.

"Do you want to dance?" a male voice asked at the same time a very large shoulder bumped up against mine.

I turned my head to find myself nose to nose with a man with big brown eyes. He was handsome and drunk, judging by the sweet scent of liquor assaulting my senses. "No thanks," I said, doing my best to be polite.

"How about me?" another voice asked from my other side.

I turned to face yet another attractive young man with a very thick accent. "No thank you, I'm meeting someone," I lied.

"A girl someone?" the guy on my right asked.

I smiled. "No, my boyfriend."

He persisted. "He's not here now."

The bartender handed me my drink, and I handed him some money before walking away from the bar without saying another word. I was used to being hit on, but these guys were really persistent. I didn't like it. I tried to blend in with the wall, standing out of the way and attempting to watch the crowd. I wasn't quite as inconspicuous as I thought. I blamed my blonde hair. It seemed to stand out a bit in the sea of dark hair tones.

I had only managed to get half of my drink down before I finally gave in. I blamed it on the jet lag. I was cranky and not in the mood for the attention. I put my glass on a table and headed for the door, bumping my way past tall, hard bodies that were purposely going out of their way to push against me. It wasn't my scene. I hadn't cared for it in college, and I didn't like it now.

I walked back to the hotel. The company was providing a steeply discounted room as part of the internship program. It was a nice hotel, and I felt safe in it. I was going to stay in the hotel for a couple of weeks and see how the job went. If I liked it and they liked me, I would look around for a cheap apartment.

When I got to my room, I checked the time. It was Sunday morning back home, my dad's one day off from work. It would be just about seven. I knew he wouldn't be sleeping in and decided to check in with him. I was homesick and needed to hear his voice.

"Hi, Dad," I said when he answered the phone.

"Hey!" he said. "What are you doing? Didn't I talk to you this morning, your time?"

"You did, but I thought I would call and tell you to have a nice day," I said with a smile in my voice.

"What's wrong?" he asked, knowing me too well.

"Nothing is wrong," I told him.

"You sound upset. What happened?"

I let out a long sigh. "Nothing. I went to a local bar to get a drink and check out the area. The guys are a little more aggressive than they are back home."

"I'll be on the next flight," he growled.

I laughed. "It's fine. It's not all that different than college, but I think it felt different because I either knew them or knew *of* them and I had girlfriends with me. You know, strength in numbers, just like you always told me."

"Are you sure you're okay?" he asked. "I will use that shiny new credit card I got and buy a ticket over there. I did not send you around the world to be accosted by a bunch of handsy boys."

"It's okay, Dad. I'm just tired. How about you? Did you get some good rest last night?"

"I did. Did you manage to sleep at all?" Concern colored his voice.

"Yep. I didn't think I would, but the bed is super comfy. As soon as my head hit the pillow, I was out."

"Good. Tomorrow is your first day?"

I felt the butterflies in my stomach that always arose just thinking about my first day on the job. "It is."

"Don't be nervous. You are going to kick ass. You're smart, talented, and this job is perfect for you."

I smiled, so happy to have him on my side. He was my consummate cheerleader, always there to give me a pep talk when I felt like giving up. He was my hero, and I couldn't imagine my life without him in it. He was getting on in years, and I worried that a lifetime of hard work and not taking care of himself all that well was going to lead him to an early grave. I refused to let that happen. I needed him around until I was ready to leave this world at the ripe age of at least eighty. Yes, I knew it was a pipe dream, but it got me through the day.

"Thanks, Dad. So, what do you have planned for the day?"

"I'm going to get that lawn mowed and then talk with the fire department about what needs to be done before the big show," he said, and I could hear the excitement in his voice.

"I hate that I'm going to miss it. I know someone will record it and

21

post it. Maybe I can watch it live." The idea bloomed in my mind. "It will be like I'm right there!"

He chuckled. "Honey, you've seen these things. Twenty-two of them to be exact. You're not missing anything."

"I'm missing the barbecue, and the dance, and the carnival in the park, and most importantly, the fireworks," I complained.

"You're in Greece," he said with a laugh. "I think that trumps anything we've got going here."

"I suppose, but I'm alone."

"Make some friends—maybe not at the bar," he said. "When you go to work tomorrow, smile. Use that friendly charm you have in spades and make a friend or two."

"I feel like I'm going back to first grade," I moaned.

"Bella, this is a trip of a lifetime. This very well might be the only time you ever get out of the country. Enjoy yourself. Have a good time. You are going to regret not spending more time exploring and walking those gorgeous beaches I saw on the internet. You love the beach. I bet it is real pretty out there right now." His voice led me to draw my own conclusions.

"I can't believe you're telling me to walk the beach alone at night," I chided.

He chuckled. "I've taught you how to defend yourself. I'm not worried about you. I'm worried about the other guy. Besides, it isn't dark there yet, and I bet that hotel you're in has beach access. Get your toes in the sand and get yourself right. You've got this."

"I wish you were here with me," I pouted.

"Bella Kamp, you are a grown woman. You cannot drag your old dad all around the world. It's time to cut the apron strings. Live. I want you to have fun and enjoy all this life has to offer. I didn't work my ass off for twenty years for you to want to come home. I've never coddled you, and I'm not going to start now. You can do anything you put your mind to, but if you keep looking for reasons to be miserable, I guarantee you'll find them."

I sighed, knowing he was right. It was just like him to snap me out of a funk before I could get in too deep. "All right, fine. I'm going to go walk the beach."

"With your shoes off. You've got to get that sand between your toes," he added. "Walk it off. Hell, I'm sure it's warm enough for you to even dive in."

"No! I'm not going swimming at night. There might be sharks out there." I squealed.

He laughed. "I doubt that."

"It's not really a risk I want to take," I said. "I don't like sharks, and I don't want to tempt my fate."

"Your fate has led you there. Don't worry yourself into making something bad happen. You have to put good vibes into the universe or some shit like that. At least that's what some dude at work always says. Of course, I think he sits around and sings by the campfire while smoking a little Mary Jane." He chuckled.

I had to laugh at my dad's very old-fashioned way of talking. He was a salt of the earth guy, very old school. "I get it. I'll do better. I'll try and put out good vibes."

"I'll talk to you later. Call me after you get home."

I laughed. "It'll be like three in the morning. I'll call you around six your time."

"Okay," he said. "I love you kid. You are making me proud. You have fun."

"I love you too, Dad," I said and ended the call.

I looked around the hotel room and realized he was right. I did not want to spend my time on what some would call a dream vacation sitting in my hotel room. I got up and slid my phone into my back pocket, along with a credit card just in case I had some kind of emergency that required money. It was something my dad had insisted on. I walked out of the hotel, going out the back and following the signs indicating beach access wasn't far.

I found the stairs and walked down in the twilight. It was stunning. I grabbed my phone from my back pocket and snapped a picture of the sea and the golden sand. It was amazing. I sent the picture to my dad, proving I had taken his advice.

He replied with a thumbs-up emoji. I giggled, happy he was getting the hang of texting after fifteen years of training. I walked down to the beach and took off my sandals. The warm sand squished between my toes. I smiled, immediately feeling happier. I could get used to living next to the beach. There were quite a few people taking advantage of the picturesque view, with plenty of them snapping pictures.

I smiled at a couple of little kids racing around the beach, their parents not far away. I liked how laid back it was. I'd been to the Oregon beach a few times, and it always felt like everyone was watching everyone. Here, it was live and let live and have a good time. I could literally feel my stress and anxiety rolling out with the tide.

Tomorrow was going to be a great day. I was going to make sure of it. I expected there to be some hiccups, but I'd roll with them. I promised myself I would come back to the beach tomorrow after work. I was going to have a drink with an umbrella in it and sit my ass in the sand. Nothing could be that bad when the view looked like this.

CHAPTER 5

ADRIAN

I reviewed emails quickly, marking those that I needed to reply to later with a little flag and deleting the others that were nothing more than spam. Even the best spam filters in the world couldn't stop some of the sneakiest spammers. I heard what sounded like a thud against my door. A second later, it was pushed open, with Rand on the other side of it looking like death. His face was pale under the dark sunglasses shielding his eyes.

I shook my head. "Asshole."

He grinned before wincing and touching the side of his head. "Ow."

"I told you," I grumbled. "Didn't I fucking tell you not to go out? When are you going to fucking learn?" I was irritated by his state when we had new interns coming in. It was not the image I wanted getting out there.

"Relax. I'm fine."

"Yeah, you look great," I said sarcastically.

"I'm here," he said. "I just need a little more coffee and I'll be right as rain."

"The dark sunglasses, pasty skin, and the mussed hair say otherwise," I complained.

He shrugged a shoulder. "It's fine. I'll be fine."

"You are not saying a damn word," I said with disgust. "Do not open your mouth. Just stand there and look like an authority figure. They're supposed to respect you."

"They will," he said nonchalantly. "They always do."

"Liar. Come on. We've got interns waiting in the conference room. Pull yourself together." I got to my feet and grabbed my iPad, making my disgust with his condition known.

I walked out of the office, doing my best to make as much noise as possible. I wanted to increase his suffering as much as I could. When I opened the door to the conference room, I noticed there were only three new faces instead of four. I would double check with HR to see if the other intern had backed out. I would make sure to never give the person another chance. My internship was highly sought after. I didn't appreciate being stood up.

I greeted the three new faces. "Good morning."

Rand was right behind me, his sunglasses still on. I shot him a glare. His phone started ringing. He looked at me as if I was the one calling him. I opened my eyes wide, growing more frustrated with his unprofessionalism.

"Oh, it's me," he said, fumbling in his pocket and grabbing the phone before stepping out of the room.

I rolled my eyes, turning back to face the three new fresh faces staring at me. "Sorry about that. You'll meet him later. I'm Adrian Gabris. I'm the CEO, founder or whatever you want to call me. Rand Mattas will be the guy you will be reporting to."

I couldn't help overhearing the conversation just outside the conference room. Rand was talking to someone rather rudely. I stepped closer to the door and realized it was a female voice, and she was talking about being lost. The missing intern, I realized.

"Look, the directions you were given were very clear," Rand grumbled. "The other three interns are here."

I heard the female apologizing.

"You don't need to bother coming in. We've got this. Why don't—"

I scowled at him and snatched the phone from his hand. "I'm sorry about that," I said, putting the phone to my ear. "No, no, he didn't mean that. Tell me where you are, and I'll tell you how to get here."

The sweet, melodic voice came through the phone loud and clear. "There's a coffee shop and a dress shop and what looks like a shoe repair place," she explained.

I racked my brain, trying to figure out where she was. Truth be told, those three shops were all over the city. "What are the names of the shops?" I asked.

"I don't know," she whined. "I think one says Zeus. Does that make sense?"

I rolled my eyes. She was in Greece. Many business owners tried to capitalize on the famous Greek gods to sell their wares. "That makes sense, but I need to know the name."

I heard her groan. "All these streets look the same. They're all old buildings and cobblestone sidewalks and the same streetlights."

"Can you tell me what street you are on?" I asked, trying to keep my cool.

I could hear the noise of people talking and car engines in the background. "Um, I don't know."

"Walk to the corner, and read the street sign," I said dryly.

I was beginning to wonder if this was the type of person I wanted in my organization after all. She didn't sound all that bright if she didn't get how to read a street sign. Every smartphone in the world had GPS on it. Why couldn't she pull up a map app and get her ass to the building?

"There's a cobblestone alley or street off to my right," she said. "And what looks like a restaurant across the street. There's a bar or pub or whatever they are called a few doors down."

I closed my eyes. "Look up. What is the name of the street?"

I heard her exhale a breath. "I don't know because it's in Greek," she confessed with a great deal of frustration. "I know that's bad, but I don't know how to read or speak Greek. I didn't think I needed to learn. When I researched the country, it said most of the people in Greece spoke English."

"It's okay, relax," I said, sensing her frustration.

"This is so stupid. I'm such an idiot. I should have found the building yesterday." She muttered under her breath.

I grinned, realizing that would certainly make it difficult. "Can you ask a local? Ask one of the people working in the coffee shop to tell you what street you are on."

"Just a second," she said, and I heard muffled sounds and the sound of her voice.

She came back on the phone and told me the street, and I knew exactly where she was. She wasn't all that far from the building. "Sit tight and I will be right there to bring you back. There should be a little café on the corner with tables outside. Grab a seat. I'll be in a black suit. My name is Adrian."

"Are you sure?" she asked. "I'm so sorry to be such a bother."

"It's fine. What are you wearing?" I suddenly felt very strange about asking a woman what she was wearing. It was a little too cheesy for me.

I heard a noise and looked up to see Rand looking in my direction with the dark sunglasses on still. I glared at him and turned my back.

"I'm wearing a pair of black slacks, black heels, and a white short-sleeve shirt," she said. "My name is Bella. I told the other guy, but I'm supposed to be there right now. It's my first day." She groaned.

I nodded, even though she couldn't see me, and put the rather vague description in my head to pull up when I got there. Bella. Her name bounced around my brain. I wondered if it was short for Isabella. Was she Italian, I mused. I dismissed the thought and focused on getting her to the office. It was the morning rush hour, and I imagined most of the people hanging out on the street would be tourists. The rest of the city would be at work. Not many tourists dressed in slacks and heels for a day of exploring.

"I'll be there in about five minutes," I said.

"Thank you so much," she said, and I could hear the relief in her voice.

I ended the call and turned back to face Rand, who was slowly shaking his head. "Seriously? You're going to go fetch your missing intern?"

I shrugged a shoulder. "Why not? She's an American and new to the city. She got lost."

"The other ones all made it," he replied.

"The other ones are locals," I reminded him.

"You're a sucker for a woman," he shot back.

"Here's a suggestion. Take off those damn sunglasses and get in there and do your job. Try not to be too much of an asshole on the first day. I don't want to get the reputation that we are a shitty company to work for. We are only as good as the people who run the daily operations. If they're unhappy and feeling undervalued, they're not going to do a good job. Pull yourself together and put on that charming smile you use to woo clients," I ordered, handing him his phone back.

He pushed his sunglasses up on his head and looked at me with bleary eyes. "I can do my job, hungover or not. You know that. Hell, I do my best work when I'm hungover."

"Bullshit. I've got to go. Don't embarrass me and don't make a fool out of yourself." I slapped him on the shoulder before heading to my office to grab my wallet and phone.

She wasn't far at all. I would walk to the café and meet her. Hell, it might be better to meet her one on one in a more relaxed setting anyway. I could hear the nerves in her voice and didn't want to make the situation worse. I knew what it was like to have a bad day and wanted to give her the benefit of the doubt. After all, I had screened every application that had come across my desk and picked the best of the best. If she flaked out, it wasn't just a strike against her. I would have to rethink my entire hiring process.

I headed out of the building, stepping outside in the warm air and actually looking forward to my morning stroll. Really, my offering to go get her was as much for me as it was for her. I was happy to get outside for a bit before I had to spend a long day in meetings inside the walls of my office.

I walked faster than usual, wanting to get to the café before my wayward intern could wander off and really get herself lost in the city. I rounded the corner, my eyes scanning the wide sidewalk. The café was on the opposite end of the block. I made my way to the tables, my eyes scanning the people at each one. There was a woman in a white shirt and black pants sitting at a table with her back to me. Her long blonde hair was hanging over the back of the chair. I assumed it had to be her and walked to the table. The moment I saw her face, my mouth dropped.

It was the woman from the bar. She was wearing sunglasses, hiding the eyes I knew were green. She looked up at me, and only then did I realize I was staring at her. "I'm Adrian, from Great Greeks," I said.

She pushed her sunglasses up and looked into my eyes. I thought I saw a hint of recognition but couldn't be sure. "Thank god," she said with a smile. "Thank you so much for coming."

I stood there staring at her like an idiot. She was gorgeous. Last night, the brief glimpse I had gotten of her had not been enough. Seeing her in the bright sunshine, her eyes bright and a healthy glow about her, was a totally different experience. She looked like a swimsuit model, minus the swimsuit.

I realized I was making things awkward and offered her a smile. "It's no problem. If you don't mind, I'm going to order a drink."

She smiled and shook her head. "I'm already late. I suppose another few minutes won't hurt."

CHAPTER 6

BELLA

Holy Greek god. If this was the kind of people I was going to be working with, I was going to have a hard time focusing on work. The man was a walking advertisement for Greece. If the women in the United States knew these were the kind of men roaming in the streets in Heraklion, there would be a mass exodus. I wanted to have his babies. No! That was crazy. I knew better than to judge a book by its cover, but holy shit! It was one hell of a cover.

I watched as the tall man, clearly a direct descendant of one of those Greek gods I had read about in middle school, walked inside the café to order his drink. His ass was fine, firm, and I could practically feel the flesh in my hands. His chest was broad, his shoulders wide, and although I couldn't see the muscles through the long-sleeved button-up shirt he was wearing, I knew they would be there. His shirt had three buttons left open at the top, just enough to give me a tease of tanned flesh with a tiny sprinkling of black hair. He was crazy tall. He was the kind of man everyone noticed when he walked into a room. It was hard not to stare.

He returned a minute later. I grabbed my purse and laptop case and got to my feet, expecting him to be in a rush to get back to the office. He pulled out the other chair at the table and sat down.

"Let's sit for a minute," he said easily.

"What? Really? Shouldn't we be getting to work?"

He shrugged a big shoulder before pushing up his dark glasses to reveal the prettiest set of light blue eyes I had ever seen. They were nearly crystal clear, popping out against his tanned face. I pushed up my own glasses, not wanting to be rude.

"We've got some time," he said. "No one will mind."

I leaned back in my chair and rambled. "I cannot believe I got lost. I feel like such an idiot. The boss is going to think he made a mistake in choosing me for the job. I swear, I'm not usually such an airhead."

He smiled, his teeth white and straight adding to the total package that was him. "I think it will be okay. Mistakes happen."

I grimaced. "He's probably going to fire me before I ever get started."

"Is this your first time to Greece?" he asked casually, as if he was in no hurry to get back to work.

I nodded. "It is my first time anywhere. I've never been away from home. I mean, I took a couple of vacations with my dad, but those were places a few hours from home. I've never been on a plane, left the Pacific Northwest, or done anything like this."

"This must be pretty overwhelming for you," he said, sipping on the dark coffee.

His English was impeccable. There was a trace of an accent but not overly so. "What about you? Are you from here?"

He grinned. "I am. My family lives in Sitia. It's where I grew up."

"Wow. I've read about that place. It looked beautiful in the pictures." I tried to imagine what it would be like to live in such a gorgeous area.

"It is nice. Have you been in Greece long?"

I shook my head. "No. I got in late Saturday night. I spent a couple of hours out yesterday but only went to a local bar and down to the beach. I slept in late, and I should have gotten up and walked the route from the hotel to the office. I feel so ridiculous. The boss is going to hate me. I hate making a bad first impression."

"I know the boss pretty well," he said, a twinkle in his eye. "I think he'll understand. I personally think he's a pretty easy-going guy and gives second chances."

"I hope so. My dad is going to kill me when I tell him what I did." I dreaded the recap of my first day on the job—assuming I had a job at all.

"Why don't we grab some breakfast? I didn't have time to eat this morning." He reached a hand in the air and signaled a waitress.

"Breakfast! We can't eat breakfast! We have to get to work!" I screeched.

"Relax. We have plenty of time. It's just the boring orientation stuff anyway. Trust me. You aren't missing anything exciting."

I wasn't sure what to think about the guy. Maybe he was my competition for a permanent position in the company, and he was trying to set me up for failure. He didn't seem like he was manipulative, but that was how manipulative people got by. They were wolves in sheep's clothing. That was what my dad would say. I sat there feeling anxious and nervous while he ordered in Greek.

"Can we make this quick? I understand you don't mind being late, but this is really going against everything I have ever known. I'm always early, and I would have been today if I hadn't gotten all twisted around. I'm not the kind of person that shows up fashionably late. I hate that." I grimaced.

"We'll eat fast. It's always better to go to work on a full stomach. Breakfast is the most important meal of the day, or at least that's what my mother always said."

He had a sexy grin that probably melted the panties off most women. My panties were made of sterner stuff than that. I was in Greece to work, not have a fling, I reminded myself.

"Fine, but will you please let the boss know why I am super late? I don't want him to think I stalled on purpose."

"I will do that. So, what's it like where you are from?" He spoke as if we had all the time in the world to get to know each other.

I didn't want to be rude, and the guy might be my only ally, or my worst enemy. It really could go either way. "Well, it was nothing like this. There are mountains and a lot of open land. We're nowhere near a beach."

"Did you live in a large city?"

I shook my head. "No, definitely not. There are lots of small towns. The town I lived in, technically I think I still live there, had a population of under two thousand."

His eyes went wide. "Really?"

I smiled, thinking of home. "Really. I commuted to college. I had to live at home to save money."

"I see. Did you get to have fun in college? Isn't that the time we're supposed to be free, party, and make lots of mistakes that we could look back on with a combination of regret and fondness?"

I giggled. "Not me. I didn't have time for regrets. I was on a scholarship and couldn't afford to have my grades slip even a little. I worked my ass—sorry—butt off to make sure I graduated at the top of my class."

"Don't Americans go on spring break holidays and get wild and crazy?" he asked with a grin.

I shook my head again. "Not this American. The school was kind of small, and it wasn't the kind of school that attracted a lot of wealthy kids. Only wealthy kids can afford to go to Cancun or some other beach for a wild vacation. I worked and studied. I had no time for much of anything else."

He looked pained. "And now you're here because of that hard work."

"I suppose so, yes. I graduated a couple of months ago, and here I am."

"What have you been doing between graduation and now?" he asked.

I thought about it. "Working and getting ready to come here."

He laughed. "You have to enjoy your time while you are here. Greece is a beautiful place to visit. There is so much history and culture for you to take in. Promise me you won't be all work and no play. I can show you around, take you to some of the sites that are worth seeing."

"I'd like that, thank you. I do want to see as much as I can, but I also really want to impress the boss. I'm sure I'm going to be very busy working on projects after I leave the office. I don't mind putting in the hard work if it will pay off in the future." I meant every word.

He offered me a smile. Our breakfasts were delivered, and I was immediately starving. I stared at the assortment of fruits and yogurt, along with a variety of pastries.

"I wasn't sure what you liked," he said by way of explanation.

I smiled, shaking my head. "It all looks amazing, but this is a lot of food."

"Ah, trust me. It isn't all that much. We can take the pastries with us." He grabbed a fork and stabbed a piece of melon before popping it in his mouth.

I followed suit, taking a few bites of the fruit and letting the flavors explode in my mouth. We ate and chatted a bit more about the places I had to check out and talked about getting together on the weekend. Once most of the food was gone, he finally made a move to leave. I quickly got to my feet, anxious to get to work and praying like hell I wasn't going to be fired before I ever got started.

As we walked to the office, I paid close attention to the route. If I got another chance tomorrow, I wasn't going to blow it by being late again. I would leave two hours early, just in case I got twisted around again.

"This is our building," he said, pulling open a door and letting me go in first.

The cool air washed over me as I looked around the wide-open lobby. It was then I realized the company I was interning for owned or leased the entire building. "Oh, I didn't realize this was all for Great Greeks."

He chuckled. "We have four floors. The top three floors are leased out to other businesses."

I nodded, in awe of the modern building. I had seen so many old buildings, I had just assumed the entire city was at least two-hundred years old. We rode the elevator up in silence. My nerves were kicking in as the doors slid open. I followed him down a long hallway. There was a conference room on my right. Large windows gave me a good view of three people sitting down, while a man spoke at the front of the room.

Adrian pushed open the door, and all talk ceased. The man at the front of the room made a big show of looking at his watch and then me. There was an obvious scowl on his face as he turned his attention to Adrian. "Glad to see you could make it," he said dryly.

Adrian looked at me and smiled. "Go ahead and take a seat at the table."

I nodded, feeling about two inches tall as I pulled out a chair, leaving a couple of empty chairs between myself and the others, and sat down. Adrian moved to the front of the room, looking at the scowling man.

"Good morning, everyone. My name is Adrian Gabris. I'm the CEO and President of Great Greeks. Thank you for coming in today. I'm looking forward to a great few weeks." His eyes met mine.

I could practically feel my jaw resting on the table, convinced drool was likely leaking out. I clamped my teeth together, making sure my mouth wasn't hanging open as I stared at the man I had just had breakfast with. He was the owner? He was the boss? Oh shit. I had really made an ass of myself, and he'd done nothing to stop me. I wanted to evaporate into thin air and teleport back home. I couldn't believe how badly I had managed to screw this thing up. My dad was going to lose his shit when I told him what I had done. Years of hard work had all gone up in flames, right alongside my dignity. I seriously debated picking up my things and walking right back out the door. I hoped like hell he hadn't brought me into the conference room just to make an example of me before he fired me in front of the others. I would die. I would absolutely die of humiliation.

CHAPTER 7

ADRIAN

With the orientation out of the way and the interns delivered to their joint working space, I headed to my office. Rand was hot on my heels. I knew he was going to question me about why I had taken so long. When I had left to fetch our lost intern, I hadn't intended on being gone so long. It just kind of happened.

I did my best to make him forget all about it by distracting him. Fortunately for me, he wasn't in his best shape, and I didn't think it would be all that hard to get him onto something else entirely. "I think we've got a good group, don't you?"

He shrugged a shoulder. "Hard to tell from looking at them."

We both nodded as we passed someone from accounting. "I meant they seemed attentive and they all seemed to have a good idea about what we expect from them."

"I suppose," he protested.

My attempts to distract him weren't working. He was going to say what he had to say, no matter what. I was glad he was going to wait until we made it back to my office. I didn't need everyone seeing him talk to me like a friend instead of the boss I technically was to him. I moved into the office, staring out the windows at the sprawling city around me. It was a good view, but the view of the sea was blocked by some of the other taller buildings.

When I turned to look at him, he had his hands on his hips and was staring at me. Nope, he definitely hadn't forgotten. I sighed, knowing there was no way around it, and I prepared to take my lecture.

"What?" I asked, feigning innocence.

"What the hell took you so long?" he snapped.

I shrugged. "We had breakfast."

His mouth dropped open. "You had breakfast?" he asked. "That's it? Just breakfast? Bullshit. I saw her. I saw the way you two were looking at each other."

I frowned at him. "We weren't looking at each other in any way," I argued.

He shook his head. "Bullshit. Did she give you a little thank you for going to pick her up? Did she try and smooth things over with the boss?"

"Shut up. Don't be a dick."

"You were gone for almost an hour. You were doing more than eating breakfast."

"You're wrong, and I don't appreciate the insinuation," I growled.

He stared at me. "Really? A woman who looks like that, and you didn't try anything?"

"No, I didn't try anything. She works here. She's an intern."

"Why?" he asked. "Why would you keep her on if she can't even find her way here? How hard is it to pull out a GPS app and find us? It sounds like a pretty lame excuse to me."

"It was the truth. She was lost, and she felt bad about it."

"Why are you keeping her on?" he asked again. "Those other three are smart and are going to be excellent employees, and they all made it on time."

"Because there's something about Bella that I think is worth giving her a chance. She's smart and driven, and I know she is going to be a hard worker as well."

"You're letting her looks sway you," he said. "We always said we would never let that shit happen here. Don't start now."

I sat down in my chair, ignoring his accusations. "It has nothing to do with her looks. My gut instincts have gotten us this far. Trust me. She's worth keeping around."

He shook his head, running a hand through his hair. "She's going to be the downfall of this company. I can see it now. You're thinking with your dick instead of your brain."

"I'm not going to say it again. It's my decision. You're being a dick. I'm going to let it slide because I know you're hungover and probably feel like hell, but she stays until she proves her position here isn't going to work out. I'm giving her a shot."

Rand was my right hand, but ultimately, the company was mine. I was the boss. He worked for me, and I wasn't going to let his assumptions push what I had a feeling was going to be a very good employee right out the door. I liked her fresh view of things. I liked that she worked hard and studied hard to put herself through school. The other interns were all from families that had influence. They did well in school, and each of them brought a little something different to the table, but there was something about Bella that none of them had. She offered a glimpse into a demographic I didn't think we'd really touched on yet. I wanted to expand and grow, and that meant finding new ways to reach new people.

"I hope you're right, but the way I see it, she's going to be the one thing that brings you to your knees and takes the company down with it," he mumbled.

There was a sharp intake of breath. Rand spun around. I moved to the side to see who it was and cringed when I saw Bella's red face. She'd heard what he had said.

"Do you need something?" Rand asked in a tone I thought was very unfriendly.

Bella's little chin went up as she took a step inside my office, her eyes locked on Rand. "Yes, I need to speak with Adrian, if he has a minute. However, first, I'd like to assure you I will not be the downfall of your company. Nor will I bring Adrian—I mean, Mr. Gabris—to his knees. I was late. I got lost. I've apologized. I really don't know what else I can say. I'm not sure how that could possibly bring down a billion-dollar business, but if that's all it takes to do so, I would think you might need to get on more solid footing before you bring on any more interns."

I couldn't stop smiling. She was not a woman to be pushed around. That made me very happy and proved she was exactly what we needed in the company. Rand turned to look at me, one eyebrow raised before he turned back to face Bella.

"You might be all right after all," he said before walking past her and out the door.

Her eyes met mine. "I'm sorry. I shouldn't have talked like that."

"It's fine. You had a right to defend yourself. Please call me Adrian. I ask that everyone does. It feels weird to be called my dad's name. What did you need to talk to me about?"

"I just wanted to come by and tell you how sorry I am for not only being late but for mistaking you for another intern or employee. I had no idea you were *the* Adrian. I feel foolish, and I am absolutely embarrassed about what I said." Her hands twisted in front of her.

I shrugged a shoulder. "It's okay. I'm glad we got to meet the way we did. It gave me a chance to see the real you and not the person meeting the CEO."

She smiled, shaking her head. "I still can't believe I did that. I really am sorry."

"Listen, you got off to a bad start. We all have those days. I just need two things from you." I looked her in the eyes.

"What would that be?"

I held up a finger. "One, get your work done on time and make sure it's good."

She bobbed her head up and down. "Absolutely. I can do that. I swear I'm good at what I do, and I'm never late. I don't miss deadlines."

"Good. That is very good to hear. The second thing I need you to do is have some fun while you are here. Enjoy the city and the beaches and everything else we have to offer. Don't spend all your time locked down in the hotel room or here with your nose buried in a computer screen. Make this a trip you won't soon forget. Make memories that will last."

She wrinkled her nose. "You're my boss. Shouldn't you be asking me to focus and work hard?"

I smiled, appreciating her stalwart dedication. "Yes, and I am, but I also don't want to ruin this for you. It sounds like you are due some downtime. I don't think it gets much better than the beach to get in some relaxation. I'm serious. Leave the laptop at home, and take it all in."

"Thank you. I really do appreciate that, and I promise what happened today won't happen again. I will be early from here on out. If you need me to stay late or work weekends, I'll do it."

I sighed. Clearly, she had ignored my second stipulation. "I'll keep that in mind, but I don't like to work every single day of the week. If I'm not here, you don't need to be here."

"Thank you again for this amazing opportunity," she said. "I promise I will not let you down, and I will not make you regret giving me a chance. I'll show the other guy too."

I laughed. "Rand is usually a lot more relaxed than what he is right now. He had a bit of a rough night. Don't take what he said too personally."

She frowned, looking very displeased. "It was hard not to take that personal. It was pretty snarky."

"It was, and I apologize for his behavior."

"It's fine. I should go. I need to get started on that assignment. I don't want to be late." She grinned.

"Thank you. I appreciate that. Bella, I'd like to think we run a friendly operation here. I don't want you to feel like you can't come to myself or even Rand if you have a question or a problem. We are here to help."

"I'll remember that. Thanks again, for everything, breakfast, saving me, and letting me keep my job for the time being." She turned around and walked out the door.

I couldn't help but admire her pretty ass in those pants. I liked that she had taken the initiative and dressed nicely. The other female intern had worn jeans, as did the two young men. While I didn't mind casual, I did appreciate someone who knew the importance of dressing the part of a professional. Bella was different. I realized I'd already made that observation, but now I knew it to be true. I had a feeling she was going to be something special. Rand had been wrong about her bringing the company to its knees, but he may not have been wrong about her bringing me to my knees. I was already ready to grovel at her feet for another one of those pretty smiles.

CHAPTER 8

BELLA

I'd had jobs in the past, but none of them came close to comparing to this one. At my previous jobs, the first few days had been boring and all about learning the ins and out, taking tours, talking about safety and what went where and so forth. Not here. Here, I felt like the gunshot had just gone off at the starting line, and it was a race to see who could make it across the finish line first. With my late start, I felt light years behind the other interns.

My cubicle was bare, minus the company laptop, a cup for pens, and a small scratchpad with the company letterhead. I put my purse and personal laptop under the desk and flopped the binder full of paperwork that needed to be completed, manuals, and various other information that needed to be gone through on the small end of the desk.

We already had our own list of tasks that needed to be done within the next few days. I couldn't help but think I had bitten off far more than I could chew. I was overwhelmed. I felt like I was drowning with no one around to throw me a life preserver.

"Hi!" a cheery female voice said.

I looked up and found pretty brown eyes with dark, sculpted

eyebrows staring at me over the wall of my cubicle. "Hi," I said, wondering why the woman didn't just walk around.

"Can I come in?" she asked with a grin.

I giggled at her obvious joke about our lack of offices. "Please do."

When she came around the edge of the cubicle wall, I got my first glimpse of her. She was petite and pretty, and her curly, dark hair made me think she was a native.

"I'm Cassia Soter," she said, extending one small hand.

I took it and gave it a shake. "I'm Bella Kamp."

"You're American?"

"I am," I said with a laugh. "What gave it away?"

"I love your accent."

I found it funny that the people I had met felt like I had an accent when I felt the exact way about them. "Thank you. I like your accent as well." I giggled.

"Today is your first day, which means you must be one of the interns Adrian hired."

"That obvious, huh?" I asked, wrinkling my nose.

She shrugged a shoulder. "Not so obvious, but this workstation is kind of where the temps sit."

"I guess as an intern, I shouldn't expect anything permanent," I said with a sigh, knowing I should feel lucky I was given a desk at all after my start to the day.

"Actually, I have a little confession," she whispered.

That scared me. "Oh?"

"I knew you were Bella. I'm going to be training you, showing you the ropes, and all that stuff. If you have any questions, just ask."

I smiled. "Thanks. I thought I was being tossed into the deep end with no one there to save me."

"Nope. You have me. I'm your shadow for the next few days, or longer if you need."

I relaxed and turned on the company laptop, taking a seat in the provided chair and waiting for it to boot up. "Okay, let me enter in my password," I mumbled, flipping open the binder I had been given and quickly typing in the username and password I had been issued.

Cassia put her hand on the laptop and gently closed it. "Not right now."

I looked up at her and then at the other interns, who were already on their computers with their shadows behind them. I didn't understand why Cassia was telling me not to start on the assignment, which included reviewing a potential client file and coming up with a unique pitch.

"Shouldn't we be getting started on creating my company profile?" I asked nervously.

She squished up her nose. "That is too easy and boring. You are going to have plenty of time to sit in this tiny little cubicle and work on the computer. Let's go for a tour. You'll need to know where the break room is, the bathrooms, and things like that."

I grimaced, not wanting to argue with my shadow, but also not wanting to be waylaid. I hated not being done first with my work. I was used to being the student or employee who was always on the top because I did nothing but what I was told. She was trying to pull me out of my comfort zone, and that freaked me out.

I didn't get up from the chair, looking at the closed laptop and then up at Cassia, who was smiling at me. "All right, um, how long do you think this will take?" I asked, already planning to skip lunch.

She giggled softly. "Adrian was right about you."

My eyes widened. "Right about what?" I asked, slightly panicked.

"He said you were going to be one of those people who worked right through lunch. You'd be here before everyone and long after everyone went home. He told me to show you around, help you loosen up a little more, and let you settle in. He said he knows your type, and you will feel more relaxed when you have your—I think he said—bearings?" She said the word as if it were the wrong one.

I grinned and nodded. "Yes, bearings, and maybe he's right a little. I got lost this morning and didn't have time to come in early and get a feel for the place. I've been to the conference room and here. I'll probably get lost just trying to get out of the building."

My dad had always told me I wouldn't be able to find my way out of a wet paper bag. I was beginning to think he was right.

"All right, shall we go?" she asked.

I felt a little better about leaving the cubicle. Adrian had personally asked her to show me around. That made me feel valued. Or he'd asked Cassia to show me around because he didn't want to have to come and rescue me again.

I followed her around the fourth floor where the main offices for the company were kept. When someone wasn't on the phone, she would pop her head in and introduce me. I met a lot of people and remembered almost no names. I was focused on remembering where the bathroom and breakroom were and the exits.

"How long have you worked here?" I asked Cassia as we leisurely strolled down a hallway lined with various framed awards and magazine covers the company had earned.

"I've been here two years now. I was hired back when things were really just starting to take off."

I caught a glimpse of her profile and was trying to guess how old she was. Her skin was very youthful and could have passed for a teenager, but she sounded and acted a little older. I was guessing my age or maybe a couple of years older. Everyone we encountered seemed to like her. They all had little tidbits of personal information to talk with her about. Asking about her cat or what she did over the weekend and stuff like that.

"It feels like a really good environment to work in," I told her.

She smiled and nodded her head. "It is. It isn't stuffy, but it isn't so relaxed that people are running around slapping each other on the ass."

I gasped. "What?"

Her light laugh filled my ears. "I forget you're American. We tend to be a little more relaxed. There is a code, but we're not so worried about offending people. If you do feel like someone is saying things you don't like or that are really inappropriate, you can tell me or Adrian."

"Thank you. I appreciate that. I'm sure things will be fine. I can handle myself pretty well." I did not want to be the squeaky wheel in a company that seemed to be running very smoothly.

"Adrian tells me this is your first time to Crete," she said conversationally.

I nodded. "It's my first time anywhere."

"When did you arrive?"

"Saturday night," I answered.

"No way!" she said excitedly. "You haven't been out to any of the clubs or the beaches yet?"

Cassia had a very outgoing, exuberant personality. I imagined it would be impossible to hate her. She had a way of making everything sound exciting and appealing. Even our tour of the building had been more like a grand adventure than a bland, standard orientation tour.

"I haven't. I do plan on getting to the beach after work or maybe this weekend. I'm not really into the club scene though." I hoped she didn't take it wrong.

She grinned. "You don't have to be into it. Maybe you've never been to one of our clubs."

"I have not, you're right," I agreed.

"Every Tuesday, most of us go out for drinks," she said, eyeing me up and down.

"Oh?" I asked.

"Yes, and you have to come. It will be a great way for you to meet everyone, and you'll get to see one of our favorite hangout spots. It's a great place to have a good drink and unwind without all the teenagers hitting on you." She winked.

I laughed. "Funny you should say that. My one and only visit to a bar here and that's exactly what happened."

"You stick with me, and I will show you a good time," she said.

"What kind of place is this? I mean, what do people wear to bars or clubs here?" I asked, cataloging the suitcase I had packed and not coming up with anything that would be suitable for any of the clubs I had been to back home.

She shrugged a shoulder. "I don't know. Just a place to have some fun. I have a dress that will fit you. I'll bring it tomorrow."

I shook my head, looking at her body and determining I was several inches taller than her. We were about the same size in other areas, but I was taller. "You don't have to do that. I can wear what I wear to work."

She turned up her nose. "No, you can't. Not to a club. You'll look like our grandmother. Dress up and let loose. No one knows you here. You can be anyone you want to be. That's thrilling! I wish for that kind of anonymity. Where I grew up, everyone knows me or my brothers. It all gets back to them. You can be free!" She squealed, raising her hands in the air and shaking her head.

I laughed. "I don't know much about being free."

"I'm going to teach you. I want to live through you."

"We'll see," I said, not making any firm commitment.

She was nodding, leaning back and studying my figure a little too closely for comfort. I felt naked under her stare. "I have the perfect dress for you."

I had no idea what that meant. "Thanks."

"Now that we've had our grand tour, let's head back and get you busy. We can't slack off all day." She grinned to show she was teasing.

I followed her back, both anxious and nervous about work and her plans for tomorrow. Part of me wanted to back out and make up some excuse about why I couldn't make it. The other part of me knew I was only going to be in Greece for a short time, and I wanted to try and have as much fun as I could. People like me didn't get these chances often. I had to make the most of it. I wanted to tell my dad I went out clubbing and had a great time with new friends. I couldn't lie to him, which meant I had to actually do it. I could put on a dress and shake my ass for a couple of hours if that was what it took to fit in and blow off a little steam with my coworkers. I was twenty-three after all, not ninety.

CHAPTER 9

ADRIAN

I stared at the man across from me, trying to size him up. I met with potential clients all day long. Usually, I went to their places of business to try and convince them they wanted my services. With the growth and success of the company, the tables were slowly turning, and now I had people lining up to get a meeting with me. It was definitely a good sign and one I was happy to see. However, I had to be careful about the jobs I took on. One bad decision could cause everything I had built to crumble to the ground. Word of mouth was important, and if I failed to please one client, he was going to shout it from the rooftops.

The reason I had been successful with few hiccups on my journey to the top was that I made it a point to learn from the mistakes I saw other social media platforms making. I took what they did, tweaked what worked, and made it my own, while avoiding the mistakes that had been made along the way. Social media could be a brand's biggest asset or biggest enemy, depending on who was minding the store, so to speak. One wrong word, one wrong hashtag, bad timing, or anything else could cause a campaign to explode in the worst way. Listening to the man pitching his ideas about what he wanted, I knew his pitch would be one of those that exploded in the worst way.

I shook my head, rubbing my jaw and reviewing the paperwork the man had brought me. "I'm not sure this proposal, as it is written, is a good fit for my company," I said, trying to be diplomatic and not offend the guy, but I didn't want his business. It wasn't something I wanted my name attached to as it was written.

He shrugged a shoulder. "I don't see the problem. It's a site meant to connect travelers with other travelers. They can share their experiences and talk about hits and misses. I want a section where people can meet up with one another to possibly share travel expenses or rent homes, boats, planes, whatever."

I grimaced. "It sounds great in theory, but what happens if someone joins your site, finds a single woman traveling alone, and takes advantage of the situation? Your site, and ultimately my company, could be held liable if something were to happen to the innocent, young woman." I was already picturing the headlines.

He scoffed. "That's a very unlikely possibility. There are plenty of other places someone could search for a single woman to take advantage of."

"Maybe, maybe not. Look at the recent problems with some of those ride services. They are being sued left and right. I'm only looking out for your best interests." I was trying to make him see the light.

He wasn't going to give up. I could see the determination in his eyes. "This is a good one. I can feel it. This could be the thing young people need. They all want to see the world, but few of them can afford to do it. The app will connect those with shared interests, and they can split travel costs ten ways. It will work."

I sighed, understanding his vision and his passion, but knowing the project wasn't ready. "Look, Curt, this is a great idea. This is something young people from all around the world could really use and enjoy. I think it's awesome that you want to try and help people see the world. I think it would do a lot for society in general if people could see and experience new cultures. However, with all of that said, this proposal is missing something. I don't know what that something is, but I think there is something here. We just have to find it."

The guy didn't look happy. I wasn't a fool, and I wasn't about to turn down what could be a very lucrative account, but I needed some time. I didn't want him walking out the door and heading down the proverbial street to my competition.

"You think you have what it takes to find what's missing?" he asked.

I nodded. "I have a great team of developers and some of the best and brightest in the business. I'll have a few of my people look it over and come up with some solutions. I'll present them to you, and you can decide if you want to move forward with us or take it somewhere else. You've got something great here, and I'd really like to see it succeed, but in the wrong hands, it could become a PR nightmare."

He chuckled. "Are you saying your hands are the right ones?"

I grinned. "I'm saying my hands are very capable, and I have a long list of happy customers who've been very happy with our work. You don't get my reputation as being the best social marketing firm in the business by not paying attention to the details. It's the details that matter, and that's what you pay me to pay attention to."

"You sure know how to charm a guy, don't you?" he asked with a smile.

I leaned back in my chair, completely comfortable with my ability to talk to a client, knowing I could generally use that charm to make a successful deal. "I know what works, and I know what a client really needs. The charm is just a little something extra."

He laughed again. "All right. When will I hear back from you? As you can imagine, you're not the only game in town, and I'm determined to get this thing off the ground."

"I'm going to ask you for a few days, maybe a week. I think you'd rather have a great app than an app that could bankrupt you." I was not afraid to pull any punches.

"Ouch. Harsh."

"Truth," I replied.

"Okay, I'll wait and see what you have to say," he said, getting to his feet.

I got up and walked out of the office with him. We talked about our plans for the weekend as we walked. I pushed the button for the elevator and nodded goodbye with the promise to be in touch soon. I turned around, already planning to give the project to my new interns and my existing research department. I wanted to see what they could come up with. If we could collectively come up with solutions to the many problems I saw with the service, it could work out very well for all parties involved.

I started walking down the hall, heading for the breakroom to grab a cold glass of water, when I was nearly knocked on my ass by Bella. "Woah, there," I said, putting my hands on her shoulders to stop her from mowing me down.

She had been looking in the opposite direction while moving toward me. I had no time to get out of her way.

"Oh my gosh! I'm so sorry! I wasn't paying attention to where I was going!" Her face turned a pretty pink color.

"It's okay," I said, dropping my hands from her arms.

"I, uh, I was headed to Cassia's office," she said, looking behind her and then toward the hall she'd just come from.

I grinned. "Are you sure about that?"

She nodded. "I am."

"Bella?"

"Yes?"

"You are nowhere near her office."

She groaned, leaning her head back to look up at the ceiling. "I'm so lost. I took a wrong turn. There are a lot of hallways. I had to go downstairs to accounting, and that really got me screwed up. I must have walked in circles for thirty minutes before I finally asked for help. Then, I got back here, but they put me on a different elevator. I ended up somewhere over by a window that overlooked the wrong street. I mean, it's the right street, but not the same street I was using as my reference with the big fountain in the center of a courtyard. And now I'm all twisted around again." She rambled, her frustration evident in her voice.

I smiled, fighting the urge to touch her arm again in an attempt to calm her down. Her green eyes were fraught with worry. It was a look

I was growing used to seeing on her face. She was high-strung and really needed to relax a bit. I understood the difficulties of a new job in a new country, but she was going to worry herself to death if she kept going the way she was.

"I will show you the way back to Cassia's office, but for your own sake, you really need to learn your way around," I said gently.

She scowled. "I know that, and I am trying. It's just the way I've always been. I don't know why, but no matter how hard I try, I get absolutely confused. I lived in a small town, the same town my entire life, and I still managed to get lost at times."

I had to fight back a laugh. She was so cute when she was frustrated. I wanted to wrap her up in my arms and take all her stress away. "I'm sorry. I didn't mean to imply you weren't trying."

She closed her eyes, using a finger to rub her temple through what looked like silky, blonde hair begging to be touched. "I'm sorry. I'm a little overwhelmed. I have to get this back to Cassia, and I have that campaign to go over and make notes on, and I'm stuck here roaming the halls like an idiot."

"You're not an idiot," I quickly replied.

She shook her head. "I swear I'm not that incompetent. I'm just out of sorts. Once I get my bearings, I won't be like this. Please don't think this is how I normally am. It's just the jet lag, a new job, trying to get around a new city and—"

I cut her off. She was unraveling before my very eyes. I didn't want her to fall apart before she could give the job her best shot. I knew she had it in her, but she needed a little encouragement. I had a feeling she was the type that would never forgive herself if she quit before she got started. I felt I owed it to her to give her that little pick-me-up she needed to get over the hump. I was convinced that was all it was. She just needed to find her footing, and then she was going to do great things—I hoped.

"Stop," I said, my voice low. "Come with me."

"Where?" she asked as I started back toward the elevator.

I didn't answer her. I wasn't sure what I was doing, but it felt right. Rand's warning echoed through my head as I stopped in front of the elevator and waited for her to catch up. I tended to forget my long legs covered a lot more ground than most people, especially when I was on a mission. I was absolutely certain he was wrong about her bringing the company down, but if I let her in too close, she would have the power to destroy me. There was something about her, a pull I couldn't quite resist, that made me feel like she had cast a spell on me. I just hoped I would be strong enough to keep my wits about me.

CHAPTER 10

BELLA

Standing in front of the elevator was making me even more nervous. Was he showing me the door? If so, I wanted to grab my purse. I had left my laptop at the hotel, realizing I would have no use for it here. My purse was a different story. My mind raced, thinking of the many different ways he could fire me.

He stepped inside the elevator, his crystal-blue eyes meeting mine. "Come on, please."

I nodded my head, fighting back the tears that were trying to fall. I wouldn't cry. I would hold my head high. "I appreciate the chance to work here, even for a day," I told him, wanting to make my exit with as much grace as I could muster.

"You're welcome. When you are feeling overwhelmed and like the walls are closing in on you, enter this code. One-three-seven-nine." He was punching the buttons as he spoke.

I looked at him. "What?"

"Enter that code, got it?" he asked.

"One, three, seven, nine," I repeated. "Where does that make the elevator go?"

"Watch, and I'll show you," he said with a smile as the doors slid closed.

My heart raced, panic setting in as I imagined him taking me into a basement where no one could hear my screams. My dad would be devastated if I were murdered or kidnapped and made into the man's sex slave! How stupid! How dumb was I to get into an elevator with a stranger—even if he was my boss?! The elevator jerked and started going up. My eyes went wide, and new horrors flooded my very overactive brain. Was he going to throw me off the roof?

"If you could see the expression on your face right now," he said with a grin, shaking his head.

His grin put me at ease. My gut intuition said he was safe. He wasn't going to throw me off the roof or lock me in a cage in his basement. "I tend to have a very vivid imagination," I confessed.

"I see," he said. "That will definitely come in handy in this line of work. It is one of the reasons I hired you in the first place. I saw some of the marketing campaigns you put together for your mock businesses."

The elevator dinged again, and the doors slid open. He stepped out and climbed the six stairs that took us to the rooftop.

"The roof?" I asked, not sure why the roof was any better than going downstairs to the sidewalk floor and getting fresh air.

"Yes, the roof. Come with me. I hope you're not afraid of heights," he said as an afterthought.

"I don't think I am," I mumbled, trying to remember a time I had ever been on the roof of a tall building. I couldn't remember because it had never happened.

"This is where I come when I'm feeling a little overwhelmed and need to get away from the ringing phones and people in general. I come up here." He stopped about five feet from the edge and pointed.

I looked out, the beach and the sea stretching out forever. The height was just enough to see over the other rooftops. A slight breeze kicked up, blowing my hair across my face. I quickly pushed it out of the way and stared. We both stood in silence, taking in the view. I did feel exceptionally better. The nervous energy I had been feeling, along with the stress and fear of failure, evaporated and floated away on the breeze.

"Wow," I finally breathed out the word.

He turned to look at me, a warm smile on his face. "Wow is right. This is my little secret and now yours."

"Really?" I asked with surprise.

He nodded his head. "Yep. You and I have the code. That's it. Well, Rand does, but he's afraid of heights, and the only way he is coming up here is if there is a zombie chasing him up the stairs."

I burst into laughter, appreciating his humorous side. "Good to know. If he's giving me a hard time, I'll come up here to get away from him."

"He won't give you a hard time. If he does, let me know. I promise, Rand is a good guy."

"I'm sorry," I said, realizing I had gotten a little too relaxed and insulted his coworker and obvious friend.

"Don't be sorry," he said, his tone serious. "Never be sorry for telling me how you feel. We may not always agree, but I need you to always be honest. When it comes time to start hashing out some marketing campaigns and strategies, I need people who will speak their mind without worrying about upsetting me or some of the other senior staff."

"I don't usually have a problem speaking my mind," I quipped.

He chuckled. "That could be a good thing."

I let out a long breath, letting the remaining bits of stress leave my body. "Thank you for bringing me up here. I can really get myself worked up sometimes."

"It's fine. I could kind of tell you were about to lose your shit." He laughed.

I burst into a fit of giggles at his choice of words. It was very American and very much something my dad would have said. "I was. I will admit it. I've been wound tight for weeks and getting lost again today was just the final straw. I was working up until the day before I left, taking extra shifts and trying to get everything ready for my time away from home. I swear I've been frazzled for a month. Before that, it was school and finals and just so much."

"I think you really need to take the weekend to relax," he advised.

I smiled and nodded my head in agreement. "I will do that. Actually, Cassia invited me out tonight. She said it's something a bunch of people from the office do every Tuesday. Do you go?"

He shook his head. "No, not really. I usually work late. Plus, no one wants to hang out with the boss. I want my people to be able to relax and have a good time without worrying about me watching them. I know there are going to be things that they need to get off their chest about me, the work, and, in general, they wouldn't be able to say those things if I'm standing there listening."

I wrinkled my nose, realizing he was right. I had been foolish to think a man like Adrian would want to hang out with interns and his employees. I was sure he probably had some model girlfriend that required his full attention.

"I understand. That's very thoughtful of you."

He shrugged a shoulder. "I wasn't always the boss. I know what it's like to bust your ass for someone else and not feel appreciated. I do try and be a good boss and let my people know how valuable they are, but no one is perfect."

"How long have you been the boss?" I asked him.

He inhaled through his nose, his eyes moving toward the spectacular view. "I feel like I've been working on this for ten years. It didn't officially become a company until maybe five years ago. Back then, it was me and Rand. It was three years ago things really started to take off, and we just kind of burst onto the social media marketing scene. Back in the beginning, it was me and Rand posting on the various social networking sites all day long. Now, we have our own platform and a slew of services. I don't think I've personally posted anything in at least a year."

"That's pretty impressive. Do you mind if I ask how old you are?"

He grinned, winking at me. "How old do you think I am?"

I groaned. "That's a dangerous question."

"The dangerous part is the answer," he said with a laugh.

I chewed my bottom lip. Guessing he was older than he actually was wasn't as big a deal for a man as it was for a woman. I threw caution to the wind and went with what I suspected. "Thirty? Thirty-two?"

He frowned. "No, I'm twenty-eight. Maybe I should take my own advice and relax a little. I don't want to age prematurely."

I laughed. "It isn't your looks that led to my assumption. I was basing my guess on how much you've accomplished. It's very impressive you've done all this before you were thirty."

"Thank you. I appreciate that."

"I should probably get back downstairs. I don't want the others thinking I flaked out and took some long break." I did not really want to leave the rooftop and the amazing view, but it seemed like it was time.

"I think you can take a few more minutes," he said. "I bet when you do go back to work, you are going to be fresh and ready to spill out all kinds of ideas."

"I hope so."

"Can I say something, and I don't want you to take offense?" he asked, turning to face me.

That was never a great way for a conversation to start, but it wasn't like I could say no. Constructive criticism was a good thing, I reminded myself. "Sure, I'd love to hear what you have to say. I could always use advice from someone who is successful."

"I think you are a very smart person. You're book smart, which can sometimes be a hindrance because it doesn't let your creative side come through. I want you to try and put aside the statistics and all that stuff you learned in school and think like a consumer. Think about what makes you take notice and go from there. You can apply the book smarts later, but I think if you live in that book-smart world, it's going to limit you. You have what it takes, I can feel it, but you have to let yourself really roll with the flow."

I smirked, not correcting his phrasing. "I know exactly what you're talking about. I had a professor tell me I saw in black and white only, but I lived in a grey world, and I needed to step out of my box."

He nodded his head. "It's not a bad thing. You're going to do great, but I feel like you have this wall in front of you. Kick it down, and you are going to do great things."

I smiled, feeling a little glow roll through me. "Thank you. The word feels inadequate, but really, thank you."

"You're welcome. I'm only telling you what I see."

"Why are you being so nice to me?" I blurted out, realizing about a millisecond after the words left my mouth that it was an internal thought, not something that was supposed to be said aloud.

He grinned, his eyes squinting in the corners as he looked at me. "I like to think I'm nice to everyone. I saw you were struggling a bit, and I wanted to help you out. No matter what you might hear tonight, I do want to be a good boss. I also like to think I have an eye for talent. I see something in you, and I'm excited to see how well we can work together. After all, I am a businessman, and I'm in this to make money and be successful. I'm only as successful as my people."

I really felt like I was on top of the world at that moment—literally and figuratively. He was a great boss and someone I could learn from. I was going to remember that the next time I felt like I was going to lose my shit, as he said.

"I hope I can prove you right," I told him, not one-hundred percent buying into it but willing to give it a chance.

"I know you will prove me right. You'll see what I see very soon. I can feel it." His eyes locked with mine.

I felt invincible. If the CEO thing didn't work out for him, he could absolutely make a killing as a motivational speaker. I felt like I could conquer the world. Hell, I felt like a Greek goddess in that moment.

CHAPTER 11

ADRIAN

I could hear the commotion in the hall outside my door, signaling it was quitting time, and everyone was chatting as they headed out for their usual Tuesday evening gathering. I was used to the energy that ran through the office on Tuesdays. They looked forward to their night out together every week. I liked that they did it. I saw it as team building. It allowed them to blow off some steam and connect on a level outside of work.

I envied them a little, but I had never really wanted to be a part of the group. It would blur the line between boss and coworker. I had to stay separated in order to maintain the respect I had worked hard to gain from each of them.

"Hey," Rand said, walking into my office.

"What's up?" I asked him, keeping it casual now that we were off the clock.

"They're all going out for a drink," he said, gesturing out the door with his head.

I nodded. "They do every Tuesday."

"You don't want to go?" he asked casually. "One of them asked me specifically if we were going tonight in honor of the interns' first night out with the group."

I shook my head, closing down the program I was working in, and met his eyes. "It isn't a good idea. This is their time. I don't want to intrude."

"They invited you and me," he reasoned.

I smiled. "Because they are good people, and that's what they do. This is no different than any other week they go out."

"Ah, but it is different. Didn't you hear me say the interns were going?" One dark brow raised.

I shrugged. "I did, and that means what?"

He grinned. "Oh, nothing. Nothing at all."

"Are you going?" I asked him with surprise.

He wrinkled his nose. "No. Not by myself. They might attack."

I chuckled. "I think you'll be fine."

"You're missing out, which means I'm missing out," he said on a disappointed sigh. "Ah well, I suppose I'll have to go home and go to bed early."

"That's probably a good thing," I said. "You could use the rest."

He scowled. "I'm not so old."

"You're not so young," I shot back.

He shook his head and walked to the door. "I'll see you tomorrow."

I watched a few employees make their way down the hall. They were chatting excitedly, likely talking about their plans for the evening. I smiled, not wanting to leave right away. I wanted to give them a chance to leave first. My phone vibrated on the desk. I glanced over to look at the screen and saw my mother's face.

"Hi, Mom," I answered.

"We want you to come to dinner tonight," she said in a way that said I had no room to argue.

I groaned, checking the time on my watch. It was technically early, but the drive would be at least an hour. "Tonight?" I questioned, hoping to get her to change her mind.

"Yes. Tonight."

"Mom, it's kind of late for a dinner invite," I tried to reason.

"Adrian, you haven't been to visit for too long. It's time."

I closed my eyes, knowing I wasn't going to win. "Fine, I'll be there in an hour and a half," I said, hoping the traffic wasn't terrible.

"Good," she said and hung up.

I grabbed my things, wanting to get out of the office without delay. I was glad I drove to work. It would save me some time. I nodded my head, smiling and telling the remaining people in the office to have a good time as I left the building.

When I arrived at the home I'd bought for my parents last year, I smiled at the new potted flowers my mother had arranged around the front entrance. I knew they loved our hometown, but I wanted them closer. They deserved a nice home, and when I had come across the private property, I had immediately bought it for them. They'd put up a little bit of a fight, telling me it was too much, but when I explained to them just how much my company was making, they accepted my gift.

I walked into the house and could smell my mother's spaghetti sauce. I did miss her cooking. While I had the means to eat at the finest restaurants in the city, nothing beat my mom's cooking.

"Mom!" I hollered, my voice echoing around the open foyer area with the living room on the right and the kitchen on the left.

"Back here," she called out.

I walked into the huge kitchen, stopped to lift the lid of the pot on the stove, and inhaled the aroma of the simmering spaghetti sauce. My mother walked into the kitchen from the back patio, carrying a glass and looking happy and healthy.

"Hi," I said, giving her a kiss on the cheek before she wrapped her arms around me.

My mom was a petite woman, but she was a strong Greek woman who took no shit from anyone, especially her sons that towered over her. She patted me on the back before stepping back. "Your father and I are enjoying a drink before dinner," she said, her English improving by the day with the classes she was taking.

She had decided to learn English last year with the intention of visiting New York City. It was a dream she and my dad had, and I had gifted them with an all-expenses paid, two weeks in the United States for Christmas. They were waiting until they both spoke better English. That was an excuse. I wasn't sure what the holdup was, but I wasn't going to pressure them.

"Dinner smells great," I told her.

"It's the only way I can get you to come and visit," she said. "You should pay more attention to your parents, especially your mother. We won't always be here."

I watched as she picked up the wooden spoon, removed the lid to the pot, and gave it a good stir. I knew my invitation had been a command, and I knew the demand for my presence was so she could lecture me face to face. I'd come anyway because I knew better than to ignore my mother.

"I promise I will come more often," I said.

She turned around, the spoon still in her hand. "You say that all the time. If you are not with your family, you should be making your own family." The spoon bounced up and down as she waved it at me.

"I know, Mom. I know."

"No, you don't know," she said. "The table is set. Call your father and we'll eat."

I walked out of the kitchen to do her bidding. To argue was futile. She was a stern woman. I assumed she had to be to raise all boys. We were a handful, but I liked to think my older brothers were far worse than I was. They felt the exact opposite.

With my dad and I waiting at the table, my mother carried in her spaghetti and meatballs, along with what I was guessing was her homemade bread and some kind of salad. She took her seat, and we all dished up. I was waiting for it. I knew what was coming.

"Adrian, your father and I want to talk to you about your future," my mother started.

And there it was. I looked at my dad, who dropped his eyes to his plate. I knew he could care less about my relationship status. This was all my mom. My dad was a big man, masculine and very assertive, but my mother wore the pants in the family.

"Mom, my future looks fine," I told her.

"You don't have a wife! You are not a young man. You need a wife!"

I sighed. "I'm not interested in finding a wife right now. I'm focusing on my career and getting my company in a good place."

"How much money do you need?" she asked.

"It's not about the money," I said. "It's about building something I can be proud of. It's about employing people and helping out other companies. I like the success."

"You need a good woman," she stated.

It wasn't a suggestion or an observation. It was a statement of fact, and she expected it to happen. "Mom, I'm not ready."

"Get ready! You will be old and alone if you don't get a move on it!"

I sighed, stuffing a heaping forkful of spaghetti into my mouth. "I'm working on it," I said, hoping to appease her.

She scowled at me. "You've been saying that for years. I've never met any of your girlfriends."

I shrugged a shoulder. "Sorry."

"I'm having a little get together next weekend," she said with a sly smile. "I have someone I would like you to meet."

"No! Dammit, Mom. I knew that's why you wanted me over here."

She gave me a dangerous stare. "Watch your mouth, young man," she snapped.

I wanted to roll my eyes, but I didn't dare. She'd just gone on about how old I was, but the moment I cursed, I was relegated to a ten-year-old boy at her table. "Mom, I don't want you to set me up. I've not had good luck with the women you've set me up with in the past."

She waved a hand, dismissing my claim. "This is different. This is a good woman. She will give you lots of fine sons and make you happy. She knows how to cook and will make you good meals."

I looked to my dad for help. He just gave me a grimace before going back to eating his meal. None of us dared go up against my mother.

"I don't care to meet anyone right now," I said.

"Why? Come meet her. If you don't like her, then you don't have to date her."

65

"I can't because I have a girlfriend." I blurted out the lie before I had a chance to think twice about it.

Her mouth was open, her forkful of spaghetti halfway to her mouth. "What?" she asked, blinking rapidly.

Time stopped. I had a chance to tell the truth. I knew lying to my mother was one of the seven deadly sins in her book. "I said, I have a girlfriend, and I don't think she would appreciate me dating someone else," I said.

I was going to hell, and my mom's foot was going to be in my ass all the way down. I assured myself it was no big deal. I'd wait a few weeks and tell her we broke up. No harm, no foul.

My mother smiled, her eyes lighting up. "Bring her! We want to meet her, don't we?" She looked to my dad.

My dad nodded his head. "Yes, dear, we want to meet her," he said, smiling at his wife.

There was a ringing in my ears as I realized I had just taken myself down a road of no return. I was so screwed. "I'll see if she's free," I said, hoping she couldn't see the lie on my face.

My mom always knew when one of us was lying.

"I'm sure you can tell her it's important," she said with a firm nod of her head. "Insist she clear her schedule."

Growing up, that nod was akin to something being carved in stone. It was so. Whatever it was, when that nod was given, it was done. There was no arguing.

"I'll ask her," I said, gulping down the lump of horror in my throat.

I was fucked. I either had to come up with a girlfriend in the next few days or tell my mother I lied. The latter wasn't an option. There was no way in hell I was going to lie to mother and live to tell about it. It looked like I was in the market for a girlfriend—and fast.

CHAPTER 12

BELLA

I looked at Cassia, and then at the dress she had brought for me to wear, and then back at Cassia. The woman had lost her damn mind. The dress would look absolutely great on her, but on me, I already knew the skirt was going to be way too high.

I didn't want to offend her. At this point, she was the only friend I had kind of made, beyond my boss, and I didn't think that technically counted. We weren't going to be hanging out on the weekends. Cassia was it, which meant I was stuffing my body into the tiny dress.

"Thank you. I hope I don't rip out a seam." I took the dress and went into the bathroom stall.

"You won't," she said excitedly. "It's going to look great on you!"

I wasn't quite as sure, but I figured the worst that could happen was I would look a little risqué. I would wear the dress, finish out my time with the internship, and go home and never see any of these people again. No one back home would ever know about the dress.

I shimmied, tugged, and pulled until the little black bandage-style dress was on my body. It was a snug fit, but the spandex material made it easy to breathe. I tried to tug down the hem of the skirt, but that only resulted in my boobs falling out. I was stuck with short.

I opened the stall door and stepped out, my feet in the heels I had brought along to go with the dress, that only seemed to make it even shorter on my body. "I'm not sure about this," I murmured.

"Damn!" she exclaimed. "You look gorgeous! I'm so jealous! Your legs are forever long!"

I could feel myself blushing as I tried to gently tug the hem down a little lower. "I don't know," I said. "Isn't this a little much for a night out with coworkers?"

She grinned, shaking her head. "Oh no. This is perfect. You look stunning. Everyone is going to want to dance with you."

I grimaced. "I'm not much of a dancer," I said and realized right away I was being a total downer. I was supposed to be having fun, and that meant shucking some of those strait-laced ways I had fallen into.

"I promise, we are going to have fun," she assured me, turning back to the mirror to apply lipstick. "This is a great way for you to meet everyone and make some new friends."

I sighed, reaching into the small makeup bag I had brought along with me, and touched up my makeup. I wasn't going quite as heavy as she was, but I did put on a little more eyeshadow and liner, along with red lipstick. If I was going to wear the dress, I needed a face to match it.

"You're going to have fun," she said again as we walked out of the bathroom.

I hoped she was right. We stashed our work clothes in her small office to pick up tomorrow and headed out of the office. Everyone else was already gone. We walked past Adrian's office, the door closed and the lights off. He was already gone for the day. I wondered if he would make an appearance tonight. Part of me hoped he did, but another part of me hoped he didn't. I wasn't sure I wanted him to see me in the dress. That might make things weird between us.

We took a cab to the bar. Cassia held my hand, leading me inside, waving at people as we walked. She seemed to know everyone.

"Guys, this is Bella. She's new at the office." Cassia introduced me to a group of about twenty men and women gathered in one corner of the bar with tables pushed together. Everyone smiled and said hello before falling back into their conversations.

We ordered drinks and chatted with a few of the people from the office before a man who wasn't part of the group approached me. He put his arm around my waist and began to drag me out on the dance floor. I looked at Cassia for help.

"Back off!" Cassia snapped, slapping at his arm.

"Oh, come on, one dance," the guy said, slurring his words a little.

I grimaced. "No thank you."

"That's not how you ask a woman to dance," Cassia said, pulling my arm and tugging me out of the man's arm.

"Thank you," I muttered, straightening the dress once again. "I think Greek men are a little more aggressive than the American guys."

She laughed. "I'm sure they are. Americans are easy to bat away because they are much smaller."

I giggled, not wanting to argue with her but knowing full well American men came in all shapes and sizes. "Some of them."

"Let's dance. We need you to loosen up." She took the drink from my hand and put it on the table before dragging me out to the dance floor.

Cassia was a great dancer. Her body just seemed to move in a fluid motion that looked sexy and pretty. I felt a bit like a pig in a blanket trying to move like her. I had my hands in the air, shaking my ass and trying to let loose when I felt a large paw grabbing my ass.

"Hey!" I shrieked, spinning around and facing a man that was a good six-feet tall and three-feet wide. He was a massive beast, and his paws were everywhere.

"Back off, buddy!" Cassia said, coming to my rescue by putting one of her tiny little hands in the man's chest and pushing him away.

The man grinned and licked his lips as his eyes roamed over my body before turning and walking away. I shuddered with revulsion. I turned to look at Cassia. She was already back to dancing like nothing had happened. I watched as a man sidled up to her, towering over her as he swayed against her. She reached a hand up to his face, still dancing before pushing him away with a laugh and turning back to face me.

"You handle all of this so well," I told her.

She winked. "Practice and never let them get to you. Let go and have fun. They don't mean any harm, but you have to have a firm hand."

I grimaced, over the dancing, and I walked away, heading back to the safety of the table. Cassia was right behind me.

"I'm sorry, but this is really not my thing," I told her, hating I was bringing her down.

"It's okay," she said. "It can be a little obnoxious. Why don't we go grab some pie at the café down the street?"

I looked around at the others from the office, all of them drinking and having a good time. I feared I would never quite fit in with them. My father's hope for me to make friends was quickly evaporating.

"You don't have to leave because of me," I said. "Stay. Have a good time."

She shook her head. "We do this every week. I'm in the mood for pie."

"All right, pie it is," I said, relieved to be getting out of the bar.

We said our goodbyes and headed for the door. We stepped into the warm, humid air outside, our heels clacking against the sidewalk as we walked away from the lively bar behind us.

"So, tell me all about you," Cassia said.

I laughed. "I'm afraid there isn't much to tell."

"What do you do when you're not at work back home?" she asked.

"I was in school full time," I said. "I worked and studied and took care of the house I lived in with my dad. That pretty much took all my time."

"That does not sound like a fun time," she commented.

"It wasn't terrible. I didn't mind. I knew what I wanted to accomplish, and I worked hard to get my degree." I did not feel like I missed out on anything. "I did go out some, but I don't know. It just isn't my thing. I prefer a walk or hanging out and talking or watching old movies. The loud, grabby scene has never appealed to me."

"You're an old soul," she said, turning to look at me.

I burst into laughter. "I am an old soul. My dad used to tell me that all the time."

"What does your dad do for a living?"

"He worked in a mine for a long time, still does, but in a different position. He has worked several jobs over the years."

"What about your mother?" she asked, pulling open the door to the café.

It was always kind of a weird conversation killer. It was hard not to be blunt, but people always reacted so strongly when I told them she was dead.

"My mom died soon after I was born. I never knew her." I did not feel sadness like people expected me to.

"Oh. I'm very sorry. Did your father remarry?"

I shook my head. "No. He had a couple of relationships, but I think he really loved my mother, and he could never find anyone else that measured up to her high standards."

"That is so sweet and sad at the same time," she pouted.

I smiled, following her to a table. We both ordered a slice of fruit pie. I felt a little out of place in the tiny dress, but I was a lot more comfortable in the café than I had been in the bar.

"What about you?" I asked, wanting to know more about her. "Are you from here?"

She nodded. "I am. Well, I grew up in Athens. I moved here about four years ago."

"I can't imagine how awesome that would be, to live in such a historical place like Athens," I said with awe.

She grinned. "When you live there and see the stuff every single day, it isn't nearly as exciting."

"I don't know. I think I would be very excited. Is your family still there?"

"Yep. They will never leave. My dad owns a shop there. They wanted me to work in it and take over the family business, but I didn't want to be stuck there. I wanted to find my own path. They are very traditional and aren't all that happy that I left them." She sighed.

"I'm sorry. My dad was just the opposite. He was pushing me out the door from the moment I graduated." I giggled.

"But you lived with him?"

"Yes. I mean, he pushed me to do better than he did. He didn't get to go to college. He didn't even graduate high school. He has always encouraged me to do and see as much as I could before I couldn't."

Thinking about him back home, alone, made me a little melancholy.

"He sounds like a good man. I think if you give yourself some time, you'll find you really like it here. I love it."

"I think I will too," I said. "Thank you so much for inviting me out tonight. I'm sorry I ruined your fun."

She waved a hand through the air. "You didn't ruin anything. If you're not comfortable at the bar, that's okay. We can go to the beach, shopping, or I can take you sightseeing. I don't always have to be drunk." She giggled.

"I would really like that," I said excitedly. "I would love to try some of the Greek cuisine and check out some of the historical sites."

"Then we will make a date," she said. "I have plans this weekend, but maybe next weekend?"

I nodded my head. "Absolutely. I am going to spend this weekend sleeping and doing very little."

She grinned. "Then we have a date."

I relaxed, feeling a lot better about the failed night out. Cassia was going to be a great ally to have, and I hoped we could become good friends. Maybe I could convince her to visit me in the United States one day.

CHAPTER 13

ADRIAN

I t had been a long day at work, and all I wanted was a good cup of coffee to get me through the last bit of work I needed to get done so I headed to a nearby café. I was used to being alone. I didn't mind it. I wasn't the type of guy who needed to be surrounded by yes men or people in general. I liked the quiet. I liked to be able to think and daydream without someone asking me what was wrong—as if thinking were a bad thing.

I opened the iPad case and pulled up an account I had been working on while I sipped the coffee. I found it relaxing to work outside of the office. I was strongly considering working from home more often and letting Rand handle the day-to-day stuff at the office.

I glanced up, noticed the sun dropping lower, and thought about heading down to one of the beach spots to watch the sunset. Something caught my eye. Not something, someone. I glanced to my right, sifting through the people leisurely enjoying a stroll along the sidewalk and saw Bella. That was what had caught my eye. A beautiful blonde woman wasn't all that rare, but Bella was different.

"Bella!" I called her name.

She turned left, then right, confusion on her face.

"Bella, over here," I said, waving my arm in the air.

Her eyes landed on me. She smiled and waved back, walking toward the small table I was sitting at. "Hi!"

"Are you lost?" I asked her.

She giggled. "No. I'm lost on purpose this time. I was just out exploring, enjoying the beautiful evening."

I nodded my head, happy to hear she was getting some downtime. "Would you like to join me for coffee?" I asked.

She grimaced. "Um, maybe tea, decaf. I don't want to be up all night."

I grinned, finding it amusing that she had a low caffeine tolerance. "I thought all Americans lived on coffee, all day, all the time?"

She shook her head. "Not this American. I'm one cup in the morning, and that's it for me, or I will be a jittery mess."

She sat down, and one of the waitresses rushed over. She ordered a peppermint tea, which I thought seemed a little odd for a warm summer evening, but who was I to say what worked and what didn't? Her hair was pulled back in a loose ponytail. The jacket she'd worn at the office was gone, leaving the blue silk sleeveless shirt exposed. Her arms were toned, telling me she did some kind of workout, but I didn't think she was the gym type. I wanted to ask how she stayed in such excellent shape but figured that would be crossing a line.

"How was work today?" I asked her.

She shrugged a shoulder. "Much better. I only got lost once."

I chuckled, sliding my finger over the screen to look at a new page. "I'm happy to hear you're learning the ropes," I mumbled, staring at the screen.

"Are you working?" she asked.

I looked up to meet her pretty green eyes. "Kind of. I'm just kind of reviewing some stuff."

"Do you ever stop working?" she asked with a grin.

I smiled in return, sipping my coffee. "I like working. Working doesn't feel like a chore to me. It's kind of therapeutic, I guess. It takes my mind off other things."

"Other things?" she asked, a grimace on her face. "Please don't think I'm being rude or too forward, but are you married? Involved?"

I slowly shook my head. "No. I'm too busy with my work to worry about any of that."

She rolled her eyes. "Lame excuse."

My eyes went wide. "Excuse me?"

It was her turn for her eyes to get big. "I'm sorry! I don't know why I just said that. I forgot who I was talking to."

I grinned, appreciating her ability to be very casual. "It's fine, although you do sound a bit like my mother."

She looked horrified. "I don't think any woman wants to hear that."

"Sorry, I didn't mean it as a bad thing."

"So, what is it you're trying to get off your mind? You're living in what I've determined must be the most beautiful area in the world, you're successful, wealthy, and quite the handsome devil. What could have you stressed?" she asked.

I liked the part about me being a handsome devil. "Well, it varies."

"Like?"

"Like today I'm a little stressed out about my mother," I said, surprised I told her anything.

"Is she sick?" she asked with concern.

I shook my head. "No, not in the least."

"You said I sounded like your mom—is she nagging you about being single?" she pressed.

I sighed, knowing I probably shouldn't divulge personal information with an employee, but there was something about Bella that made me feel like I could talk to her. She was very genuine and didn't put on airs. She would have made an excellent therapist, I decided. I found myself wanting to tell her everything.

"I went to dinner at my parents' house last night," I said. "My mom all but demanded I go. When I got there, the usual conversation came up—the fact I am single."

She smiled and nodded her head. "Hence the comparison of me to your mother."

"Yes, but I'm not saying it's a bad thing. It's just kind of funny your words were so similar to what she said."

"I take it this is a conversation that's been had before?" she asked.

"Yes, it has, and it's always the same thing. I'm the youngest of three brothers. I'm not sure why she picks on me so much, but she does. She is always pushing me to date, and when I say I'm too busy, she sets me up on dates! The women she chooses for me are not quite what I would say was what I was looking for."

She grinned. "I see. It's sweet that she cares and that she is looking out for you. I don't know if I would want my dad setting me up on dates, though. That could definitely end badly."

"It does. Trust me. Stay away from anyone your parent recommends."

"Is that all that's got you stressed out?" she asked. "I mean, it sounds like you are kind of used to her asking you about your relationship status."

I grimaced, a little embarrassed to admit just what it was that had me stressed out. "That isn't what has me stressed. It's my response to her attempt to set me up that has me debating moving to America."

She burst into laughter. "It must be serious if you're thinking about leaving this behind."

"You haven't met my mother," I griped. "Trust me. A man would move to Antarctica if he had to in order to escape her wrath."

She was still laughing while looking at me with obvious pity. "It sounds rough."

I nodded. "It is. I told her I had a girlfriend and that's why I couldn't go out with the woman she was trying to set me up with."

She winced. "And you don't have a girlfriend?"

I shook my head, holding her eyes with mine. "No."

"Ouch."

"Yes, ouch," I mumbled. "If I tell my mother I lied, she will kill me. I will be dead or wish I was."

"So, find a stand-in," she replied easily.

I looked at her. "A stand-in?"

"Yes. I could pretend I was your girlfriend if you want. We go meet your mom, and she will see you're already spoken for and will hopefully stop setting you up. Then, you can tell her we broke up or I moved back to the States or something like that."

I thought about her idea. "You would do that for me?"

"Yes. I owe you for not firing me immediately on my first day. I don't mind." She shrugged a shoulder.

As much as I wanted to jump at the quick and easy solution, I couldn't do it. "You don't want to get mixed up in this. Trust me. If my mom finds out we lied to her face, it won't be good. She's small but mightier than any mythical goddess."

I could see Bella trying not to laugh. I knew I probably sounded like a scared little boy, but my mom was no joke. She could be terrifying. It wasn't a threat of violence that kept us boys in line, but it was the implied threat. There was something about my mother that could make any man quake in his shoes. She was a fierce tigress. To be on her good side was a great thing. To get on her bad side was the stuff of nightmares.

"Well, it's up to you. The offer is on the table. I don't mind doing it. I won't pressure you." She took another drink from her cup before putting it on the table.

"Thank you. You're very kind and very generous, but I can't ask you to do that."

"You're not asking. I'm offering."

I smiled, appreciating her willingness to go out of her way for me. "I appreciate that, but I think I'll have to pass."

"Suit yourself. Thank you for the conversation and tea. I'm going to head back to my hotel and get some reading done before I go to bed."

I watched her stand and quickly got to my feet. "Thanks for hanging out with me for a bit. It was nice talking with you."

"You're welcome. Try not to work too much or think too hard on your little problem. I'm sure it will all work out."

She turned and started to walk away. I couldn't help but smile. "Bella?"

She stopped walking and turned to face me. "Yes?"

"You're going to your hotel?" I clarified.

"Yes."

I pointed behind me. "It's the other way."

She groaned, her shoulders drooping as she shook her head. "Thanks," she mumbled and walked past me, heading in the right direction.

I couldn't help but chuckle as I sat back down at the table. I was going to have to put a GPS collar on her neck. It was only a matter of time before she ended up truly lost. I supposed it was a good thing we were on a relatively small island. It was hard to say where she would end up without a fence to keep her contained.

I mulled over her solution to my problem. Truth be told, I had considered doing exactly what she suggested, but it felt too risky. Fooling my mother was no easy task. I wasn't sure I wanted to put Bella in that situation.

For now, I would have to try and figure out another solution. I had gone through the contacts in my phone, mulling over names of women I had dated in the past, but the idea of taking any of them to meet my mother was not appealing. I knew my mother wouldn't like any of them. Things could only get worse if my mother managed to ferret out the truth of the lack of relationship between myself and my so-called girlfriend. The woman I chose to take would have to understand it was only a one day relationship. I didn't want the woman to get the wrong idea.

I shook my head, quickly nixing the idea again. It was too risky.

CHAPTER 14

BELLA

I was tapping away on the keyboard of the laptop, my mind whirring as I wrote up my ideas for the new campaign. Cassia was sitting across from me at the long table in the smaller conference room we had taken over. We wanted quiet and a space we could talk freely without interrupting the others busy working on their own projects. I quickly finished the document and emailed it to Cassia for her to review.

"I just sent it," I told her, pulling up another file to begin working on it.

"Damn, you're fast!" she exclaimed.

I laughed, staying focused on the project while she reviewed what I had sent. "I like to get my work done."

"You are picking up on this job faster than anyone I have ever worked with before," she said with a smile. "You are speeding through this, and it's actually very good. I'm impressed."

"Thank you. It's something I've always done. I knew I had a choice: be good at what I wanted to do, which was marketing and creating, or be forced to work in the mines with my dad or some kind of hard-labor job like that. I didn't want that for my life, and my father certainly didn't want that for me. I learned how to absorb knowledge and how to focus at a very young age. Seeing your dad come home bone tired and hearing of families losing their loved ones to tragic accidents or lung disease is a motivating factor to find a different line of work." My eyes stayed on my screen as I reviewed the file.

"Wow, you are really driven," she said with a small laugh.

"I'm very motivated to not do manual labor," I said. "I'm not big on sweating and physical exertion."

"I could definitely understand that. I wouldn't want to get dirty and sweaty either, at least not in that kind of environment," she added with a giggle.

I opened my mouth to reply but felt a presence in the room. I turned around to see Adrian standing just inside the room.

"Hi, ladies," he said.

"Hi," we both said at the same time.

"What brings you in here?" he asked.

"It was quieter and easier for us to talk about the project we're working on without disturbing the others," Cassia answered.

He nodded. "I see."

Cassia pushed a file across the table. "Check out what our young intern has done."

Adrian took the file, pulled out the chair next to mine, and sat down. His presence was hard to ignore. I could smell a faint hint of his cologne and found myself quietly inhaling through my nose to get more of it. It was manly and sexy and was triggering all kinds of responses in my body. I looked over at Cassia and found her watching me intently. It was then I realized I had leaned toward Adrian. I felt ridiculous and quickly leaned away.

"This is great!" he exclaimed, turning to look at me.

"Thank you," I replied sheepishly.

"Bella, you're doing amazing work. Really, this is great. I'm glad to have you on board." He reached out to touch my hand resting on the table.

I gulped. "Thank you. I'm happy to be here." His hand practically seared my flesh.

I couldn't move or breathe with his hand touching mine. I had no idea what was happening, but the reaction to his touch unnerved me. I schooled my features, not wanting to look like I was freaking out. When inside, I was melting and quivering.

"I'll let you two get back to work. I just wanted to check and see how things were going. I'm looking forward to seeing what the two of you put together." He rose from his chair and walked out of the room.

His departure left a sucking hole in the room. It was like the sun being blocked by clouds after basking in the warmth. I heard myself sigh and quickly reminded myself I wasn't alone. I turned to look at Cassia and found her staring at me with a grin on her face.

"What?" I asked.

She nodded her head at the door. "What was that about?"

"What was *what* about?" I asked innocently.

She was still smiling, shaking her head. "You two could have started a fire with the sparks flying between the two of you."

I rolled my eyes. "You're imagining things. It's nothing."

"I don't know about that," she said. "It certainly looked like something. Something hot."

"Stop," I chided. "He's my boss."

"Whatever you say, but I know what I saw, and I know what you felt," she said with a knowing look.

I put my eyes back on my computer. I didn't want to think about Adrian like that. I wasn't here to get myself into some kind of office romance, especially with the boss. That would only lead to trouble. I didn't need trouble. I needed experience and a good recommendation so I could get a great job back home.

I didn't answer her, but while I attempted to work, I couldn't help but think about what she had said. Was there chemistry? I felt it, but I didn't think he did. He'd been very casual and friendly.

I felt a little foolish for having a tiny crush on the boss. I wasn't going to admit it, even if Cassia had guessed it. It would never go anywhere between us. I was from the US. He was from here. He was a billionaire with the entire world at his fingertips ready to do whatever he asked. I was a small-town girl, struggling to get by with no culture and zero worldly experience. I imagined Adrian had been there, done that, on just about everything, everywhere.

"Hungry?" Cassia asked after we'd been working a while.

I nodded. "Starving!"

She giggled. "You could have said something."

"I didn't want to stop working. We're on a roll."

"You're seriously too much," she said. "Come on. There's a small deli around the corner. I'm buying."

"No, I can't let you do that," I protested.

"You are kicking ass in there and saving me a ton of time and energy," she said. "I want to buy you lunch to thank you."

"Thank you," I said, accepting her compliment and very willing to accept her offer for lunch.

We walked the block to the small restaurant, ordering salads and diet sodas.

"Do you like it so far?" Cassia asked.

"The job?"

"The job, the city, the boss?" she asked with a grin.

"Stop," I said with a shy smile. "I do like it—all of it."

"He's a good guy to work for. Rand is nice too. He's funny and a little dramatic, but all of us like him."

I knew I shouldn't ask, but I was going to do it anyway. "So, what's Adrian's story?"

She grinned. "I knew it!"

I shrugged, feigning nonchalance. "I'm only asking out of curiosity. I mean, he's gorgeous, rich, and successful. Why hasn't a woman snared him?"

"Oh, many have tried. I think he's picky. I don't know. He reveals almost nothing about his personal life. I don't know where he grew up. I don't know anything about his family. I don't know what he likes to do in his free time—nothing. The man is a closed book. I don't think anyone at the office has ever had a real conversation with him. He's very friendly, and he asks about all of our lives, but he reveals almost nothing about himself. It isn't that he's been rude, but he's extremely private. Hell, maybe he does have a girlfriend and none of us knows." She shrugged a shoulder.

"He doesn't talk to anyone?" I asked with disbelief.

"He and Rand are really good friends, and Rand talks about his weekends and stuff, and sometimes it involves Adrian, but he never gives out too many details about Adrian. I think that's because Adrian has asked him not to. It's kind of strange, but I respect his privacy. I'm sure a man in his position has a lot of people that try to get close to him because of his wealth and influence."

I nodded in agreement. I realized then I probably knew more about Adrian's personal life than Cassia did. It made me feel special. I wasn't going to tell her we'd talked a couple of times outside of work. I wasn't going to tell her I knew about his family or what he liked to do in his off time. I realized I was one of the few people that knew that about him. I wouldn't betray his confidence and go blabbing to the world.

"That must be difficult for him," I said, suddenly understanding why he'd been alone the other night. "I imagine it must be very isolating as well."

My heart went out to him. I had a feeling his mother realized how isolating his wealth was, and that was why she was so determined to get him married off. She wanted him to have someone in his life he could trust and depend on. It was the sweetest thing.

If I got the chance to talk to him again in a private setting, that was exactly what I was going to tell him—in a roundabout way. I didn't want him to know I had tried to get information out of Cassia about him. That would go over as well as a lead balloon.

"I'm sure he does fine," she said with a cheeky grin. "If he were lonely, all he would have to do is snap his fingers, and he'd have a line of women ready to warm his bed."

I rolled my eyes, taking a bite of the salad that had been delivered and making it a point to change the subject. I didn't want to get caught gossiping about the boss. I felt like I was still on shaky ground, being the new girl and all.

We finished our meals and headed back to the office. Cassia was called away, leaving me alone to walk to my little cubicle. I was about halfway down the hall when I ran into Adrian coming out of the breakroom, a bottle of water in his hand.

"Did you have a nice lunch?" he asked.

"I did. Did you stay in the office to eat?"

He shrugged a shoulder. "I usually do. I have phone calls to return, and sometimes with the different time zones, I have to work right through lunch."

"I see. I mean, I have no business lecturing you about taking time for yourself and all that." I laughed.

"Speaking of, have you been able to explore more of the city?" he asked.

I wrinkled my nose. "I plan on it—soon."

"Bella." When he said my name, I got chills up and down my spine.

"Hmm?" I murmured, the sound of his husky voice had made me feel all warm and tingly, and I didn't want it to be ruined with the sound of my own voice.

"I want you to meet me tomorrow morning," he said.

I looked up, his blue eyes gazing at me. "What? Here? At work?"

"No. I want you to meet me at the beach. I'm going to show you around. I want you to have some fun."

"Okay." I squeaked out the word.

Really, who was I to argue with my boss, or better yet, why would I want to argue with a man that looked like Adrian? He was kind and hot. Those were two qualities that made spending a day at the beach with him right at the top of my list of things to do on a Saturday morning. I wanted to scream and jump up and down with excitement, but that wouldn't be cool. I'd make a fool out of myself.

"Great, I'll see you tomorrow," he said. "Are you an early riser by chance?"

I bobbed my head up and down. "I am."

"Should we shoot for six?" he asked. "We can watch the sunrise."

"That would be amazing!" I said, not hiding my excitement. "I've seen it from my room a couple of times but watching it on the beach would be awesome!"

"Perfect. Can you give me your number, and I will text you the pinpoint? I don't want you to get lost." He gave a small laugh.

I wanted to tell him I wouldn't get lost, but that was a lie. I would. Hell, I'd probably get lost even *with* the directions.

CHAPTER 15

ADRIAN

I had been restless all night. By the time four o'clock rolled around, I had given up trying to sleep and gotten up. I rambled around in my large house before deciding to go to the beach early. I could use the serenity and peacefulness of a beach sunrise when most of the world would be sleeping in on their Saturday morning.

I put on a pair of shorts and some boat shoes, tossed a few beach necessities in a bag, and headed out for my little sports car. The morning was perfect. I couldn't wait to get to the beach, but mostly, I couldn't wait to see *her* on the beach.

I kicked off my shoes, leaving them on the blanket I had spread out, and strolled along the sandy beach. It felt good squishing between my toes. A little cool but refreshing. There were a few other early risers enjoying the quiet morning. I kept my head down, not wanting to be recognized or engaged in conversation. I just wanted to be alone.

I was staring at the water when out of the corner of my eye, I saw her. I turned to watch her stroll down the beach toward me. She was wearing a long white dress and carrying a bag over her shoulder. Her feet were bare, and her hair gently blew in the breeze. She looked like an angel. There was an ethereal quality about her, downright heavenly.

I put up my hand, waving to her. She waved back and continued toward me. I had to fight the urge to run across the beach like a damn fool.

"Hi," I said. "You're early."

She giggled. "You're early too."

"I couldn't sleep, and I thought I'd come down and watch the full sunrise."

"Me too. I'm used to getting up early back home. My dad was always up at four and off to work by five."

"I have a blanket over here." I pointed. She fell into step beside me. I steered the conversation back to her home life. "You said you lived with your dad?"

"I did," she replied. "It just made more sense for me to stay at home while I went to school."

"How so?" I asked, gesturing at the blanket.

We both sat down, facing the water and the rising sun.

"He worked a lot. I worked as much as I could to help cover the costs the scholarships didn't. I couldn't afford a rent payment, and I know he needed me. At least, I liked to think he needed me." She laughed.

"I'm sure he needed you. I bet he misses you."

"I think he does, but I think he is also enjoying his freedom a little. He's been my sole provider for twenty-three years. He hardly had time to go out with his friends or do much of anything. This is his time. I keep telling him to live it up because when I get home, I'm going to put him back on a diet. I tried to make sure he ate right when I was home, but I bet he's eating hamburgers and pizza every night with me gone."

I found it sweet that she took care of her dad. She was a natural caregiver. I liked that. "I think that's very admirable of you."

She shrugged a shoulder. "He took care of me forever, and now it's my turn to take care of him. He needs it, and he deserves it."

"I can't imagine what it must be like for your father," I said. "My mom and dad, while they fight a lot, they are also completely dependent on one another."

"They are lucky to have each other," she said. "Are you close with them?"

"I am. I know I complain about my mom, but I love her." I was not the least bit embarrassed to say it.

"And she loves you, which is why she wants you to have someone. I understand it. She doesn't want you to be alone."

"No, she doesn't, but her tactics leave something to be desired," I said dryly.

She giggled softly, turning to look at me. A thick strand of her blonde hair blew across her face. She pushed it away, tilting her head and looking into my eyes. "I think it's very sweet that you have a close relationship with your parents."

"I am happy to have them around. I moved away and then realized I missed them."

"You said they live fairly close?" she asked.

"Yes. I wanted them close, and I wanted them to be able to retire and live out their golden years in a comfortable home."

One eyebrow shot up. "You moved them *closer* to you?"

"Yes. I bought them a house not too far out of the city."

She grinned. "I think you and I are a lot alike. When I get established in a good job, I'm going to buy my dad a house. I want to pay him back for all those years he busted his ass to keep me clothed and fed."

I stared out at the water. "Was it difficult when you were a child?"

She let out a sigh, not looking at me as she watched the sunrise in the sky. "It was, but it wasn't. My dad always made it seem like we were okay. I didn't have the newest fashions or get a fancy phone or iPad or even a car. We simply couldn't afford it. He struggled and struggled and struggled every day just to make sure I had the necessities. I grew up with nothing worth having, but I never really noticed."

"Your dad sounds like a really good man," I commented.

"He is, which is why I'm going to make sure he gets to live out his golden years in comfort and close to me, kind of like what you've done for your parents. I know he would love to live in a place like this with the ocean surrounding him and endless miles of beach. I know I never want to leave here." She sighed.

"It is a beautiful place to live," I told her. "A little crowded, but I love it."

"I'm glad that you can appreciate it. Sometimes, people get so used to seeing or having something every day, they can't really see how lucky they are to have it. Back home, my friends that had moms who nagged them or made them clean their rooms and pick up all their clothes, I used to be so envious of them. I would have loved to have a mom nag me or enough clothes to be scattered all over my bedroom floor. Don't get me wrong. I'm not really complaining, but I just hate when people can't see what they have right in front of them."

I nodded my head in agreement. For a young woman, she was extremely wise. "You're very grounded."

"Thank you," she replied. "My dad raised me to be humble, and I hope to stay that way. You're very grounded as well. Your parents raised you right."

"I liked to think they did. My parents believed in hard work. They gave us nothing. We had to work for everything we wanted. They weren't well off, but they were comfortable. My mom, she's the one who hated the idea of spoiling us. When I was a kid, I used to resent it, but now I understand it. I understand why she wanted us to understand what it meant to earn something rather than have it handed to us." I smiled.

We sat in silence for a while, both of us lost in thought as we stared off into the sunrise. I liked the comfortable quiet. I didn't feel like I had to fill the void.

"Have you given any more thought to what we talked about the other day?" she asked in a soft voice.

"What did we talk about?"

She nudged my shoulder with hers. "Your mom situation. Do you want to take me up on my offer to be a fake girlfriend for a day?"

I chuckled, shaking my head. "Let's focus on today."

She laughed in response. "Way to deal with a problem head-on."

89

"I have an idea," I said, quickly changing the subject.

"About how to deal with your mom?"

"No. I'm not talking about my mom. This morning is about me showing you a good time. My problems with my mom will wait."

I got up and offered her my hand to pull her up to her feet. "Should I put on my shoes?" she asked.

I grinned. "Nope. Follow me."

We walked down the beach to a surfboard rental shack. "Uh, what are we doing?" she asked hesitantly.

"I'm guessing you've never been surfing."

She shook her head. "No, I haven't. I don't know how. I'm not dressed for surfing."

"You're wearing a swimsuit under that." I nodded toward the dress.

"How do you know?"

"I can see the strap," I said with a wink.

She reached up to her neck. "Oh. I wasn't sure how long we were going to be hanging out and figured if I was at the beach, I may as well test out the water."

I nodded. "Good. I'm glad you did. You can wear that, or I can get you a wetsuit."

"Do you wear a wetsuit?"

I shrugged. "Sometimes, but I don't plan on being in the water all that much. We'll just go through the basics for now."

"Then I'll stick with my suit."

"Perfect. I'll get us a couple of boards."

"You surf?" she asked.

"Yes."

"Do you have your own board?" she asked.

"I do, but I didn't bring it."

I left her looking at some of the surfing accessories while I quickly handled the rental of two boards. We carried them out, Bella looking absolutely terrified as we walked back to the blanket.

"I'm not sure about this," she said, looking out toward the water where there were already a couple of guys taking advantage of the waves.

"I'll be right there with you. The water is nice and calm. We'll start with just paddling around."

She scrunched up her nose. "Do you know how to swim?"

I laughed, nodding my head. I used my arm to wave at the ocean. "I grew up next to the water. Yes, I know how to swim. It was something my dad insisted on. All of us boys spent a lot of time at the beach. Do you know how to swim?" I realized she might not.

The grimace on her face was very telling. "Yes, and no. I mean, I took swim lessons, and I've gone swimming in public pools and the river, not the ocean."

"I've got you," I promised. "I'll keep an eye on you."

"Okay," she said with resignation.

I watched with rapt attention as she unbuttoned her dress and pulled it over her head. God have mercy. She was wearing a two-piece that wasn't anywhere near as revealing as what I saw on the beach usually, but it was far sexier. Her body was incredible. I was going to have a hard time keeping my focus. I wouldn't mind giving her mouth to mouth if she happened to drown a little.

CHAPTER 16

BELLA

I was having more fun than I could remember having in a very long time. The water was comfortable, not too cold, nothing like I remembered the Pacific Ocean being. I was straddling the board, my feet dangling in the water, with Adrian right alongside me on his own board.

"Ready to try standing up again?" he asked.

I'd been struggling to concentrate on the surfing lessons. He'd taken off his shirt, revealing numerous tattoos and a chest that had left me wiping the drool from my chin. He was tanned and muscular, and the tats were a stark contradiction to the strait-laced suits I always saw him wearing. It intrigued me. I wanted to ask him what they meant, if there was any meaning. I had a feeling he would only get ink on his body that held some kind of significance.

"I will try," I answered, not looking forward to another faceplant into the water.

Any makeup I had put on this morning was long gone. I had tied my hair back in a ponytail after the first few times of getting dunked in the crystal-clear water.

"One more try, and then we'll grab some lunch," he said with that sexy smile I was growing very accustomed to seeing. "I'm starving."

"All right, here goes nothing," I said, paddling out and hoping there was a chance I could actually ride a wave.

It was futile. Surfing was never going to be my sport. While I had fun trying, it wasn't ever going to be my thing.

"Let's get lunch!" he exclaimed, running out of the water, his board under his arm.

I followed behind him, laughing at his gleeful, boyish exuberance. He was a completely different man on the beach than he was in the office. I really liked this side of him. We walked back to return the surfboards. He pulled on his shirt while I used the towel he had thought to bring and dried off before pulling on my dress.

"Ready?" he asked.

"Should we put this in your car?" I asked.

He shrugged. "It's just a blanket. Leave it for the next person who wants to enjoy it."

"Okay."

"There's a place just a short walk away. We can drive if you prefer?"

"Walking works for me. It's a nice day, and I could use the walk to dry my hair a bit." I imagined I probably looked like a drowned rat.

We sat at a table outside on a cobblestone patio, each table with an umbrella to provide diners protection from the sun. I could hear and smell the ocean. I felt completely relaxed.

"You okay?" he asked, his head tilted to the side as he stared at me.

"Yes, fine, why?"

"You have a look on your face, like you're... tired," he said as if he wasn't sure that was the right word.

I smiled. "It's contentment. Complete relaxation. I'm relaxed."

He grinned, nodding his head. "I see. I'm glad to see it."

"Thank you for helping me achieve it," I said. "I have truly never felt this relaxed. I know I'll feel guilty about it later, but for now, I'm going to enjoy it."

"Why feel guilty?"

"Because I feel like I should be doing something, working or calling my dad, or—I don't know—something productive."

He chuckled. "This is why you work. So you can have these moments. Did you work all the time back home?"

"I suppose I did. If I wasn't working or studying, I was usually cleaning the house or volunteering at the animal shelter. I always felt like there wasn't enough time in the day. Since I've been here, I feel like I have a lot of time on my hands."

"What brought you here? It doesn't sound like your life in the United States was bad."

"It wasn't bad!" I defended.

"I'm sorry," he said. "I didn't mean *bad*. I guess I wonder why you chose to come all the way around the world for a job. You're talented, and you have excellent people skills. You could work anywhere you wanted. Why come here when you so obviously miss your father?"

It was a good question. "I did a lot of research. Your company is at the top. I wanted to know what it was you were doing that was working so well. When I saw you were offering an internship, I figured that was a great way to get inside and learn from the best."

He was studying me, watching me closely. "That's a great answer, but I don't think it's the real answer. Why are you really here?"

I squirmed. My dad was the only one who knew me well enough to know when I wasn't telling the truth. "I came here because I wanted one shot at living this kind of life."

He nodded, leaning forward in his chair. "What kind of life?"

I put my hands up, gesturing to the water and the beach and all of it. "This. Eating a delicious lunch on a beach in a foreign country. This life where I wasn't the girl who didn't have a mom and lived in the tiny house that was falling down around her. I wanted to be one of the girls I had read about on blogs, traveling the world and just being completely free."

"That right there is exactly what makes you so special," he said, picking up the cold drink that had been delivered to our table.

"What? Special?"

He nodded. "Yes, your true talent lies in your people skills. You have an innate charm about you. People are drawn to you."

"Except your friend, Rand," I replied.

He smirked. "Rand is just as impressed with you like everyone else. Cassia can't stop talking about you. You've really impressed her, and that is no easy task. She's a tough person to get in good with."

"Thank you. That means a lot coming from you."

"I'm serious. You're very good at your job, but I think we're wasting your true talents by locking you down in a tiny cubicle, hiding behind a computer screen."

I raised an eyebrow, not sure where he was going with his compliments and not entirely sure I wanted to stop him. "What are you referring to?" I asked, hoping I wasn't going to have to dump the diet soda I had in my hand all over his pretty little head.

My father raised me to be a respectable woman. I wasn't going to be propositioned over lunch by my boss, no matter how handsome he was.

He held up a hand. "I was referring to your people skills. You would be really good with clients. I have a meeting in Athens this coming week, and I would really like you to go with me. You have an honesty and an innocence about you that I think clients will appreciate. They don't want to hear my spiel. They want to hear from someone who they feel they can trust and relate to."

I shook my head. "I don't know. I don't think I'm any good at dealing with people."

"You're great with people. You have a warm smile and a way about you that puts people at ease. I'm at ease. I'm never at ease with anyone. That should tell you something right there." He laughed.

"I guess it was all those years of waitressing and working in the nursing home," I said, shrugging a shoulder.

"A nursing home?" he asked.

"Where old people live. I don't know what you call them here, but back home, it's like a hospital, but it's for old people who don't have anyone to care for them. They go into a nursing home. I started volunteering with my friend when I was fourteen."

His brows raised. "Really? What did you do? You were a nurse?" The skepticism on his face was laughable.

"No, no. I would read to them, play Bingo with them, sometimes help them eat and stuff like that. I wasn't a nurse." I found it interesting that he didn't know what the homes were.

"I see. I think that definitely helped you relate to people. When I talk to clients, many of them are small-business owners that want an edge. I hate to admit it, but I don't think I have that personality that puts them at ease. They see me, and sometimes, I get the feeling they think I don't really care about their struggles to run a small business. I do. Trust me, I do, but they see me as the successful CEO of a company." He sighed.

"And you think I can persuade them to hire the company?" I asked, wanting clarification.

"Yes. You're exactly what I think will persuade them. You'll be my secret weapon." He grinned.

I laughed. "That's flattering."

"It's the truth," he said, his eyes holding mine. "If there is one thing about me you need to know, I don't lie. I don't like to dance around a point. I say what I feel and don't waste time with empty compliments."

I felt like I was in a business negotiation with him. He was a formidable man and could be very intimidating but in a nice way. "Okay. I'm your employee, and I'll do what you think is best."

"I think this is best, and I appreciate you being open to trying something different. This is going to be great for you, for me, and for the company."

I couldn't stop smiling. I felt like I was on top of the world. I couldn't wait to tell my dad. I wasn't sure it was a promotion, but it certainly felt like it. Not only was I going to get out from behind the computer, but I was going to get to go to Athens. That had definitely not been on my agenda. My dad was going to be so excited.

A waitress came by and took our orders. I was absolutely starving and was already telling myself not to stuff my face and embarrass myself in front of not only my boss, but probably the hottest guy on the planet.

"How often do you surf?" I asked him, changing the subject.

"Not a lot, and I will never be a pro, but it's great exercise, and I try to get out here at least once a week. It doesn't always work out like that." He shrugged.

"I still cannot get my head around living here and having the beach right there," I said. "Like, you get out of bed and there's the beach!"

He nodded his head. "It's not quite that close, but my house does have private beach access," he confessed.

"No way!"

"Yes, way."

"Wow. It is going to be really hard to leave this place. If I was a native, I don't think I would ever move away. I would live here until the day I died," I said on a breath.

When I turned back to look at him, I saw him watching me. The way he was looking at me made me feel breathless. My heart was pounding in my chest. I wanted to ask him what he was thinking but stopped myself. I wasn't sure I wanted to know. I wasn't sure I could handle it. There was a very good chance I would melt.

"I don't think I will ever leave," he said.

I thought I sensed sadness or maybe regret. I wondered what the story was behind it. Adrian was a man who only offered small tidbits of personal information. I would wait. He would tell me if he wanted me to know. I wouldn't press. I was going to enjoy the time I had with him in this beautiful city.

CHAPTER 17

ADRIAN

The weekend had been too short. I could have spent an entire week hanging out with Bella, showing her around the city and maybe taking a road trip down the coastline to visit some of the other cities crowded on Crete. I'd had one day with her, and I was hooked. I wanted there to be more days just like Saturday.

Maybe there was a way I could extend our trip to Athens by a day. I knew it was risky, but I kept telling myself it was just two people hanging out. I was being nice and showing her around, being a friend for someone who was in a new place and knew no one. I was being a good guy—nothing more.

There was a soft knock on the door, pulling me from my thoughts about working out a way to spend more time with Bella. "Come in," I called from where I was seated at my desk.

"Hi, are you busy?" Bella asked, popping her head in the door.

"Not at all," I answered, jumping to my feet. "Come in."

She walked inside and quietly closed the door. My eyes roamed over the skirt and sleeveless blouse she was wearing. It was professional, sexy, and made me think of a bad porn movie. All she was missing was the glasses on the tip of her nose. Even her hair was up in a loose bun, with little strands falling around her face. She was sexy as hell no matter what she wore.

"I wanted to ask you about what you mentioned on Saturday," she said, looking over her shoulder as if she was afraid someone would hear her.

"Have a seat," I said, anxious to have her stick around a bit.

"Were you serious about the Athens trip?" she asked.

I smiled, nodding my head as I took my seat again. "I was. Why? Do you not want to go?"

"No, I mean, I do, but if you weren't serious, it's okay," she said, her hands twisting in her lap. "I'm only asking because I need to plan my week here."

"I was absolutely serious," I told her. "It's an important meeting, and I think your presence there could really sway them to sign with us."

"Okay, great," she said with a smile. "I'll let Cassia know. When do we leave?"

My phone ringing was her answer. I grabbed it, seeing my mother's face on the screen and grimaced. "I need to take this."

She nodded. "No problem," she said, getting to her feet.

"No, stay. It'll just take a second."

She sat back down while I answered the phone.

"Hi, Mom," I said into the phone.

"Adrian, I need to know if you are coming on Saturday," she scolded.

I sighed, my shoulders slumping forward. "Mom—"

"Adrian, it is one day, half a day. You can make it. I know you are the boss. You don't have to work if you don't want to work."

"I know, but I—"

She cut me off before I could come up with a clever excuse. "No, no *buts*. I want you here."

I closed my eyes before leaning back in my chair and staring up at the ceiling. "I'll be there."

"And your girlfriend?" she asked. "Will you be bringing her?"

"Mom," I started, not sure what I was going to say.

"Adrian," she snapped.

"Actually, you know what?" I looked at Bella. "She's here right now, and we were just talking about it."

Her eyes went wide with surprise. I offered her a small smile. I probably should have asked her first, but it was done now.

"Oh great!" my mother exclaimed. "Let me speak to her. I will personally invite her."

"Uh, not now. We both have to run. We've got work to do. I'll see you Saturday." I quickly disconnected before she could pressure me into saying or doing anything else I might regret.

I put the phone on my desk and looked up to see Bella staring at me. There was a small smile on her lips. "Your mother?" she asked.

I nodded. "Yes."

"Are we going to a barbecue or whatever it is called here on Saturday?" she asked, that playful smile still resting on her lips.

I let out a groan. "Yes, please?" I asked.

She giggled softly. "I already told you I would. I don't mind. I've always wanted to meet a big Greek family, and now I get to."

I slowly shook my head. "You might end up regretting this."

"I doubt it. I'm looking forward to it."

"I'm only accepting your offer because you owe me," I teased.

"Oh, good god, for what part? The job? Rescuing me? Hanging out with me?" She laughed. "I think I owe you a lot, and one little lunch with your family doesn't quite seem like it will even the scales."

"Trust me," I said with a grimace. "I'll be in your debt after this lunch with my family."

"I think you're overreacting. It will be fine. I can get along with most people. I'll do my best not to embarrass you."

"You couldn't embarrass me, and it isn't *you* I'm worried about. My family? They can be kind of, um, obnoxious, I think is the word I would use."

She burst into laughter, obviously amused by my discomfort. "I cannot wait. You always have this calm and cool thing going on. I cannot wait to see you out of sorts and uncomfortable."

"Thanks," I grumbled.

"So, this Athens thing," she said, getting right back to business. "When and where and for how long?"

"We leave tomorrow morning," I told her.

"What?" she exclaimed, panic in her voice. "Already? Oh my god! I have so much to get done!"

"You don't need to worry about your work here. It will get taken care of. I was serious when I said I wanted to pull you out from behind the scenes. I want you up front where the action is. I want you to be the one that talks to clients and makes them feel comfortable about hiring us. You have the benefit of knowing what goes on in a campaign, and you have the creative edge that can't be taught—it's a gift. I want clients to see that and hear it from you."

"You sure know how to be persuasive," she replied.

I grinned. "Together, we'll make a hell of a sales team."

"Okay, I will be ready. Are we flying?"

"Private jet. I'll pick you up at the hotel around seven. Does that work?"

She nodded. "Of course. How many days should I pack for?"

I thought about it. I was going to do what I could to try and get an extra day in Athens. I was sure Rand could handle things in the office, and I didn't have anything pressing on my schedule for the week.

"Let's plan for three days," I said. "We can always come back early if our business is taken care of early."

"Okay." She nodded, but I could tell there was something on her mind.

"Bella, did you have something you needed to be here for?" I asked.

"No, it's just, I was going to live stream my dad's show on Friday morning," she said, a hint of sadness in her voice.

"Your dad's show?" I asked with confusion.

"It's the Fourth of July back home on Thursday," she replied. "His show will be going at seven or so our time on Friday morning. I was hoping to be able to watch the live stream."

"What kind of show?"

"Fireworks," she explained. "My dad is kind of the local pyro guy in our small town. He does a big show every year. Everyone from around the area comes out to the park to see it. It started out just us having a little thing in the park for the other kids in the area whose parents couldn't afford to buy fireworks. It just kind of took off from there. Now, he works with the city council, and they budget money to pay for the fireworks. There's always a really big potluck picnic in the park, and the last few years, a few vendors have set up booths. It's just a lot of fun, and I've never missed a year."

I could see the sadness in her eyes and felt bad for her. She had to be homesick. I knew I wasn't strong enough to leave my family. She was a strong person, whether she realized it or not.

"Well, I'll make sure you are somewhere where you can watch the show," I assured her.

"It's okay. I don't want it to interfere with my work. He's going to have someone record it. Every year, people record it actually. I'll see it, and as he said, I've seen more than twenty. I'm just being a little melancholy. It's really not a big deal." She waved a hand.

"It is a big deal to you," I said softly. "It's a special day. I'm sorry you're going to miss it, and I appreciate you sacrificing that special day to be here with us."

"It's me who is lucky to be here," she said, chewing her bottom lip. "I should probably get back to work. I need to update Cassia on the project we've been working on. I hate that I'm going to be dumping it all in her lap."

"You're not dumping anything," I assured her. "We're a team. We're all working towards the same goal. I'll assign someone to pick up where you left off. Cassia will be just fine."

"All right. Thanks again for the opportunity. I really hope I won't let you down." She got to her feet.

I stood up and watched her walk out of the office before taking a seat at my desk. I didn't think she fully understood how gifted she was. She said she worked hard and studied hard, but she had a natural inclination for creative design. Her people skills were special and unique. It wasn't often I came across someone who had the head for design and had the same kind of charm Bella did. She was a rare find.

I made the call to the pilot I regularly used and arranged for the next day's trip. Then I booked a hotel room and arranged transportation. I could have had my assistant take care of the arrangements, but I had a few extra requests that I didn't feel like relaying through a third party. With the travel plans made, I focused on my schedule. I needed to work extra hard to free up some time later in the week. I planned on making our trip to Athens fun. It didn't have to be all work and no pleasure.

I felt like I was going to be indebted to her after the coming weekend with my family. If I could show her a good time in Athens and we got to know each other a little better, it was going to be that much easier to fool my mother into believing Bella and I were truly a couple. Plus, I didn't think it would be all that bad to go through the motions, even if it wasn't real. I was looking forward to the practice and then our performance. It would give me a good excuse to touch her. Hell, maybe I'd even be able to steal a kiss or two.

CHAPTER 18

BELLA

Work had been a blur since I'd left Adrian's office. I couldn't believe I was getting a trip to Athens. I was thrilled to be given the opportunity to branch out a bit, and I hoped I had the "it factor" that Adrian was convinced I possessed.

I wanted to make him proud. I wanted to impress him and wow him with my ability to woo a company into investing their hard-earned money in Adrian's business. I wasn't sure why I wanted to impress him. I was chalking it up to my Type-A personality that drove me to be the best, no matter the work it took to get there.

It was close to quitting time when Cassia stopped by my cubicle. "So, are you ready for your big trip tomorrow?" she asked in a hushed voice.

"I don't know if I am or not," I muttered.

"You're going to do great," she assured me.

I groaned, pushing back a strand of hair that had fallen into my face. "I don't know. I have to pack, and I have no idea what I should wear. I'm kind of stressed about all of this."

"I'll go to your place with you and help you get ready to go," she offered.

"You will?"

"Sure. I don't have anything going on after work."

"Thank you!"

I was hoping I could talk with her as a friend once we were outside of the office. In the office, she was technically my boss. I didn't want her to think I was taking advantage of our friendship at work, and I didn't want to risk being overheard.

"Give me five minutes, and I'll be ready to go," she said before walking away and heading for her office.

I quickly finished up, looking around my desk to make sure everything was in place. It felt strange to be leaving my desk for days when I had only just started. If by some chance Adrian decided to fire me, I didn't want to leave anything behind that I would need to come back for. Cassia came back, and we left the office together.

"This is a really big deal," she commented as we rode the elevator up to my room.

"What's a really big deal?"

"Adrian inviting you with him on this trip," she said. "He's never taken anyone with him before. Rand has gone along a few times, but usually, it's only Adrian."

"Oh," I replied, not sure how to answer.

"I think you've impressed him—in more ways than one." She giggled.

I dropped my purse on the small table in the entry and turned to face her. "It isn't like that. He's been kind."

"There is chemistry between you. You cannot still be trying to deny that."

I shrugged a shoulder. I wasn't sure how much to tell her about my relationship with Adrian outside the office. I wasn't sure he wanted anyone to know, and I didn't feel like it was my place to say anything. I didn't want to risk him firing me or not wanting to hang out with me anymore.

"I think there is chemistry, but neither of us has acted on it," I said. "He's just one of those people I feel like I click with."

She grinned. "I click with you, but I have no intentions of whisking you away on a private jet for a romantic getaway."

I rolled my eyes. "You know what I mean."

"I do. He's a pretty good guy, and if something were to happen between the two of you, I would be happy for both of you."

That made me feel a little better, but I was certainly not going to admit my crush on my boss—not yet. I was going to stay focused on the work. That was what I was in Greece for, and that was where I was going to focus my energy.

"All right, so what do I wear to a meeting with a potential client?" I asked, walking into the single bedroom in the hotel suite.

She opened up the closet and stared at the very minimal clothing I had hung up. I grimaced, a little embarrassed by my lack of wardrobe. It had never made sense to me to spend a lot of money on clothes I might only wear a couple of times a month.

"For the meeting you'll be attending with Adrian, you want to step it up a notch. Adrian, as you might have noticed, is a fantastic dresser. He really turns it up when he wants to impress someone. You're going to want to complement his look." She pulled out a two-piece business suit I had bought at the Goodwill last year. It had a skirt and blazer and always felt a little too fancy for school. I wasn't sure if I wanted to wear it to the office.

"He does dress very well," I agreed, thinking about what he'd been wearing today.

And I was still in awe of the way he had looked on the beach that day. He commanded the attention of all when he walked into a room wearing one of his tailored suits. There was an air about him that drew a person in, but when he was stripped down, that air was gone, and it was all him. I wasn't sure what to call it—charisma? Animal magnitude? Whatever it was, he had it in spades.

"We need to add a touch of femininity," Cassia said as she laid the skirt suit on the bed. "Pink—do you have a pink top?"

I walked to the chest of drawers and pulled out the silk short-sleeved blouse in pale pink. "This?"

"Yes! Perfect. Now we need sexy, confident, and yet sensible shoes. Do you have a pair of black or nude pumps?" She looked around the room as if she had overlooked them.

I grimaced, standing on one foot and holding out my leg. "These," I said, a little embarrassed I had only one pair of heels with me.

"Perfect! This is the outfit. Now, I suggest you put your hair up, a slick ponytail or maybe a messy bun." She leaned back as she stared at my hair.

I turned my head to the side and lifted my hair into a ponytail, holding it with my fingers. "Like this?"

She studied my face as I turned from left to right, sucking in my cheeks playfully. "No, I don't think that works. You look too stern. Adrian told me he likes you because you have that down-to-earth thing. The ponytail makes you look like a lawyer."

"Messy bun?" I asked, twisting my hair up and letting some strands hang.

She shook her head. "Nope. I think loose and free works better for this situation. If it were a business meeting, I think up is the way to go, but for this meeting with this set of potential clients, relaxed is best."

I agreed, and I had a feeling Adrian would as well. "Then it's settled. I should probably take a backup outfit in case there is a second meeting."

"I would go with another dress," she said, turning back to my closet and pushing the hangers as she examined the articles of clothing.

I had only one other skirt, and I wasn't overly fond of it. We spent some time mixing and matching until we had put together two outfits for business meetings, a dinner option, and a casual set for any exploring Adrian might decide to do.

"Thank you for your help," I told her. "I can't tell you how much this sets my mind at ease. I'm very nervous about the meeting and hope I don't let him down."

Cassia smiled, putting her hand on my upper arm. "You're going to do great. Adrian won't let you be anything but spectacular. Trust him."

I walked her to the door. "I will. I'll see you on Thursday or Friday. I'm not sure what his plans are."

Once she was gone, I checked the time and decided to call my dad to tell him my big news. I hadn't told him when I talked to him yesterday because I hadn't been entirely sure Adrian had been serious about taking me along for the meeting. Now that I knew he was, I couldn't wait to tell my dad.

"Hi!" I exclaimed when he answered the phone.

"Good morning, or evening, I guess," he said with a chuckle.

"Guess what?"

"That sounds like a *good* guess what, so I guess you're not fired," he teased.

"No, not yet. My boss is taking me to Athens tomorrow! He wants me to go with him to talk with a company that is interested in our company's services. He thinks I might be able to persuade them to sign on. He says my talent is wasted behind the scenes." I smiled as I thought about Adrian speaking the words.

"That's great. I knew you were a triple threat. You can do the computer stuff, use your charming personality to win over clients, and your brains to run your own company. I'm so proud of you." His voice was full of emotion.

"Thanks, Dad. I couldn't have done any of this without you."

"Nope, this was all you," he said firmly. "You put in the time, and you deserve all the credit for your success."

"I'm hoping we get to spend some time looking around Athens before we have to come back."

"You like it there." He said it as a statement and not a question.

"I do. Of course, I do."

There was a long pause. "Do you think you'll stay?" he asked in a somber voice.

We had talked about the possibility of me getting hired on full time and staying in Greece for a while. I had never actually expected it to happen, but now that I was here and working with Adrian and the others, I believed there was a chance I could be given the opportunity to become a permanent employee.

"I don't know, Dad. I haven't really thought about it."

His soft laugh filtered through the phone, making me miss him and home more than ever. "You're thinking about it. I don't want you to let me be the thing that holds you back. This is an opportunity that only comes around once in a lifetime. Don't let it pass you by. I'll be here. We can talk and visit if you want to give that job a real shot."

"I'm not even sure it's an option," I told him.

"If it does become an option, don't let me hold you back, got it?"

"Got it." I steered the conversation back to a lighter topic. "Now, tell me how the firework show is coming along. Did you talk to George or Tammy about recording it and doing a live stream?"

"I did, and they will. I told George to text you what he was doing because I haven't got a clue." He laughed.

"Good. I can't wait to see it, and I hate that I won't be there to feast on Tammy's potato salad."

"You can have her salad anytime," he said. "You live in the moment while you're there. Don't take any of it for granted."

"I know, I know," I told him before he could get started on the same old lecture.

We talked a bit longer before he had to go. I missed him. As much fun as I was having in Greece and as often as he told me to enjoy myself, I felt like I was abandoning him. He worked so hard and had devoted the last twenty-something years to me, and I up and left him. The guilt I had felt when I first applied had been pretty heavy. He had assured me all was okay, and I thought it was, but now that I was here, having a good time and getting to see the world, the guilt was back in full force.

I kept telling myself I was doing all of this for him, but I had to admit it was just as much for me. I had longed to get out of the small town back home and see the world. I had always wanted to know what it was like to experience new cultures. My dad had an old set of encyclopedias. We used to spend hours poring over the books, looking at pictures and talking about all the places we wanted to see. It wasn't fair I was getting the chance while he stayed home, working every damn day.

I was going to change his fate. I was going to give him a chance to travel. A little more work, and I knew I could get there. All I needed to do was prove to Adrian I was too good to let go after the internship was over.

CHAPTER 19

ADRIAN

I strolled into the lobby of the hotel where Bella was staying as part of the internship package. My company got a discounted rate, which made it easier for us to attract interns, especially those from out of the area. It was a nice hotel, and I hoped Bella was enjoying her stay.

I looked around the seating area and didn't see her. I checked my watch and realized I was a little early. I moved to take a seat in one of the chairs facing the elevators and waited.

"Oh my gosh, I'm so sorry!" I heard Bella exclaim.

I looked up to find her rushing toward me, a small suitcase rolling along behind her, her purse over her shoulder, and her laptop bag in her free hand. She looked a little harried.

"It's fine, I'm early," I said, rising to my feet.

She shook her head. "My alarm didn't go off. Usually, my internal clock is faultless, but this morning, it fails!"

I smiled, looking down at the casual jeans and tennis shoes she was wearing. "It's really okay. It's a private jet. We leave when we get there."

She looked down at herself and then back up at me. "I'm wearing jeans because I didn't want to get all wrinkled on the flight."

I smiled, shaking my head. "It's fine, Bella. The meeting isn't until tomorrow. I scheduled us to go up a day early, hoping to take advantage of the free time to show you around a bit."

Her mouth dropped open. "Really?"

"Yes, really. You're dressed perfectly for a day of sightseeing. It's me who isn't. I'll change on the plane." I would be happy to shuck the suit for a day.

I took the suitcase from her and pulled it along. The driver opened the back door of the limousine when he saw me coming.

"That's your car?" she gasped.

"It's a hired car," I told her.

"Oh, I've never ridden in a limo before," she murmured.

"Then this will be your first," I said, handing the suitcase to the driver to be stowed.

She stood in front of the open door, not moving. I put my hand on the small of her back, giving her a gentle nudge. She looked at me, her innocent green eyes sparkling with excitement before she crawled inside. I got in and smiled, watching as she checked out the interior of the car.

"I would have never imagined I would be riding in a limo, in Greece, on my way to catch a flight on a private jet. This kind of stuff doesn't happen to girls like me. This is the kind of thing that I couldn't even dare to dream about, and yet, here I am." Her smile was contagious.

"I'm happy to be a part of the dream."

We arrived at the small landing strip where my jet was stored. We quickly boarded, taking our seats in the luxury chairs. We were given mimosas for our flight. I could see Bella was nervous. Her hand was gripping the armrest of the chair, and I feared she might tear it off.

"Are you okay?" I asked.

She looked at me, a grimace on her face. "The first time I ever got on a plane was to come here. I don't think I'm quite used to the idea of flying."

"I'm sure this will be a smooth ride. It's only an hour-long flight."

She shook her head. "I told my dad I was afraid of the plane crashing. He told me to put my head between my legs and kiss my ass goodbye."

I burst into laughter. "That is horrible advice!"

"I know!" she exclaimed before she started laughing.

"We'll be fine. I have an excellent pilot, and this thing is kept in great shape."

"Good to know," she breathed as the plane started to taxi down the short runway.

Once we were in the air, she seemed to relax, drinking from her glass and staring out the window. Usually, when I was on the jet, I was working. I had no desire to pull out my computer and review notes or accounts. I wanted to be in the moment. I found that happened a lot when I was with her. Work was what I thought about all the time, but when I was with her, I didn't want to think about work at all. I wanted to learn more about her.

"Did you tell your father about our trip?" I asked.

She looked at me, her eyes lighting up. "I did. He's thrilled for me. Have you talked to your mom anymore?"

"No."

"Are you worried about Saturday?" she asked.

I shrugged a shoulder. "I'm not worried necessarily, but I am a little preoccupied with the situation."

"The situation? As in, you don't have a real girlfriend and you're bringing your intern?" She smiled.

"Yes, that about sums it up. No one lies to my mother and gets away with it. I don't want to think I'm lying. Technically, we are seeing each other. I don't need to mention that it's only been once, and we are only coworkers."

"Twice. Once when you came to save me and again at the beach. I think that is officially seeing each other."

"I hope she sees it that way. If, by some chance, she figures out I exaggerated our relationship, it will get ugly. I will do my best to protect you, but I make no guarantees."

She threw her head back, her slender neck exposed as she laughed. "You make your mother out to be this monster."

I shrugged. "She isn't a monster, but she is a different beast. Your father and my mother are nothing alike. While I know my mother loves me and she wants what is best for me, her way of showing support leaves a little something to be desired."

"I'm not going to lie. My dad is pretty awesome."

"You're lucky to have him."

"I am very lucky, and I try to tell him that as often as I can," she said.

"I envy and admire that."

We talked a bit more about our families before it was time to land. The car I had ordered was waiting on the tarmac to take us to the hotel.

"This is so impressive," she gushed. "I feel like I'm in the Lifestyles of the Rich and Famous or something."

I smiled, happy I could show her something new and impress her while doing it. I liked seeing her smile, and I liked seeing the excitement and wonder on her face. We strolled through the lobby of the posh hotel, Bella's head whipping back and forth as she tried to take it all in.

"Adrian Gabris checking in," I said to the man behind the reception desk.

He tapped on his keyboard before looking up at me, something akin to fear in his eyes. "I'm sorry, sir. It looks like there's been some kind of mistake."

Bella stood beside me. "Mistake?" she asked.

"Yes, we had a late check-in last night, and someone accidentally gave away the second room. I do have the suite available."

I looked at Bella, not wanting her to think I had somehow set up the whole thing. I didn't want her to think I had intentionally worked it so that we had to share a room. Before I got the chance to demand there be another room made available, Bella put her hand on the tall counter and smiled at me.

"We'll take it," she said confidently.

"We will?" I asked with surprise.

"Yes, we will," she said with a smile.

I looked at the clerk, who was visibly relieved. "Great, let me get your keys, and you can go right up."

I didn't say anything, not sure what to say. When he slid the keys to us, Bella turned and headed for the elevators. The bellhop waited to follow us up with our luggage. I had no idea what to expect. The suite only had a king-sized bed in it. I wasn't interested in sleeping on a cot, and I wouldn't ask her to, which left the bed. I didn't want to jump to conclusions. I was going to let her lead the way. I was up for anything if it involved her.

"We can get the bags," Bella told the bellhop.

He looked at me, shocked and with what looked like hurt on his face. I quickly reached into my pocket and handed him a generous tip before sending him on his way. I stepped into the elevator behind Bella, the cart taking up too much room for our rather small amount of luggage.

"You're sure about this?" I asked her, wanting to give her a way out.

"I'm positive."

I left the cart in the hallway, Bella and I carrying our bags down the hall to the room. I quickly opened the door and pushed it open. Bella squealed when she walked inside the spacious room, dropping her bags in the middle of the walkway and rushing to the massive windows lining one wall. I dropped my suitcase and briefcase and joined her.

"Nice view," I commented.

"It's amazing!"

She turned to face me, looking up at me and making me want to pull her into my arms. I couldn't remember ever feeling so drawn to someone. I prided myself on my ability to stay in full control of my emotions. She was stripping away that control and taking me back to a time in my life when I had been carefree and willing to throw caution to the wind. It'd been a long time since I'd been able to shed the cloak of wealth and fame and just be me.

"I like spending time with you," I blurted out.

Her eyes dropped to my mouth before meeting mine again. "I like spending time with you, too. Spending time together is going to help us be more convincing when we have to pretend to be together for your mom."

I nodded. "Practice makes perfect," I said, my voice husky.

"I agree, which means there's something else we should practice," she whispered, stepping closer to me.

I was afraid to ask what that something was. Afraid to ruin the moment if I said what I wanted to practice. "What would that be?" I asked instead.

"This," she whispered, rising up, her hand going to the back of my head and pulling my head down.

Her lips brushed over mine, sending a flash of desire through my body so intense I jerked forward. I heard her gasp as our bodies connected. I dropped my arm around her waist and pulled her against me, closing my eyes and letting myself fall into the moment. I focused all my energy on the kiss, applying a little pressure and silently asking her to part her lips for me to taste her.

I moaned the second my tongue slid past her lips, tasting the orange juice from the mimosa. I inhaled, taking in the scent of her, appreciating the smell of fresh flowers clinging to her skin. I was quickly losing control.

My body was demanding more. I wanted more. I wanted all of her. I wanted to taste her and touch her and hear her cry out in pleasure when I filled her body with mine. I demanded myself to slow down, rein it in before I scared her away.

I pulled back, our noses nearly touching as I looked into her eyes. I was asking without speaking.

"Don't stop," she whispered.

They were the sweetest two words I had heard in a very long time.

CHAPTER 20

BELLA

I was going to live in the moment, just like my dad had told me to. Part of living in the moment was being with Adrian. I had never had a fling or an affair. I was throwing caution and good sense to the wind and letting myself experience something I had only heard about through other people. Adrian was too good to pass up. Even if I couldn't have him forever, I wanted to know what it was like to be held in his arms as our bodies joined together.

He started to move backward. I trusted him to guide me. I wasn't sure where we were going, but getting naked in front of a very large window was probably not a good idea. I was glad he had the presence of mind to move us away from the full exposure.

"Bed," he mumbled, his hands reaching down to yank up my shirt.

"Okay," I said, kissing his jaw as I walked backward.

I started working the buttons on his shirt, irritated when my fingers stopped working. Then, because I was really in the moment, I grabbed his shirt front and pulled in opposite directions. All but one of the buttons flew off.

He stopped moving, looking down at me. I was immediately embarrassed by my rather enthusiastic gesture and hoped I hadn't just ruined things.

"Fuck me, that was hot," he said, yanking the shirt off his body and revealing the sexy chest I had ogled just a few days ago.

I pressed my palm to his chest while he worked to unhook my bra. I had a brief moment of "what the hell are you doing" but quickly pushed it aside. I wanted him too much to let my conscience get in the way. This was all about getting laid. I could afford one slip in my very moral life. By the time he pushed me through the double doors leading to the bedroom, we were both only wearing our underwear.

I reached down, grabbing his dick in my hand, and was pleasantly surprised by the girth. "Damn," I murmured.

He growled, his mouth slamming over mine again, his tongue plunging inside while his hands roamed over my body. My hands were doing the same. It was like seeing through touch, taking in every bit of skin as we tasted each other.

He jerked his mouth away from mine and pushed me onto the bed. I fell to my back, my hair fanning out around me as I stared up at his large body. He was most definitely a god, and I couldn't believe my luck that I was going to get to be with him.

I lifted my arm, reaching toward him. He didn't seem to notice, or he didn't care. His eyes were glued to my breasts. Feeling incredibly daring, I reached my hand to my breast, cupping it and lifting it in offering. His nostrils flared, his blue eyes darting up to mine before he dove in. I gasped when his mouth closed over my nipple, sucking it between his teeth as he massaged. He moved to the other, while my hands ran up and down his back.

"God, I want you," he rasped, his mouth closing over mine.

I answered with my body, wrapping my arms around him and squeezing him against me. "Take me."

He rose away from me, standing and yanking down my panties. I lifted my hips, letting him take them off and watching as he ditched his boxers. I bit my lip when I saw him. He was a big man in every way. I felt completely wanton getting naked with a man who was practically a stranger in the middle of the day. I was going to live it up and enjoy every last second of it, though. There would be time for regrets later.

"You're beautiful," he said, his eyes swallowing my body inch by inch.

I did the same, looking at the tattoos and letting my eyes linger on the center of him before taking in his strong thighs. He was built. I reached up to him, sitting up and grabbing his hand to pull him back down to the bed. He rolled to his side, and his chest pressed against me as his arm reached down to the top of my thigh. I held his eyes as the hand moved to my inner thigh, gently opening my legs. Like a heat-seeking missile, his hand drifted up, his knuckles brushing over me, pulling a gasp from my lips.

I moaned when his finger slid over my slit, parting my folds and touching the most sensitive part of my body.

I could feel the heat spiraling through my body as he moved his fingers over me, parting me but barely touching me. I craved pressure. I wanted the fullness that only he could bring.

"You're wet," he whispered.

"I want you," I managed to get out.

My body was weeping, demanding his. When his finger probed my opening, I let my knees fall wide, completely opening myself to him. The finger slid in deeper, aided by the passion already coursing through my body after his intense kisses. His finger toyed with me, giving me immense pleasure with what felt like very little effort.

"I want you to let go," he ordered, his finger pushed high inside me.

"I can't. I want you inside me." I whimpered, my body on the verge but unable to find release.

"Not yet. Let go, Bella." He said my name, and it was the last push I needed to fall into sweet oblivion.

I whimpered and moaned, clenching the bedspread in my fist as my body arched and clenched around the finger deep inside me. His mouth touched mine, gentle at first and then with more intensity as he pushed a second finger inside me, stretching me and sending my body into another fit of spasms that rocked me from the tips of my toes to the ends of my hair.

In a flash, his fingers were gone, and he was rising up over me, bracing his weight on his elbows. His mouth slammed over mine. I groaned under the delicious weight of his lower body pressing me into the mattress. I reached down and grabbed a handful of his tight ass, jerking and pulling him against me. I could feel his heavy cock pressed against me. I wanted to feel it inside me.

He reached between us, guiding himself between my legs, slick with my own juices. His head probed my opening. I felt swollen, ripe for the plucking as he pushed inside a little at a time, stretching me and reigniting the pleasure that had just swept through my body a few minutes earlier.

"Oh my god," I groaned, my head going back as he pushed in deeper.

He stopped moving. "Are you okay?" he rasped.

I opened my eyes and moved my head to look at him. "Better than okay. Don't stop."

He reached a hand down, his fingers threading through mine as he put my hand on the side of my head before grabbing the other one. I was completely at his mercy. I liked the feeling of him being in complete control as he rose up, using those glorious abs of his to hold himself off my body and pushing himself deeper inside me.

I cried out, my body filled with so much exquisite pleasure I felt like I was going to shatter into a million pieces. "Oh god," I said again, not knowing what else to say.

He grunted as he pushed himself all the way inside, his body fully seated inside mine.

I struggled to draw a breath. I was going to orgasm again. I was a little embarrassed, but my body didn't give a shit about my embarrassment.

"Move, I'm close," I ordered, not wanting to go alone.

"I can't hold back," he ground out the words as if he were in pain.

"Don't!" I shouted when he started to move inside me. When his body froze, I clarified. "Don't stop!"

"God dammit, this isn't enough. I need more." His body rocked against mine, pushing me across the bed.

"More, more, more," I groaned, eager at the very idea.

"I can't. I have to." He garbled the words.

I knew what he meant. I was right there with him, ready to let myself fall into that oblivion I had visited just a short time ago. I arched my back, taking him impossibly deeper and triggering a cataclysmic release for both of us. Our shouts of pleasure mingled together as his body collapsed on top of mine, arching and bucking against one another.

He rolled to the side, one arm flung over his face as he dragged in heavy breaths. "Holy shit," he whispered, and that was when it hit me.

"Holy shit," I repeated. "Did I just screw things up?" I asked him, but it was more about me asking myself.

"Screw what up?" he asked.

"Us. This. Work."

He reached up and put a hand on my cheek, leaning forward to kiss the tip of my nose. "Not at all. This doesn't screw anything up. This was amazing."

"I don't normally sleep with my bosses," I muttered.

"Hey, I think we're a little more than boss and employee," he said with a laugh.

I looked at him. "We are now."

"This isn't going to ruin anything," he said with a smile. "It might actually help."

"Help what?" I asked with confusion.

I didn't see how having sex with my boss was going to help my career, besides the obvious, and I refused to use a sexual relationship to get ahead in the world. I had too much self-respect to do that.

"It will help convince my mother we're a thing," he said with that sexy grin of his, which I now knew for a fact could melt panties away.

I rolled my eyes. "We know each other in the Biblical sense," I said with a laugh.

"Indeed, we do, but I think there might be a lot more to learn," he whispered, trailing a finger between my breasts.

I smiled with contentment. I didn't feel the slightest bit of shame lying on the bed with the man wearing nothing but my birthday suit. I didn't want to get dressed because I didn't want him to get clothes on. I quite liked the look of him naked.

"Should we go over the meeting tomorrow?" I asked.

He sighed. "We should, but I think I would rather do this."

"I can't say I would mind doing this, but can we order some food? I ran out the door and didn't have a chance to eat anything."

His eyebrows shot up. "Why didn't you say something? I could have fed you before—well, before we did this. Although I didn't know this was even on the menu."

I laughed. "I don't think I knew either, but when the mood strikes, the mood strikes!"

He sat up, getting to his feet and helping me stand. "Get dressed. We'll go get a late breakfast and try to do a little sightseeing before we have to think about work."

"That sounds like a great plan," I said, watching with a hint of sadness as he pulled on his underwear.

I really, really liked looking at his body. I hoped I got the chance to see him naked again—and soon.

CHAPTER 21

ADRIAN

Waking up with Bella in my arms was probably right at the top of the best mornings of my life. I didn't do sleepovers. I wasn't a virgin or a saint and I'd had my fair share of women in my bed, but it never ended up in a sleepover. Waking up with her soft body against me, the fruity scent of her shampoo filling my senses, and the sound of her soft breathing was all very comforting. I rolled my head to the side, being careful not to disturb her as I checked the clock on the nightstand.

It was time to get up and get ready for the meeting. I wanted to stay in bed with her forever. I knew I was probably crossing about a million boundaries, but I didn't care. She'd made the move. I could have tried to tell her it wasn't a good idea. I didn't because it was all I had been thinking about since I first laid eyes on her back in the bar that first night. I was drawn to her. There was some kind of magnetic pull I couldn't ignore.

"Hey," I whispered, not wanting to startle her.

I didn't know much about her dating life back home in the states, but I didn't get the impression she spent a lot of time in any man's bed. I didn't want her waking up disorientated and freaking out when she saw me next to her.

"Hmm?" She groaned, not opening her eyes or moving her face away from my chest.

"It's after seven. We need to get ready for the meeting at nine." I kept my voice soft.

There was a pause, and then she rolled away from me. "Oh shit!"

"Relax," I assured her. "We have plenty of time."

She turned her face to look at me, offering me a sheepish smiled. "Good morning," she whispered.

"Good morning." I returned her smile.

"I need to shower," she said with a disappointed sigh.

I was happy to know she was just as reluctant as I was to get out of bed. "I'll order some breakfast."

She yawned, nodded her head, and rolled out of bed. I got the chance to admire her beautiful body as she walked naked into the bathroom, closing the door behind her. I felt like pinching myself. I couldn't believe I had actually spent the night with a woman like her. It was unexpected, yet exciting.

I heard the shower turn on and figured I better get a move on. I quickly ordered breakfast for us and unzipped the garment bag containing my suit for the day. When Bella emerged from the bathroom, a fluffy white towel wrapped around her, I felt like I had been kicked in the gut. My breath escaped me as I watched her move toward me. She was stunning.

"Your turn," she said with a smile.

I nodded, my mouth hanging open. "Breakfast will be here soon," I said before walking away and directly into a cold shower.

It had taken a great deal of willpower to keep my hands to myself. I wanted to pull the towel away and feast my eyes and mouth upon her naked, wet body. After the cold water did its trick, I quickly moved it to hot, cleaned up, and pulled on my clean underwear before walking out of the bathroom.

Bella was in front of the mirror, putting on makeup. "So, what should I say today?" she asked, her eyes meeting mine in the mirror.

"I'll do most of the talking. I want you to watch and observe and see how it all works. I'll ask you direct questions when it's time for you to chime in."

"Great, I can do that," she said with confidence.

We ate breakfast first and then finished dressing, my eyes constantly moving toward her. She looked amazing in the short skirt and jacket. I couldn't wait for us to get the meeting over and done with. I wanted to spend the rest of the day with her, enjoying her company and not worrying about business.

When we arrived at the client's offices, we were escorted into the conference room to wait. I could sense Bella's nervousness. "Relax," I said in a low voice.

She nodded. "I am. I mean, I'm not, but I will."

I smiled at her. "This is just a trial run. This particular client worked with us before, fired us, and now is considering rehiring us but has some reservations. It's a good account, and I want it back. We're here to prove our services are worth what we charge."

"Got it."

A few minutes later, several men in suits walked into the room, sitting across from Bella and me at the table. I smiled at them, letting them know I wasn't the least bit intimidated.

"Good morning, gentleman," I started, immediately taking control of the meeting. "This is my associate, Bella Kamp."

The three of them looked at Bella, and I saw the very second they were taken with her. It was a slight advantage in my favor.

"Good morning," Aaron Keeler, the owner of the company, said before turning his eyes back on me.

"I understand you have concerns about coming back for another quarter," I said, getting right to the heart of the matter.

Aaron nodded his head. "I do. As you know, you've done great work for us in the past, but the proposal we were given last week? Well, to be frank, it seemed a little exorbitant."

"My company has grown, and we have become the leader in the industry," I told him. "I've hired new talent, and our services are in high demand. The cost for our services has increased because we've gotten better. You're paying for talent. You're paying for the best in the business, and that isn't going to come cheap."

Aaron scowled. "As a customer that has been with you from the beginning, I should get some kind of discount."

I scoffed. "We are both businessmen. We are both here to make money. My fees are nothing compared to the money you will make from our marketing talents."

He shrugged a shoulder. "I don't know if there is much difference between what you do and what other companies do. I need to understand why your company charges so much more than the others."

I looked over at Bella. I could see she wanted to say something but was holding back. I cleared my throat. "Because my company does it better," I said matter-of-factly.

Bella interrupted. "Aaron—can I call you Aaron?"

Aaron offered her a small smile. "You can."

She nodded. "Aaron, I think what Adrian is trying to explain is that Great Greeks isn't your average social marketing company. There's so much more to it than a few tweets or posts or getting your company to trend on some of the most popular sites. I work on marketing campaigns, and I'll tell you, the team at Great Greeks is amazing. They are the most creative minds I've ever worked with. They're young and in tune with what is happening in the world. They know the latest trends, and better than that, they know what hits and what fails because they are tapped into the various social groups."

Aaron nodded his head. The other two men looked intrigued as well. I realized she was reeling them in. I sat back in my chair and let her go. She had them in the palm of her hand, and I had been pushing them away.

"But is the cost of the service really worth it?" Aaron asked. "Don't other companies have young, talented people who are just as creative?"

Bella smiled. It was the kind of smile that lit up a room. "Possibly, but how many other companies are bringing their CEO to your door? How many of those companies are promising you results that you've seen in action before? You said you've been happy with the services you got before. Isn't that worth a little extra money? When you go with someone new, you start over. You don't know them, and they don't know you. Adrian told me all about you before we came in here today. He told me about your little boy and about how your company got started. He took the time to get to know you. Have the others?"

I watched Aaron softening, turning to putty in her very skilled hands. "I suppose not," he murmured.

"I'm telling you, from someone who has interviewed with other companies in America and a few other places, this is the company to be involved with. Every person I've met has integrity, and they truly care about their work. They love their boss and want to make him happy. A good working environment is always going to produce good results, but I'm sure you know that because your company is a place people want to work at." Her smile was just enough to drive home her point.

I waited, keeping my mouth shut, afraid I would undo all the progress she had made. It was pretty clear she'd been very persuasive. Aaron was thinking about it.

"All right," he said with a sigh. "You bring up a lot of good, valid points. I will admit I've talked with a couple of other companies and I was unimpressed. While they were cheaper, I didn't get the same level of confidence that their work would be as good as yours."

Bella was smiling and nodding her head. "You have to pay for quality. Your suit, it isn't off the rack is it?"

Aaron shook his head. "No, of course not."

"Because you appreciate quality and all of the things money can buy you. Our services are no different."

He grinned. "I see. You've sold me."

"Great. I will let you and Adrian hash out the details." She leaned back in her chair, effectively removing herself from the conversation.

Aaron looked at me, shaking his head. "That wasn't fair."

"Pardon me?"

Aaron nodded toward Bella with a grin. "She is very convincing. You need her on your staff. I like her."

Bella blushed a little. "Thank you."

"She's my secret weapon," I told him with a small laugh. "I only bring her out for the most important clients."

"Smart man," he said. "We'll accept the proposal you sent over on Monday. I'll have my people take care of the paperwork. I want to get started right away. The few weeks we've been without promotion are already taking their toll on the business."

"I'll call Rand as soon as we're finished here and get him moving on your account," I assured him.

"I appreciate that, and thank you for coming all the way here to meet with us in person. You did go the extra mile. That does make a difference." He looked at Bella again.

"You know you can call me direct if you have any questions or concerns," I told him. "Your account is important to me."

He chuckled. "I can see that. I didn't think I'd get the main man in my office. I've heard you rarely left Crete."

I shrugged a shoulder. "I used to travel a lot more, but the business keeps me in the city."

I got to my feet. Bella followed my lead. Aaron extended his hand. I shook his hand, along with the other two gentlemen's. Bella did the same.

"Keep her around and I think you might one day run the world," Aaron said in a low voice.

Bella had already moved down the hall, the two men eager to keep her company while Aaron and I lagged behind.

"Thanks, I'll keep that in mind," I said, watching her laugh at something one of them said.

The men were fawning over her, clearly enamored with the pretty, blonde American. I felt a tiny twinge of jealousy and quickly excused myself, making my way to where Bella was standing. I put my hand on her elbow, guiding her away from the men and toward the elevator.

She was mine. I didn't feel like sharing her laughter or smiles.

CHAPTER 22

BELLA

I waited until the elevator doors slid shut before I looked up at Adrian. I couldn't stop grinning. He looked very serious. When he finally looked at me, I grinned even bigger. He smirked, shaking his head as he punched the button for the ground floor.

"Don't say it," he playfully warned.

"Oh, I'm going to say it," I told him.

He let out an exaggerated sigh. "Let's get it over with."

"I saved your bacon," I announced proudly.

He raised one dark eyebrow. "You saved my what?"

"Your bacon," I teased. "You were drowning in there. Aaron was about ready to throw you out and take his business elsewhere, but I saved you. I saved the account. I think you should be the one who sits back and learns from me."

The elevator jerked to a stop, the doors sliding open. Adrian slid on his dark sunglasses before stepping out. I put on mine as well. We walked toward the glass doors without him saying a word. I hoped I hadn't pushed him too far.

We stepped outside, the heat of the day in full force. I quickly took off my jacket and draped it over my arm while we stood on the curb, presumably waiting for the car.

"You kicked ass in there," he finally said.

I turned to look at him, unable to see his eyes behind his dark sunglasses. "Thank you."

"You impressed me."

I felt my shoulders go back a little, pride filling me. "Thank you," I said again.

"Seriously, that was a great job," he said in his smooth baritone voice. "He was going to walk away. I don't usually have such a hard time keeping a client, but he was rubbing me the wrong way. I'm glad you were there."

I felt like a peacock, strutting as I walked to the car that had pulled up. I had done well and was going to bask in the glory of that for a short time.

"So, are we headed back now?" I asked, a little disappointed at the thought of going back to reality.

"I had thought it would take me at least two meetings to get Aaron back on board," he said. "I didn't think he'd be that easy to persuade. Why don't we go back to the hotel, change into something a little more comfortable, and do a little sightseeing?"

"Really?"

"Sure," he replied easily.

"That sounds fantastic. I would love to!"

"Great, we'll grab lunch while we're out. We'll see how the day goes, and we can have dinner out." His voice grew husky. "Or order in."

He pushed up his sunglasses. I quickly did the same, giving him my eyes as we were driven back to the hotel. I could stare into his eyes for days. There was something so deep, so soulful when I looked into his eyes. I felt like I saw something other people didn't, like he was letting me see something he kept hidden from everyone else.

When the car stopped in front of the hotel, I was anxious to get changed and back out into Athens. Athens was one of the oldest cities in the world. There was so much history. I wanted to take pictures of everything and show my dad. I had a sudden understanding of the people back in the old days who had slideshows of their vacations. I was glad my phone had plenty of storage. I was going to take a million pictures.

I had a brief thought of sex as I stripped out of the dress suit, but the excitement and allure of exploring Athens was too great to put too much thought into getting naked with Adrian. We could do that later. I was convinced this was my one shot to see Athens and the rich history that came with it. I wasn't a history buff, but how could a person not be drawn to the monuments and historical sites that had been around for thousands of years? It was mind-boggling.

"Ready!" I announced, sliding on one of my low-rise tennis shoes before dropping the other one on the floor and sticking my foot in.

He looked up from the chair he was sitting in and tying his own shoes. "I didn't know women could get ready to go anywhere that fast," he teased.

I walked to him and put my hand on the back of his head, being careful not to muss his hair. His arm wrapped around my waist, pulling me closer, my stomach at his eye level. "This is Athens. I could have been ready three minutes ago."

I bent down and kissed him. It was the first kiss since last night. I hadn't been sure if that was allowed or okay, but I had to get one small kiss in. I knew whatever it was that had happened between us was probably a one-night, possibly two-night, thing, and I got it. I really did, but it was hard to not touch him. I wanted to touch him and have him touch me. When his arm went around me, I took that as my approval to kiss him.

He pulled me down onto his lap, one hand on my hip and the other moving through my hair and holding the back of my neck as he deepened the kiss. I sighed into him, happy to know he was still interested in me after last night. I knew the risk of giving it up. The man might decide he'd had better and move on. Adrian was still here—or rather, I was still here—and it could all be about convenience and being in the right place at the right time. I'd think about that later. For now, I was going to enjoy the moment and pretend to be someone else while I was in Athens.

"We should go, or we might never leave this room," he whispered against my lips.

"Okay," I breathed, kissing him again and reigniting the spark he was trying to put out.

He smiled against my lips. I pulled back and looked into his eyes and felt supreme contentment, like there was nothing wrong in the world. Everything was all right.

I disentangled my arms from around his neck and my legs from his, and I got to my feet. He stood and gave me another quick kiss, being careful not to get too close. When he turned to walk away from me, I swatted his ass. He turned to look back at me, one eyebrow arched. "It's like that, huh?"

I grinned. "Maybe," I said with a giggle before taking a wide berth around him and stuffing my phone into the back pocket of my cutoff jean shorts.

When we arrived at the Acropolis of Athens, I was absolutely awestruck. I couldn't believe I was seeing it in person.

"Over here," Adrian said, taking my hand in his.

I let him lead me away from the long line of tourists and toward another small group of people standing around. It was then I noticed a man holding a sign with Adrian's last name written on it.

"What's this?" I asked.

"I hired a private tour guide," he said.

I had no words. I sometimes forgot he was rich, like crazy rich, and people bent over backward to make him happy. "Oh."

"So we can skip the lines," he reasoned.

"I see," I murmured.

"Is that okay?" he asked.

"Absolutely!" I said with a laugh.

"Good, there's so much to see, and we have so little time," he explained. "I want you to see as much as you can while we are here."

I could feel tears threatening to well in my eyes. I quickly blinked them back. His thoughtfulness made me feel all warm and fuzzy inside. "Thank you."

We were escorted through the ruins, our tour guide providing plenty of information and interesting facts. I could feel the history and thought about the people that had once roamed the place when it was functional.

"What do you think?" Adrian asked in a low voice.

The guide had moved away and was talking to another guide, giving us a few moments to ourselves. "I have no words. I'm overwhelmed at the moment."

"Is that a good thing?"

I smiled, squeezing his hand still holding mine. "It's a *very good* thing. I'm just in awe. I cannot imagine growing up here and seeing this all the time, hearing stories that I bet only true Greeks know. You must have had an amazing childhood filled with culture and history."

He shrugged a shoulder. "I suppose I did. You didn't?"

"Not like this. History in the states is nothing like it is in other parts of the world. Our history only goes back a few hundred years. This? Standing in a site that dates back further than anyone even really knows? That's amazing. It's so hard to wrap my head around the fact I'm really here. I never thought I would see this stuff in person. I never thought I would get to experience a true vacation around the world, and here I am. You're making this all possible, and I really don't know how to tell you just how important this is to me." I felt emotional and ridiculous for gushing, but it was all the truth.

"I am happy to be a part of this," he said in a low voice.

"This is truly a first for me," I told him, looking up to meet his eyes. "I feel so free, so normal, so... so... free!" I shook my head. "Back home, I always felt like I had all these ropes holding me back. I couldn't do a lot of things because it was financially impossible. I couldn't take a day off because I had to study or work to make sure I was able to afford to live. This? This moment? I feel like I'm really living."

There was a warm smile on his face as he nodded his head. "Good. Let's not stop here. There are a few other places you'll want to see while you're here."

I nodded, swallowing the lump in my throat, and let him lead me away.

The day was a whirlwind of activity. I was too amped to be tired. My feet hurt a little by the time we made our way up to our room at the hotel, but it was all worth it. I had blown up my dad's phone, sending him a ton of pictures. I knew it was the middle of the night for him, but I felt like I had to share it.

"I'll order dinner," Adrian said, kicking off his shoes. "Do you want to take a bath?"

I was dying to get into the huge jacuzzi tub and soak my weary legs and my poor feet. I nodded. "Do you want to join me?" I asked in a soft voice, a little unsure if that was crossing a line I wasn't aware of.

He grinned. "I would. I'll order some champagne as well."

I nodded, energy still zinging through my body after the adrenaline rush of the day. I could think of no better way for the day to end than crawling into a hot bath with a hunk of a man like Adrian. I knew it was all a dream world and I would soon wake up and land back in reality, but I wanted to live in the moment. The memories we were creating were going to get me through the rest of what I expected to be a mundane life, compared to what it was like in Greece with Adrian.

"Are we going back tomorrow?" I asked him, knowing the answer but hoping for the best.

"No."

My eyes went wide as I spun around to look at him. "No?"

He smiled, slowly shaking his head. "I've made some plans for tomorrow."

"You did?" I squeaked out the words.

"I did. Go get that bath started," he gently ordered. "I'll be in there in a few minutes."

I nodded and walked away, feeling like I was floating.

I never wanted it to end.

CHAPTER 23

ADRIAN

Bella was pacing the living room, anxious to get to where we were going, with no idea where that place was. I had kept it a secret, wanting to surprise her. I learned pretty fast she wasn't a patient person. She'd pinched and begged and pleaded and offered to do all kinds of things to my body—some good, some not—in an effort to get me to reveal our plans for the day.

"Are you ready?" I asked, half teasing because I knew she'd been ready for an hour.

She glared at me. "Are you? I'm beginning to think this is all a hoax."

"It's not a hoax," I said, walking to her, putting my hands on her hips, and pulling her in close.

She tilted her head back to look up at me. "I'm ready."

I dropped a kiss on her lips before stepping away and heading for the door. The car was waiting to whisk us away to a vineyard I had reserved for the entire day. No visitors besides myself and Bella. Only the staff and owner would be there.

The limo was waiting for us when we walked out the front doors of the hotel. Unlike the first time she'd seen the magnificent car waiting, Bella strolled to the car and climbed in the backseat like a pro. I loved that she could quickly acclimate to anything sent her way.

"I think you're really going to like this," I told her when the car turned off the main road, traveling away from the city.

"I can't imagine I wouldn't like anything you show me," she replied, her eyes focused out the window. "It's all wonderful."

I took in the long legs, crossed at the knees. The tiny shorts she was wearing made her legs look even longer. She'd put on a T-shirt, covering her shoulders after getting a little too much sun yesterday. I tended to forget not everyone was acclimated to the heat of a Greek sun.

When the car stopped, Bella looked at me, then back out at the massive sign indicating we were at a vineyard. "A vineyard?" she asked.

I smiled. "Very good," I teased.

She didn't look all that impressed.

I knew there were vineyards all around the world, but this was special. "Yes, a vineyard. It's just me and you and the workers of course."

That caught her attention. "Yes. We'll get a tour and do a little wine tasting. They have a chef on staff that is world renowned. The restaurant on the grounds is one of the best in Athens."

"Oh no! I'm not dressed for that!"

"You're dressed just fine. As I said, it's just us. We're not impressing anyone. Besides, I'm wearing shorts and a T-shirt as well."

The back door opened, and before she could worry anymore about her attire, we were escorted into the vineyard tasting room where the owner was waiting for us.

"Hello," he greeted with a warm smile.

"Hi, Alesandro," I said. "This is Bella. Bella, this is Alesandro. He owns the vineyard."

Alesandro stepped forward and gave Bella a quick kiss on the cheek. "It is so nice to meet you. Your man has taken care of everything. We hope you enjoy your visit."

"Thank you," she said a little shyly.

"Thank you for letting me do this," I told him.

He cocked his head to the side. "For you? Anything. You've done amazing things for our little family vineyard. Business is booming. My staff was very pleased to have a day off." He chuckled.

"Hey, you hired the best," I joked. "I had to see for myself what it is you're offering."

"Of course, of course. We have the villa ready for you if you would like to rest first."

"The villa?" Bella asked.

"We'll be staying here tonight," I announced. "I've rented the entire vineyard—all of it, including the villa."

Her eyes were as big as saucers. "Are you serious?"

I smiled and almost told her the rest of my surprise but managed to keep it to myself. I couldn't wait to see her reaction when she did see it. I wanted to impress her. I wanted to make her happy, and fortunately, I had the money and the means to do it. I could make her smile and bring a tear of joy to her eyes. That was my new goal in life. I didn't care about making more money or increasing my company's value.

I wanted to see her smile.

"I'm very serious," I said.

"But we didn't bring our bags," she said.

"It's taken care of," I assured her. "Our things will be here within a couple of hours."

"Oh. Wow. All right then. Let the wine tasting begin. I've always wanted to do one of these tours but never seemed to have the time."

"Now you do."

"We are ready to start with the first samples, and then we can move over to the wine-making area for you to make your own wine," Alesandro said.

"We're going to make wine?" Bella asked with astonishment.

"It's part of the package," I said with a wink.

She shook her head, her hand covering her mouth. "I cannot believe this. I'm—I'm at a loss for words. This is so awesome!"

We spent the next few hours tasting wine and touring the massive vineyard before we were taken up to the main showroom to have lunch.

"Alesandro, join us," I invited.

The older man looked at me and smiled before gently shaking his head. "No, no, this is your time."

Bella chimed in. "Please do. I have so many questions about your vineyard."

Alesandro's face softened. "If you don't mind my intrusion, I would love to share a meal with the two of you."

The three of us sat down. Alesandro looked from me to Bella, and then back at me with a gleam in his eye. I headed him off before he could say anything that would make Bella or myself feel awkward. We hadn't talked about what was happening between us, and I didn't want to. I just wanted to go with the flow of things.

"How is business?" I asked him.

His face lit up. "We are booked for the summer. People want to tour the vineyards, and with your team's ideas, we have opened up the dining area to accommodate more guests. We have sent in our first order for merchandise with our brand on it and will soon start shipping our wine via our new online storefront."

"Really? Good to hear!"

"I owe it all to you. You helped an old man when others were trying to tell me I would never get this small winery on the map. You made it happen. I am so grateful to you." He smiled before turning toward Bella. "I was one of his first clients. Did you know that?"

She shook her head. "I didn't."

Alesandro smiled and got a wistful look in his eye. "It was almost three years ago. I had just lost my wife of forty years, and the winery wasn't doing well. I was ready to sell and give up. Adrian told me he could help me. He convinced me he could revive the business and breathe new life into it. I didn't think it was possible, but within six months or so, things were looking up. It's only gotten better from there. My wife would be so happy to see her dream finally coming true. I only wish I could have met Adrian sooner."

I reached out and put a hand on his shoulder. "You had it all right here. You just needed someone to put it all in a pretty little package."

He grinned. "And you did. I know you did more than I paid you for. I cannot tell you how much it means to me to see my business thriving. I owe it all to you."

I looked over to find Bella staring at me. The way she was looking at me made me squirm a little. I could see the admiration and adoration in her eyes and didn't feel worthy. I had done my job with Alesandro. Maybe I had given him a little extra, but he had taken a chance on me, and I wanted to make sure he got his money's worth from my services.

"I'm going to use the restroom," Bella said, getting up from the table.

When she was gone, Alesandro turned to face me, a serious look on his face when he reached out and touched my arm. "She's a good one. You have to hold on to the good ones."

"She is a very good person," I said, not wanting to admit she was my intern.

It felt wrong to think of her as my intern and nothing more. I was staying in his villa with my intern. It was pretty clear there was something going on between us. We'd spent the day exchanging kisses, holding hands, and with me keeping her close with my arm around her. I felt ashamed of myself. I wasn't going to tell him we were just sleeping together or that it was just an affair while we were away from the office.

"And I will keep that in mind," I mumbled, looking away, afraid he would see my guilt.

"Ah, I see you aren't sure," he said. "Take it from me. That kind of affection comes around only once. The way she looks at you? That only happens once. You grab on to that one and don't let go."

"She has proven herself to be invaluable to my company and maybe to me," I confessed in a soft voice before finally meeting his all too knowing eyes again.

"Ah, yes," he said. "My wife, she was the company. She was the one with the vision and the energy to make it happen. When I lost her, I gave up. I didn't think I could do it. I wasn't sure I *wanted* to do it without her, but then you convinced me I could honor her by making this place a success."

"I'm glad it is working out. I truly am happy to see the success you're having."

"Thank you," he said, rising when Bella returned. "I will leave the two of you alone to enjoy your dessert. Your bags have been placed in the master suite at the villa. You can retire whenever you would like."

"Thank you so much for this lovely lunch and allowing us to tour your winery. It was a wonderful experience." Bella gave him a warm hug.

"You're very welcome," Alesandro said before turning and winking at me as he walked away.

I looked back at Bella. "Would you like to do a little more adventuring?"

She let out a tired sigh. I felt the same way. Yesterday had been exhausting, and today was just as tiring. "Sure," she said half-heartedly.

I chuckled. "I agree. Why don't we retire to the villa? I could use a little downtime, and I need to check email."

She bobbed her head up and down. "Absolutely. I am anxious to see what the villa looks like. I've seen them on TV but never in person."

"Do you want to walk, or should I call for one of the golf carts?"

"Let's walk," she said with a small laugh. "I think we have that much energy let in us."

"Barely."

We got up and walked away, following the path I knew led to the villa. I had seen it once, but that had been a while ago. When we approached the large home, I heard Bella gasp.

"Wow, it's better than what I've seen on TV," she exclaimed, taking in the two-story white home.

"Good," I said, opening the door and letting her go in first.

Her sharp intake of breath as she stepped into the open, airy living space made me smile. The villa was perfectly romantic. I couldn't wait until later when the real surprise happened.

CHAPTER 24

BELLA

While Adrian checked in with work, I took advantage of the huge bathroom and the lovely garden tub that had huge windows overlooking a private garden. Adrian assured me I had complete privacy and didn't need to worry about anyone peeping on me while I bathed. After spending more time just hanging out and relaxing, there was a knock on the door.

Adrian smiled, a look in his eyes that said he was up to something.

"What's going on?" I asked with curiosity.

"You'll see," he said.

I rose from the place on the couch where I had been cozied up to him, surfing the internet on my tablet while he read a book on his. It was incredibly peaceful in the vineyard, and settling in with Adrian had been easy.

I watched when a cart, the kind used for room service, was wheeled in. Adrian directed the young man pushing it to leave it in the kitchen. I smelled a familiar aroma coming from the cart and walked toward it. Adrian stood next to it with a huge grin on his face.

"What is it?" I asked in confusion. "It smells like… barbecue?"

Adrian winked and pulled off one of the dome lids to reveal a pile of barbecued ribs. "You have a good sense of smell."

"No way!" I squealed.

He pulled off a few more lids. I could feel tears springing to my eyes as I stared at all the familiar dishes. It was a barbeque. Although gourmet, it was a good old-fashioned American barbecue right in the middle of our Greek villa.

"You talked about how much you were missing home and the barbecue, so I thought I would bring it to you," he said nonchalantly.

I shook my head in complete awe. "This is crazy. I can't believe you did this."

"It *is* the Fourth of July," he said with a shrug.

I giggled. "It is. Too bad we won't be able to live stream the fireworks show."

He smiled. "About that," he said, leaving the words hanging.

"This is plenty," I assured him, anxious to dive into the meal. "This has made this trip absolutely perfect!"

"It isn't perfect yet," he insisted. "Let's get plates and head out to the balcony."

I clapped my hands together, unable to hide my excitement. "I'll grab one of those bottles of wine Alesandro gave us."

The wine we had made together was bottled and waiting for us to take home and open in a few months or years if we wanted. For now, we'd been given a couple of bottles of our favorite varieties from our tasting tour. With our plates heaped with coleslaw, potato salad, ribs, baked beans, and fried chicken, we moved to the patio to enjoy the beautiful night. After stuffing our faces with the perfectly cooked meal, we stretched out on the lounge chairs with a glass of wine to do a little stargazing.

"Look over there," Adrian said in a low voice, pointing out something I couldn't see.

I wasn't sure what I was looking at. "Um, I—"

The sky erupted into brilliant colors—red, blue and green—as fireworks began to fill the sky, bursting into vibrant colors before fading away.

"Surprise," Adrian whispered.

My hand was over my mouth, staring at the sky with a myriad of emotions. "You did this?"

"Happy Fourth of July," he said.

I got up from my chair and crawled in next to him on his lounger. "You're amazing. I can't believe you did all of this for me. Thank you."

"You're welcome," he said, wrapping his arm around me and squeezing me closely against him.

We watched the fireworks show for fifteen minutes until the last one had erupted in the sky. I lifted my face to his and kissed him.

I felt raw and vulnerable. My emotions had been running high, and all I wanted to do was fall into him. I rose up, moving over the top of him and straddling him in the chair. My hands moved to the hem of his shirt and pushed it up his body. He was watching me without saying a word as I undressed him before moving off the chair and stripping off my own clothes.

I stood beside the chair staring down at his naked body in the moonlight and felt something so intense I couldn't explain what it was.

I crawled up his legs, my hands running over his muscular thighs before I leaned down, gently grabbing his hard length and taking the first taste of him. He sucked in a huge gasp of air as I slid my mouth down his shaft, moaning with the pleasure of tasting him.

I bobbed my head up and down, scraping my teeth over his sensitive flesh. I loved hearing him groan in pleasure, his fingers threading through my hair. A cool breeze brushed over my naked flesh as I knelt over Adrian's equally naked body, his cock buried in my mouth. I moaned, the sound apparently too much for him. His hands reached under my arms and jerked me forward, knocking me off my knees. I landed on his chest, my breasts pushed against his hard muscles.

"You're so beautiful," he whispered, a second before he pulled me up higher, sliding my body over his and sending a series of shock-waves through me as his mouth covered mine.

I reached between us, grabbing his cock in my hand once again and guiding him to my opening. I pushed away from him, tearing my mouth from his, and wiggled my hips, taking the tip of his engorged head inside me. I gasped, wincing a little as I struggled to make him fit inside me.

"Slow," he whispered, putting his hands on my hips to steady me.

I was anxious and ready, but my body wasn't—yet. I rotated my hips, feeling my body opening to his invasion and slowly pushing down on him. I leaned back and looked up at the stars high overhead as I slid down the rest of the way, letting him fully impale me.

I didn't move or breathe. I closed my eyes, all of my energy focused on the area where we were joined together. Spasms of electricity jolted through me, causing me to jerk and igniting new delicious sensations.

"Heaven," I whispered the word.

"What?" he rasped.

"Heaven. This must be what heaven is like." I leaned forward and put my hand flat against his chest.

He offered a small, tight smile. "I agree. Move. I need you to move."

The feeling of sublime vanished and was replaced with intense passion and need. We'd skipped a few steps to get to where we were in that moment, but I didn't miss any of it. Having him buried inside me was too good. I craved his touch, his body and, most importantly, him. I rode him hard and fast, both of us panting and encouraging more from one another. The lounge chair was presenting some logistical problems. I couldn't get there.

I slapped at his chest with frustration. "I can't!" I cried out.

He sat forward, using those killer abs, and wrapped his arms around me, pulling me close to him. My mouth went to his, our tongues dueling as he throbbed inside me. The skin-on-skin contact was what I needed. I sighed with contentment at the feel of his crunchy chest hairs rubbing over my sensitive nipples.

"Get up," he ordered, yanking his lips from mine.

I scrambled off the chair, his absence from my body leaving me feeling empty. He got to his feet, taking his sweet time, his eyes locked on mine. I could sense the crackling energy in him and braced myself for what I hoped would be a very exuberant taking of my body. I waited, staring up at him, willing to do whatever it was he asked of me.

"Turn around and put your hands on the table," he ordered in a stern voice.

I shuddered. The domination I heard in his voice nearly made me orgasm without him even touching me. I moved the few steps to the patio table and placed my palms on top of the cool slate. He moved behind me, one large hand spread out to run over my back, squeezing my ass before pushing my legs wider. His hand slid between my thighs, his fingers tracing over my swollen flesh and parting me. One finger pushed inside without warning. I yelped, going up on my toes as he pushed it in deep before pushing in a second finger. The rough invasion sent me spiraling. I cried out, moaning for him to give me more.

He pushed me down, my face going flat against the surface of the table. His hand between my thigh, guiding his heavy cock between my legs, excited me. I was on the verge of exploding. He pushed inside me, grunting as he filled my body with his hard, long length. I moaned with satisfaction. When he pulled out and slammed into me, my face sliding across the table, my moans turned to gasps and little whimpers mingled between cries for more.

He spoke his native tongue. I didn't understand the words, but they were said in a way that told me he was losing control. His hand was pressing my chest against the table, his other on my hips and holding me against him while he rocked against me. I slapped my open hand against the table, the pleasure torturous as he took me to a place I had never been. It was the stars and the moon and the clean, fresh air with the hint of earth and fruit wafting over us as we made love on the balcony of a Greek villa.

I felt a smile spread across my face as the orgasm slowly spun out of control, starting low in my belly and flooding me with heat and ecstasy. It was beautiful and sweet and oh so good.

"Oh fuck," he groaned, the words signaling his pending release.

I arched my back, taking him a little deeper and giving him the last bit of ecstasy he needed to find his release. He gasped, his body going stiff against mine before he moved his hips with deep thrusts that tickled every last nerve ending in my body.

I moaned, relishing in the feel of him pumping inside me.

He stopped moving, dropping to one elbow beside me on the table, his body still embedded inside mine. I opened my eyes and smiled at him, completely sated and happy to stay right where we were all night.

"You okay?" He gasped out the words.

"I'm so much better than okay."

He grinned, leaning forward to drop a quick kiss on my nose before standing up, leaving me feeling empty without him pressed against me. I pushed myself off the table and turned to face him, letting him envelop me in his strong arms.

"Should we go in?" he murmured over the top of my head.

I sighed against him. The heat from his nude body felt good against mine. "I kind of like it out here, just like this."

He chuckled. "As do I, but maybe we could be just like this inside the bedroom on the big, comfortable bed."

"Okay," I sighed, happy to go anywhere with him.

We strolled through the large, open villa and made our way to the master suite, crawling into bed and holding each other close.

"I don't think it's going to be all that hard to fake it for my parents now," he said in a dry tone.

I burst into laughter. "I suppose not."

CHAPTER 25

ADRIAN

Landing back in Heraklion was a little disappointing. I had enjoyed my time with Bella, and I wasn't ready for it to be over. It was, and now it was time to get back to the real world.

We walked to the waiting car on the tarmac, both of our moods subdued. I slid into the backseat and reached for her hand. I knew me touching her like that couldn't happen at the office. It was going to be a bit of an adjustment for me to get used to keeping my hands and eyes to myself. I certainly didn't want rumors getting started.

"Why don't you take the day off?" I suggested.

"What? I'm sure I have a lot of work to do."

I shrugged. "It's almost lunchtime. I doubt you're going to get much done anyway. Take the rest of the day off, and I'll see you tomorrow morning."

"Are you sure?"

"I'm sure," I insisted.

"I guess I can't really argue with the boss," she said with a small smile.

"Get some rest. You're going to need your strength to deal with my family tomorrow."

"You're not going to scare me away," she said. "I said I would do this, and I will keep my promise."

"Good," I told her. "Thank you. It will make my life easier—even if only for a short time."

I leaned forward and told the driver to take us to Bella's hotel. Neither of us spoke during the ride. I knew I was already thinking of what next week looked like with us. I had let myself fall into a weird sense of comfort and stability with her the past few days, even though I knew it couldn't last.

When the car stopped in front of the hotel and the driver got out to get her bags, she leaned over and gave me a quick kiss as if she didn't want anyone to see or know about us. I understood it—but hated it.

"I'll see you tomorrow morning," I told her.

"I'll be ready," she said and jumped out of the car before I had a chance to say anything more.

I watched her go inside, feeling like I was losing something, but I couldn't really say what that something was. It was just an absence I felt. Instead of going home, I had the driver take me directly to the office. I *did* have a lot of work to catch up on, and I didn't feel like being alone.

When I walked through the halls of the office, I was warmly greeted by all. It felt good to be back, but there was an emptiness. Bella had only worked in the office for a week, but I could feel her absence. I imagined what it would be like after she worked here a little longer and then left. I would be looking for her, wandering the halls lost and confused for a long time after she was gone.

I got to my office, took off my jacket, and was just settling in when Rand knocked on my door once before letting himself in. "Long time no see," he said, strolling in and taking a seat in one of the chairs.

"How have things been here?"

"Good," he replied. "Nothing exciting. What about Athens?"

Our daily check-ins had been restricted to bigger issues, and the little things had been left for a time when we could actually talk —like now.

"Good," I said, shrugging a shoulder nonchalantly.

"Good? You told me you closed the deal on Tuesday, but you're only just now back. I would say it was better than good," he said with a knowing smile.

"Actually, I didn't close the deal. Bella did. I was sinking. If I would have kept talking, he would have taken his money and business and left."

"What?" he asked with shock. "Bella? The shy little intern?"

I nodded. "That's the one."

"Really?" he asked, shaking his head. "I thought she was in the marketing and creative area?"

"I told you I saw something special in her," I said, grinning. "She's a pro at talking to people. He was like putty in her hands."

"You're just saying that so you can say you were right about her," he protested.

I shook my head. "No, I'm not. She's talented, and what's even better—people *like* her. She's smart and kind and easy to be around."

"Really?" he asked, staring at me in a way that made me a little uncomfortable.

"Yes, really. I told you she would be good for the company."

He nodded, scrutinizing me as I spoke. "Good for the company for the short time she's here."

"Yeah, of course," I muttered.

"Shit," he said with what sounded like frustration.

"What?"

"You—you're walking a dangerous path, my friend."

"What are you talking about?" I asked, not ready to admit to anything if there was a chance I could deny it.

"I warned you," he said with a sigh. "I knew it the minute she was late for work, and then when I saw her and the way you looked at her, I knew this was going to happen."

"Knew what was going to happen?" I asked, hedging.

He smiled. "Exactly what is already happening. You never extend a business trip. You were gone all week for something that could have been handled in a few hours. You could have come back Tuesday night, but you didn't. You wanted to spend time with her. I'm not even going to ask what happened between the two of you. I don't have to ask because I can see it all over your face."

"You can't see shit," I retorted.

"I've known you the better part of my life. I know the look you get when you're interested in a woman. This is different though. I can feel it, and if *I* can feel it, that must mean it is pretty damn serious."

"Stop," I said, not looking directly at him.

"You need to be careful with this," Rand warned.

I looked at him. "Careful? What do you mean by that?"

"She's an intern. An American intern who is several years younger than you."

"So?" I snapped. "What's that have to do with anything?"

"You're a wealthy man, Adrian," he said. "You know how badly this could go for you, for the company if she gets pissed when you dump her or tell her it was a fling."

"You don't know that I will."

"Even if you don't, she's not here to stay," he warned. "She's staying in a hotel. She doesn't even have an apartment. This is temporary."

I shrugged. "I know that."

"Do you? You spent several days with her. You have feelings for her," he stated it rather than asked it.

"I don't know if I do," I told him.

"I do. Like I said, I know you, and this isn't like you. She's changing you, and she's only been here a week. What happens when you let yourself fall for her, and she up and leaves you in a few weeks? This company needs you at the top of your game. Have fun with her, but remember. This is temporary. She will go home once she's bored with all of this. She's young and having fun."

I sucked in a deep breath. "You don't know her. She's not like other women her age. Bella is different."

Rand slapped a hand to his forehead. "You didn't just say that."

"I did, and I've been saying it because it's true. You would know if you gave her a chance. You're too busy making assumptions about her to let yourself get to know her."

"I'm not getting to know her or any of the interns. Why would I?" He shrugged a shoulder. "They're here to do a job, nothing more. They come, they do, they go."

"I'll keep that in mind," I muttered. "If you don't mind, I need to return some of these phone calls you left for me."

"I'm only looking out for you," he said from the doorway. "I don't want you to get yourself in a situation that causes problems. I know you. You don't fall easily, and this one is getting to you."

I nodded my head. "I get it. I do. Thanks for looking out for me, but I'll be fine."

He shrugged a shoulder. "All right, see you later."

Once he was out of my office, I breathed a sigh of relief. I didn't want to tell him about tomorrow and the fact we were going to pretend we were a couple to get my mom off my back. There was very little pretending on my part. I knew we weren't an official couple, but I wouldn't mind pursuing something along those lines.

Was it worth the effort if she was only going to be gone in a few short weeks? I didn't want to get involved with someone that wasn't interested in sticking around. I couldn't move to the United States, and she didn't seem interested in leaving her father. I had seen how homesick she was the other night. I had done what I could to appease that loneliness, but it wasn't the same. She was the woman she was because of her relationship with her father and the grounding he provided.

I wasn't sure who she would be without him. I wanted to try with her, but deep down, I knew she had no intention of making Greece her home. I couldn't do a long-distance relationship. It would never work with my responsibilities with the company. She would likely get a job in a heartbeat and find herself encumbered with work. The time difference would be an added problem.

It wouldn't work. I had to accept that the woman wasn't mine to keep.

She'd won me over and made me feel things I had never experienced before, but it was only temporary. It was going to be hard to see her tomorrow, now that the reality of our future was staring me in the face. Somehow, I had managed to forget all about her only being a temporary addition to my life. The past few days had been amazing, so freeing and so full of excitement. It led me to believe there was a chance for a future with us together.

"Dammit," I muttered, running my hands through my hair with frustration.

I pushed it all aside and focused on the work in front of me. I couldn't afford to neglect my clients. Like we had learned earlier in the week, I wasn't the only game in town, and a client could fire me and move on to the next guy without looking back.

CHAPTER 26

BELLA

I was bored. I wasn't used to not having a list of things to get done. Maid service stayed on top of the picking up and cleaning. I hadn't worked for days and had nothing to do there. My dad was in bed. I was a little tired after all the exploration we'd done in the past few days. I sighed, tossing my arm out to the side as I lounged on the white sofa in the spacious hotel room. It was a big room, but I felt claustrophobic. I wondered what Adrian was doing just then.

There was a knock on the door, startling me. I wasn't expecting any company. I grinned, jumping to my feet, thinking it might be Adrian. I yanked open the door. "Oh," I said.

Cassia rolled her eyes. "Gee, I feel loved."

"Sorry." I giggled. "You surprised me. Come in."

"What are you doing?" she asked, breezing past me.

"Nothing, absolutely nothing," I told her.

"Put on your swimsuit," she ordered.

"What?"

"Put on your swimsuit," she said with a smile. "We're going to the beach."

"Right now? It's kind of late, isn't it?"

She rolled her eyes. "It's four o'clock. It's Friday night. You're not that old."

I laughed. "You're right. What am I thinking? Give me five minutes." I rushed past her to change into my swimsuit.

I stuffed a few things in the beach bag I had bought in Athens at one of the tourist traps, against Adrian's advice. I knew it was cheesy, and I didn't care. I needed a beach bag, and it was cute.

"Ready?"

"I am," I announced, putting on my dark sunglasses.

She groaned. "You look like a tourist with that bag."

I grinned. "Perfect, because I am."

Once we had found a patch of sand to lay out our towels, we both stretched out on our backs. It was warm, and I wasn't convinced I was going to be getting a tan in the waning sun, but it felt good to lay on the beach, listening to the sounds of people playing and frolicking on the beach around us.

"How was your trip?" she asked.

"It was awesome!" I exclaimed.

"You guys must have had a lot of, uh, business meetings," she said.

I wasn't sure what I was supposed to say or admit to. "Adrian allowed me to do a little sightseeing."

"I see. Did Adrian do this sightseeing with you?"

"Yes."

"Hmm," she said, turning her head to look at me.

"What does that mean?" I asked.

She was still grinning. "Nothing. I'm glad the two of you had a good time. He works a lot. I think a few days away was good for him. He was in a really good mood at work today. He told me he told you to take the day off."

"Yes, he didn't think there was a lot I could get done in the few hours I'd be there," I said, backing up the story.

She turned away, both of us quiet as we relaxed on the beach. "You know you can talk to me, right?" she asked in a quiet voice.

I did want to talk to someone. I couldn't talk to my dad, but I also didn't want to talk to my immediate boss about *her* boss and me sleeping together.

"I have a friend, and she's found herself in a bit of a weird relationship with her boss," I started. "She isn't sure what it means or if she should even talk about it."

"Is this friend an American?" she asked.

"Yes," I quickly answered.

"I think Americans and Greek people have a different outlook on things like that. We're not so uptight. Greek women are strong. We don't feel like we have to prove ourselves or try to be better than the men we work with."

I shook my head. "What does that mean?"

"I mean, if your friend and her boss have a relationship, I don't think it is so bad."

"Really?" I pressed. "What do you think the other people in the office will think about that?"

She scoffed. "Who cares? It isn't their business. I think if your friend and her boss enjoy being with each other, that's what matters. Obviously, I don't think your friend will want to flaunt her relationship. I'm sure the boss is an attractive man, and some of the women might be a little jealous, and we know how women can be."

"Jealous? Do you think this has happened before? I mean, do you think her boss does this often?" I was a little horrified to think of Adrian making his way through all the new women in his employment.

"No, definitely not," she quickly replied.

I turned to look at her. We were speaking in hypotheticals, so technically she wouldn't be able to be sure of that. I was pretty sure my little hypothetical game had failed. She knew damn well I was talking about me and Adrian. I wasn't going to admit it, but at least I knew she was giving me her inside advice.

"What if the boss is just using her because he knows the relationship will never go anywhere?" I asked softly.

"I think your friend will probably know the difference between a man looking for a piece of ass and a man that is genuinely interested."

My mouth dropped open. "Cassia!" I exclaimed.

She giggled. "You know what I mean. When you pick up a guy at the club or on the beach, you kind of expect it to be a one and done. Maybe you hook up a couple more times, but then that's that. There are no promises of anything, and it's just sex. There's a difference. Please tell me you've had that experience?"

I shook my head. "Not really, no. I lived a sheltered life, and I lived with my dad. I couldn't exactly bring a man home. I'm not a virgin, but I was a little more restrained than any of my friends."

"Ah, I understand now," she whispered.

"Understand what?"

"Does your friend like her boss?" she asked.

"Of course!"

"I mean, does she like him in a way that she wants to see him again?"

I nodded. "I think so, but she doesn't know if it can ever go anywhere. She doesn't know if she should ask or even try. She's worried about getting laughed at for being naïve enough to think there could ever be something between a plain American and a wealthy, uh, her boss." I didn't want to reveal too much.

The whole conversation seemed a little ridiculous. We both knew I was talking about Adrian, but I couldn't say it. I felt like the naïve woman I had just described.

"These are questions your friend should talk about with her boss," she replied. "I bet her boss is a good guy who would be willing to talk about these very important matters."

"What if he doesn't want to talk to her outside of the office?"

She made a choking sound. "Then, you—I mean *she*—makes him talk. Your friend needs to be strong."

"I know. I agree."

"Good. I think you should tell your friend she should follow her heart. If your friend feels a connection to her boss, she should pursue it, not let the working relationship interfere with what is in her heart. Life is too short to let a good man get away. Love is up to fate. You never want to mess with fate. If this is meant to be, it will be." She turned to look at me again and pushed up her sunglasses.

I raised mine as well. "But is it wrong?" I whispered.

"Wrong? How could it be wrong?"

"I don't know," I said. "I mean, they're two different people. They come from very different backgrounds. How does someone know when it's right? When it's fate, like you said?"

"I think only the person in that relationship can know," she said with a smile. "Everyone else is on the outside, looking in. It's only the boss and your friend who know what's happening between them."

"I suppose."

"Bella, what are your plans?"

"My plans?" I asked.

"When your internship is over, what do you plan to do?"

I inhaled, turning to look up at the sky. "I don't know. Go home?"

"What were your plans before you got here?" she pressed.

I grinned. "My dream was I was going to get here and blow all of you away with my skills. You were all going to be so impressed, you were going to insist I open an office in Seattle and run it. I was going to have my dream job and get to be close to home."

She burst into laughter. "Wow, think much of yourself?"

"Hey, you asked." I giggled.

"Okay, now that we've got that established, what are your plans now? If you could have your dream come true, what would that look like? Do you still want to go home and open an office?"

I grimaced because I didn't know, and that worried me. I always knew what I wanted. I always had a goal to work toward. I was always on the road to somewhere, and that road had faded before my very eyes. I didn't know what I wanted to do.

"I don't know."

"Your internship is over soon," she said. "Will you go home? Do you think there might be a reason to stay?"

I hesitated. "I honestly don't know."

She smiled. "Then I suggest you have a conversation with someone. I think you might have a reason to stay for a little while longer."

The thought of staying made my heart hurt. I couldn't leave my dad alone for months or longer. If I did stay in Greece much longer, I was going to have a hard time leaving Adrian. I wasn't sure if I could handle that. I didn't want to fall for Adrian and then have to leave.

Who was I kidding? I had already fallen.

"Let's get a drink," she said, sitting up. "I have a feeling you might need one."

"Yes, I could. Maybe more than one."

"Follow your heart," she advised. "My mom always told me to follow my heart, even when my head was telling me something different."

"That's the problem. My heart is kind of split. I have a foot in two different worlds. I didn't expect to come here and like it. I expected to come here, do my work, get something really cool to put on my resume, and then go home. It's not so cut and dry anymore. And what's worse, I know my dad would want me to stay. He's already encouraging me to apply for a permanent job. I know he's trying to be encouraging and support me, but I don't think he actually wants me to do it."

"Of course not. It's a parent's job to push their children out of the nest. They know that we have to spread our wings and fly, and we can't do that under their close supervision. They hate to see us go, but they know they have to push us away."

"You seem to be talking from a place of personal experience."

She nodded. "I am. You've told me a little about your dad, and I have a feeling he would be happy for you if you chose to stay. You really never know what might happen. Don't you think you owe it to yourself to at least follow this new path and see where it may lead?"

I groaned, putting my head back and looking up at the sky. "You're not making this easy."

"Nothing worth having is supposed to be easy," she said, grinning. "It has to be hard in order to make sure you weigh all the options. If it was easy, you wouldn't give it much thought. You need to think this over very carefully before you make a decision. This is a big deal."

I rolled my eyes. "Gee, you think?"

She burst into laughter. "Let's get you that drink."

I remembered my plans for tomorrow. "I can't stay out late. I have to get up early. I have a busy day tomorrow."

"Really?" she asked with a teasing tone. "How odd. I thought I was your only friend in the city. Well, me and one other person. I know *we* don't have plans, so I guess that means your busy day must be with a certain other someone?"

"Stop. I am admitting nothing."

"You don't have to. I'm happy for you and the someone. You can't ignore the chemistry. When it's hot, it's hot." She winked.

"Oh, it's hot," I said, unable to keep myself from making one little naughty comment.

She squealed. "You vixen!"

CHAPTER 27

ADRIAN

I'd stayed late, long after everyone had gone home for the night. I had overheard the conversations, people talking about their plans for the weekend and telling one another they would see each other on Monday. Even Rand had plans. I was going home, alone.

Since meeting Bella, I realized I was alone. It had never been an issue for me until now. I had the pleasure of spending time with a woman who I felt compatible with. I had felt adored and appreciated, and truth be told, I was a little addicted to the feeling. I liked the touches and kisses throughout the day.

I especially liked what happened when we were alone in our room at night and once in the middle of the day. I smiled.

"Fuck it," I grumbled, reaching for my phone.

Got plans? I sent the text to Bella.

She answered a few seconds later. *Nope. Just got back from the beach.*

I was tempted to ask her if she'd worn a bikini and if it was still on. I loved looking at her body.

Hungry?

For? she replied.

I chuckled, loving her cheeky comeback.

Dinner. Food. And maybe some dessert.

I wasn't great at flirting—I knew it—but it didn't stop me from trying.

Sounds good. I'll be waiting.

See you in thirty minutes.

I shut everything down and headed out the door. I had plans. That was a rarity for me. As I walked to the elevator, I pulled up the app for one of my favorite Chinese restaurants and quickly ordered plenty of food to be picked up in twenty minutes.

I didn't bother calling a car, choosing to hail a cab instead. It was much faster, and I was in a hurry. I was having withdrawals after being away from her for less than eight hours.

With the food in hand, I had the cab take me to the hotel. I found myself speed-walking to the elevators, anxious to see her. The smell of the Chinese food in the bag I was carrying reminded me I had skipped lunch and was very hungry.

I knocked and waited. When she opened the door, I literally lost my breath. She was so damn gorgeous, even wearing a pair of leggings and a baggy T-shirt. She was beautiful.

"Hi," she said, standing back and letting me walk in.

"Hi. I hope you're hungry," I said with a laugh. "I may have gotten a little carried away when I ordered."

"I'm very hungry, and that smells delicious," she said. "We can eat at the little table in here or out on the patio."

"The patio sounds good to me," I said, reminded of the last time I'd been on a patio with her and how that had worked out. "I want the fresh air."

We dished up, each of us taking generous helpings from each carton before settling in on the patio chairs.

"How was work?" she asked.

"Fine. I don't think they missed me at all while I was gone." I smirked.

"You have the best team in the business," she said. "I would hope they could keep things afloat while you were gone. You deserve some time off. You and my dad are a lot alike, you know?"

"We are? How so?" I was genuinely curious.

"You are both dedicated to your work. You're both convinced the world will fall off its axis if you take a few days off. You both have a real dedication to the job, to your people, and I find that admirable. I've heard a girl tends to be drawn to guys who have a lot of her father's traits. I guess it's true." She laughed.

"Tell me more about your dad," I said, wanting to learn more about the woman that was capturing my heart.

She smiled, her eyes lighting up. "He's a great guy. I don't feel like words are enough. My dad grew up poor. Like really, really poor. He dropped out of school to get a full-time job to help support his family. He always says he wasn't cut out for school, but that's wrong. He's so smart, and most of it is self-taught. He always sacrifices for everyone else. He doesn't make a big deal out of it. He just does it, and when you try and thank him, he shrugs it off. He is always sacrificing for others. Everyone loves him."

"What kind of sacrifices?" I asked out of curiosity.

"Oh, gosh. I could go on forever. He is the kind of guy who will give his last dollar to the guy on the street asking for help for his family, even when we had nothing to spare. I remember when I was little, and we came out of the grocery store with our bags. There was a young woman with two little kids with her, holding up a meager sign asking for help. My dad stopped, rummaged through our groceries, and put together a bag for her and the kids. The little boy was terrified. Apparently, she'd escaped a horrible abuse situation with nothing but her kids and the clothes on their backs. Not only did my dad give them our food, which we really couldn't afford to spare, but he insisted she load up in our car, and he drove her thirty miles into the city where there was a women's shelter. I think I was probably six or seven at the time. From that moment on, I knew he was a superhero." Her eyes beamed with pride.

I nodded my head. "No shit. He sounds like he should be up for sainthood."

She giggled. "If I had my way, he would be. He wasn't big on religion, but he did give me the standard stories to live by. He told me I always had to give. Even if I didn't think I had it to give, do it anyways because no matter how little I had, someone else had less."

"Holy shit, I feel so inadequate," I said, shaking my head with disgust at my opulent lifestyle when guys like her dad were giving all they had when they had so little.

"Don't feel inadequate," she said. "My dad is kind of different than the rest, and that's why he's special. If everyone was like him, he wouldn't be so special."

I shook my head. "Still, he sounds amazing. I'd like to meet him one day."

She scoffed. "I don't know if my dad would ever get on a plane. You'd have to go to him."

"You never know. It could happen."

"It would be worth your trouble to meet him. I don't want to brag, but my dad is frickin' amazing. He's my everything. I've already decided he's never going to get sick or die. He's going to be around until I die."

I laughed. "You sound pretty certain about that."

"I am."

"Well, I envy you," I said. "I have to prepare you for tomorrow. My family is nothing like that. You're not going to want to anoint any of them. They will make you rethink everything you think you know about me."

"Stop," she said, laughing. "You're exaggerating."

I shook my head. "I'm not. Not in the least. My family is loud and boisterous, and they all just say whatever pops into their heads. They have no filters. I don't think they try to be intentionally rude, but it just happens."

"I'll be okay. I've dealt with people all my life, and I can handle rude. I'm not a wilting flower."

She looked so sweet and innocent. I knew my mother would eat her alive if she got it in her head she didn't like Bella for one reason or another. I couldn't imagine what fault my mother would find, but I knew my mom well enough to know she could see fault in just about anything, and she didn't hide what she thought. Her opinions tended to be loudly expressed.

I shook my head. "If someone says or does something that makes you uncomfortable, tell me. I won't tolerate them mistreating you."

She reached across the table and touched my hand. "Adrian, I think you're worrying about nothing. I see you and I can't imagine you were spawned from monsters. Your mom loves you and wants what's best for you. I get that and I appreciate that. I'll be on my best behavior. If she gives me any shit, I'll be quiet and demure and walk away. I don't want to cause any problems for you. I've dealt with people looking at me with the side eye for most of my life—trust me, it's nothing new."

I shook my head again. "No, that isn't okay. If my mom gives you any shit, tell me."

She winked. "I'm a big girl. I can handle my business."

I chuckled, trying to imagine her as a redneck woman. I'd seen movies and the American television shows that showcased the stereotype. "Can you shoot a gun?" I asked, remembering the differences in our cultures and laws.

"I can, but I don't go out shooting all the time, and when I do, I don't wear tiny little shorts and cowboy boots," she said dryly.

I grinned, picturing the image in my mind. "I wouldn't mind seeing that."

She giggled. "Thanks, but don't expect to see that anytime soon."

"Not even once, if I ask really nicely?" I teased.

She shrugged. "I didn't pack my cowboy boots."

"Damn."

"Seriously, stop stressing about tomorrow. We'll have fun. Tell yourself it's about the fun, and it will be fun. If you go in there all stressed out and waiting for your mom to say something that pisses you off, you'll find it stressful. It's all about the mindset. Think happy thoughts."

"I'll keep that in mind. Right now, I have some happy thoughts that you can help bring to life." I waggled my eyebrows.

She got up from her chair and moved toward me. Her hand reached out and ran through my hair, her nails stroking over the skin on the back of my neck. I tilted my head back, looking up at her from where I sat, and felt like the luckiest man in the world. I had her. I had her touch, and I was about to have her body.

"Do your happy thoughts have anything to do with us being naked?" she whispered.

I leaned my face into her hand that had moved to my face. "They do."

"Hmm, I think like those thoughts, but tonight, I think we need to go inside. We don't have the privacy, and I'm not interested in showing the world all my lady parts." She leaned down to drop a kiss on my head.

"I don't want you to show the world your lady parts. I'd prefer we kept that between us."

I got to my feet, her hand sliding down my chest. I loved the way she touched me with the slightest bit of hesitation. I knew where to touch her, where to put my lips to steal away all hesitation and turn her into the fierce little wildcat I knew she could be.

She giggled softly. "I'll happily show you my lady bits."

"I like looking at those lady bits," I said, following her into the room.

She stopped walking and turned to face me, pulling off the shirt and showing me she was braless underneath. It took less than two seconds for my dick to grow hard. She cupped her breasts. "These lady bits?" she asked provocatively.

I nodded, my mouth hanging open. "Yes. Those bits. Can I touch?" My voice was husky with desire.

"I've shown you mine," she said. "It's time for me to see yours."

I groaned. The woman was going to kill me with ecstasy. I had to admit, it was a hell of a way to go.

CHAPTER 28

BELLA

I giggled as I watched the large man in my hotel room rip off his own clothes as if they were toxic. He stood in the center of the room wearing nothing but his underwear and a raging hard-on, staring at me with eyes that were devouring me bit by bit. I very slowly started to shimmy out of my leggings, inching them down a little at a time, revealing the tiny black thong I was wearing underneath.

"I want you," he said in a deep voice.

I smiled. "I'm offering me."

He shook his head. "No, I want all of you. I want to taste you."

The way he was looking at me, like I was the most exquisite dessert he'd ever seen, nearly made me orgasm right there in front of him. I licked my suddenly dry lips. "Okay," I breathed.

"Naked," he said, not moving toward me. "I need you naked."

I stood just inside the doorway of the single bedroom inside the hotel suite. It wasn't nearly as fancy as the suites we'd stayed in while we were in Athens, but it was luxurious to me. Without hesitating another second, partly because the look in his eyes told me he might shred my panties if I didn't get them off in a hurry, I pushed them down my legs. I looked up, waiting for his eyes to meet mine. His were busy roaming over my body, studying every inch.

I rubbed my legs together, feeling a tiny bit self-conscious under such an intense visual inspection. He sprang forward like a tiger lunging at his prey. The look in his eyes was dangerous. A smarter woman would have run, but not me. I opened my arms, ready to be preyed upon.

His mouth slammed against mine, his arms wrapping around me and yanking me against his hard body, skin on hot skin as he tried to eat me alive. He was a fierce, passionate, and unbridled man, starving for carnal pleasure. I was happy to feed him.

I groaned, wrapping one leg high around the back of his knees, pulling him closer to me, rubbing myself against his hardness.

He lifted me up and strolled across the room with me draped against him, his mouth still on mine before he deposited me on the large king-sized bed. He stood over me, my legs bent at the knees and hanging over the bed. He was breathing hard, his chest heaving up and down and his nostrils flaring as he gazed at my nude body splayed out in front of him.

I shuddered. My entire body burst into heat and chills at the same time. I knew something intense was coming. It was a prickling of excitement, fear, and lust rolled up into one crazy feeling. My skin felt tight under his lustful stare.

"Adrian?" I whispered his name, asking for the touch I craved.

"I want to look at you. I want to know everything there is to know about you."

I reached my arm up, hoping to entice him to come to me. He dropped to his knees beside the bed, shocking the hell out of me when he grabbed my legs and yanked my body forward. I fought the urge to close my legs and scoot away from him. It was so intimate, so daring, and nothing I had ever done before.

"Adrian." I said his name again.

His eyes met mine as I stared down my flat stomach to where he was positioned between my legs. "Shh, lie back, and let me feast upon you."

My eyes went wide as I watched him move his mouth toward me. His tongue lapped over my folds, and I gasped, my back arching and my eyes squeezing closed. Hot streaks of ecstasy zipped through my body. He licked again, one of his hands sliding up my thigh and pushing my legs apart. I was completely open, exposed, and vulnerable to him.

The hesitation and fear I had felt seconds ago evaporated, replaced with euphoria. My body was singing as he ran his tongue over the sensitive folds, tickling and teasing and making me feel things I had never experienced before. I felt like a stringed musical instrument that he was plucking with expertise. Every stroke of his tongue created a beautiful melody in my head.

When that same tongue pushed inside me, the melody erupted into a full-blown orchestra. My body went as tight as a bowstring, arching against his mouth and pushing his tongue deeper inside me.

I screamed, the only thing I knew to do to release the tension that spiraled through my body. The orgasm was explosive, sending me into the heavens. Little pinpoints of light burst in front of my closed eyes. I felt numb and overly sensitive at the same time as I slowly drifted down to reality. Adrian was kissing over my belly, taking a path to my breasts, where he lapped and suckled them. I finally managed to open my eyes and looked at him with wonder.

"You good?" he asked.

I moaned. "My god. So much better than good."

He grinned, lifting me by my arms and sliding me onto the bed. "Good, because I'm not finished with you yet."

An aftershock tore through my body. "I'm not sure I have anything left."

"You do. Trust me, you do. Roll over." His voice was firm and commanding.

I now knew to trust the man. Everything he told me to do led to great pleasure. I was his sex slave. Whatever he asked for, I was more than happy to oblige. I was the one who benefited in the end. His big hand roamed over my shoulders, squeezing and applying pressure before sliding down my back. His hand moved over one ass cheek, then the other, before moving between my legs and spreading them. I felt his knees on the bed on either side of me, the mattress indenting as he crawled over me. He jerked my hips up, my chest still pressed against the mattress.

My heart was pounding. The anticipation of what was to come made me breathless. I fisted the blanket in my hand, waiting for the first touch of him between my legs. I felt his knuckles brushing over my thighs a split second before the bulbous head brushed over my swollen folds. Then, it was gentle pressure pushing inside me. I adjusted my position, arching my back and spreading my knees wider to give him full access to my body.

"That's it," he encouraged. "Oh god, you're so tight and wet."

I closed my eyes, sinking into the feeling of him filling me. It was too good. I could already feel my body winding up, wanting more of the ecstasy that only he could give. He stretched me completely, filling my body with his. His hands moved up and down my sides, scraping over flesh that felt raw. He gently pushed me down flat on my stomach, with his heavy body over mine. He reached down and pushed my legs closed.

"Oh god," I moaned, squeezing his heavy cock inside my body.

He groaned, and his mouth dropped to the back of my neck. His teeth scraped over my flesh before he nibbled and sucked. He didn't move his lower body. He didn't need to. Him being inside me, cradled tightly within my sheath, was far more arousing than anything I had ever experienced.

"You feel so good around me," he whispered. "I have to move. I have to fuck you."

I gasped. "I want you to fuck me."

He rose to his knees, his arms supporting his weight as he began a slow glide in and out of my body. His pace was slow and steady, dragging out the pleasure.

"More," he grunted, pulling me back to my knees, my head still down.

His body rocked against mine. Our flesh slapped together as he moved fast and hard. Our mingled grunts and gasps and the occasional curse word filled the air. He was fierce. I reached behind me, digging my nails into his ass, encouraging him to fuck harder.

"God dammit!" he shouted.

I squeezed again, pushing my body against his and taking him deeper. The eruption of ecstasy took me by surprise. I shouted out with pleasure, my hand dropped to the bed, fisted in the blanket and held on as he moved faster than a jackhammer—until he was the one shouting out his release. His body spasmed violently against mine, pulling groans of what sounded like pain from him as he lost all control.

When he collapsed beside me on the bed, shaking the mattress, I dropped to my stomach again, struggling to catch my breath.

"Good god," I gasped.

"You're okay," he murmured.

"I'm fine. Better than fine. Are you okay?"

He chuckled. "I don't know yet. I'll let you know in a couple of minutes. I might be dead."

I giggled, turning my face to look at him, my head too heavy for me to hold up. "You look alive, maybe a little dead."

"I feel a little dead, but in a good way."

I found the strength to put my hand on his chest. I pressed my palm over his strong, beating heart and smiled. "Definitely alive."

He didn't say anything for several long minutes. I could practically hear his thoughts and knew he was worried about tomorrow.

"You're sure you still want to go tomorrow?" he finally asked.

"I'm sure. I'll be okay. You'll be okay. Don't worry about it."

"Okay, but if—"

"Adrian, things will be fine. Why don't we get some sleep?" I hoped to get him to relax a little.

"Do you want me to stay?"

"Yes, will you please?" I asked, not wanting to sleep alone.

The man had spoiled me in Athens. I didn't want to go back to sleeping alone. I liked being curled next to his big body and feeling the quiet strength that pumped through his veins. I felt so connected to him when we were sleeping, like our souls were resting together.

"I will. Hell, I'm in no position to go anywhere," he said with a small laugh.

"That's very good for me."

I scooted off the bed and reached down to pull him up. We climbed under the covers together and assumed our usual sleeping positions, with my head nestled against his chest, his arm protectively around me. As I laid there thinking about tomorrow and how stressed the man was about it, I started to have some doubts.

He was making a really big deal out of things. I wondered if there was something to be worried about. I had never really met anyone that didn't like me. I wasn't entirely sure how I would handle that. It probably wouldn't be so bad if I were on my home turf, but I was going to be at their mercy.

I had to be careful what I said and did. It was his family. Ultimately, he was my boss. If I did something that offended them, I would probably end up fired and on the first plane back to the United States with a huge black mark on my resume.

Maybe meeting his family wasn't such a good idea. It was a little late for that now. I had pushed and encouraged him to take me, promising him all would be okay.

I really, really hoped I didn't shoot myself in the foot with my offer to be his fake girlfriend.

CHAPTER 29

ADRIAN

I had gotten up early and gone back to my place to shower and change for the family gathering. I knew my mother said casual, but that meant business casual. I could skip the suit, but I still needed to wear my slacks and a button-up shirt. I just hoped it wasn't too hot.

By the time I made it back to the hotel, Bella was ready to go. She met me in the lobby of the hotel to save time.

"You look stunning," I said, walking across the large lobby and directly into her waiting arms.

She was wearing a pretty pink and white summer dress with wedge sandals. It was feminine and pretty, just like her. She'd pulled her hair back in a low ponytail, showcasing her beautiful neck that I loved to feast on.

"Thank you. I hope it's enough. I don't want to be underdressed, but I don't want to look like I'm trying too hard."

I laughed and gave her a quick kiss. "It's perfect."

"I'm the one who's nervous now," she griped.

"We can't both be nervous at the same time," I told her, taking her hand and walking through the hotel lobby.

I noticed the people looking. I knew they were looking at her and thinking I was a lucky man to have her on my arm, or my hand rather. I *was* lucky. I was proud to go anywhere with her, and I hoped my mother approved—even if it wasn't the real deal.

With her tucked into the front seat of my Mercedes, I got behind the wheel, took a deep breath, and put the car in drive. No matter how things went with my family, I knew it would be something I remembered for a long time. If they loved her, they would never let me live it down when we broke up. They wouldn't know it was fake. If they hated her, they were going to constantly remind me of the girl I brought home that one time.

"Hey, it's not your turn yet," Bella said with a smile, stretching her hand out to rest it on my leg.

"My turn?" I asked, glancing her way before putting my eyes back on the road.

"To stress," she said. "I'm still stressing about how your family is going to accept me. It's still my turn."

I chuckled. "I see. Let me know when it's my turn. We could just turn around and head in the opposite direction. I'll call and tell her something came up."

"We can't do that. I've got you, and you've got me, right?"

I looked at her and realized we were a team. No matter what our relationship status was, I knew she would have my back. "Right."

I was shocked, irritated, and overwhelmed all at the same time when I pulled my car into the driveway of my parents' home. It looked like her get together was a full-blown family reunion. I looked over at Bella, who was eyeing the many cars parked in the driveway and up and down the street.

"This is your family?" she asked.

"My extended family, I'm guessing," I complained.

I shook my head, turning off the car. This was not what I had expected. My family was loud and boisterous on their own. Add in the cousins, uncles, and aunts to the mix, and it was sure to be a recipe for disaster.

"It will be fine," Bella said, and I wasn't sure if she was talking to me or reassuring herself.

I reached over and grabbed her hand, giving it a good squeeze before I got out of the car. I opened the passenger door for her, and with her hand in mine, we walked to the front door. My mother answered the door. I cringed the moment I saw her face. I could already see the disapproval, and she hadn't even met Bella.

"Adrian, I'm so glad you could make it," my mother said before turning to look at Bella.

She turned her nose up at Bella, and it wasn't just because Bella was several inches taller than her. I sighed, knowing we were not getting off to a great start. My mom was determined to hate any woman I chose. She was convinced every woman was after my money and didn't care about me—the man. In my mother's eyes, there would never be a woman good enough for me, unless she handpicked the woman.

"Thanks for the invitation. I didn't realize you were inviting the whole family," I said dryly.

She shrugged a shoulder. "We thought it would be nice to get everyone together."

"I see. Mom, this is Bella. Bella, this is my mom, Helen."

My mother gave Bella a cursory look. "You can call me Mrs. Gabris," she said in a haughty tone.

"Mom," I said in a warning voice.

"Come inside. I have guests to attend to." She ignored my tone and walked away.

I looked at Bella and saw the look of hurt on her face. My mother had dismissed her, not even giving her the chance to say a word. Sometimes, my mother really pissed me off. I had hoped she would be better. I had some stupid idea in my head that she would have been polite at the very least. I only hoped the rest of my extended family were much kinder.

"You okay?" I asked Bella.

She smiled. "I'm fine."

"Bella, I'm sorry. I shouldn't have let you do this. My mom, she can be a handful at times."

"It's okay, really. I can handle it. So, she doesn't like me. I'll survive." She shrugged a shoulder.

"Stick with me, and I'll protect you in there," I told her.

She giggled. "It cannot possibly be that bad."

I grimaced. "I'm not so sure about that."

We moved into the house, closing the door behind us. I followed the sounds of voices and laughter. There was a group in the living room, some of my distant cousins. I kept moving, heading toward the backyard where there would be a bit more space and we wouldn't feel quite so trapped.

"Adrian!" my father greeted me.

"Hi, Dad."

"I didn't think you would come," he said with a laugh.

"I said I would. Dad, this is Bella. Bella, this is my father, Stavros."

"Hi Stavros—I mean, Mr. Gabris," she said, fumbling her words.

"You can call me Stavros," he told her, putting her at ease, unlike the way my mother had handled her.

"Thank you. It's nice to meet you. I see where Adrian gets his height from." She smiled.

My dad smiled and nodded his head. "All of my boys are good, strong men."

"I bet they are," she agreed.

"Adrian, get Bella and me a drink," he said to me.

I looked over at her, making sure she was okay with that. "Anything diet or water will work for me."

I nodded my head. "I'll be back."

I trusted my father to be decent toward her. I would have never left her alone with my mother. I could already sense the tension between Bella and my mother, and it wasn't Bella's doing. I was going to give it some time, but if she continued her rude treatment of Bella, I would say something. She might not be my real girlfriend, but she was someone I respected, and she deserved to be treated better than what my mom was doing.

I quickly fished around in the ice chests, retrieving two sodas and a bottle of water before making my way back to where my dad and

Bella were still talking. I was waylaid by an aunt I hadn't seen in a while. I kept my eyes on Bella, looking for any signs of distress. I was feeling guilty as hell for bringing her to this thing. My family would eat her alive, given the chance. They were all proud Greek men and women and didn't particularly approve of any of those in my generation dating Americans, or anyone else who hadn't been born and raised in the Greek traditions.

I managed to extract myself and make it back to Bella, who had been joined by one of my cousins. "Hi, Amanda," I greeted my cousin, who was two years younger than me.

"Adrian!" she said. "We didn't know you had a girlfriend. I thought your mother would be shouting it from the rooftops."

I rolled my eyes. "Yes, I'm sure she will."

"I'm stealing her away," Amanda said. "I want to introduce her to everyone. Besides, Uncle Stavros is probably boring her to death."

"It was very nice talking to you, Stavros," Bella said quickly.

"Here's your drink," I said, handing her the icy can.

"I guess I'll be back," she said as Amanda pulled her away.

I turned to my dad, who was grinning ear to ear. "Walk with me. I need to get something from the study."

That was code for: he wanted to have a private conversation. Anytime he wanted to talk to one of us away from my mother's ears, he would suddenly need something from the study. The *something* always changed, and we always walked out of the study empty-handed.

"What's up?" I asked him.

I sat down in one of the leather pub chairs, waiting to hear what he had to say. He took a seat in the other chair and looked at me, smiling. "I like her."

"Bella?"

"Yes, Bella," he said with sarcasm. "Did you bring another woman?"

"No, I didn't. I'm glad you like her."

He nodded. "I like her, but she's an American."

I shrugged. "So?"

He looked at me with confusion. "Why would you bring an American here? You know your mother wants you to marry a proud Greek woman."

"Because my mother isn't the one who would be spending the rest of her life with the woman I chose to marry," I said. "Bella is my girlfriend. We aren't talking marriage."

Hell, we hadn't even talked about a relationship, let alone a committed one. I wasn't about to tell him it was all a sham just to get my mother off my back. That would only make things worse—or better perhaps.

"She's a nice girl, but she's American," he repeated.

"Dad, I know where she's from. She's a good woman. You said you liked her. What's the problem? Do you mean to tell me you would really deny my happiness with a woman because of where she was born?"

"I think there are lots of girls from right here that would make a suitable wife for you. Girls that would know and understand our ways and appreciate our traditions and customs."

"How do you know Bella wouldn't?" I asked. "You're not giving her a chance, and it's pretty clear Mom isn't either. Please don't disappoint me and judge her based solely on her citizenship. You guys are better than that."

"Maybe we are. Maybe we aren't. I think it was a mistake for you to bring her."

I narrowed my eyes. I was disappointed in him. I thought he would be the one person who would be an ally in the situation. I hadn't expected my mom to welcome Bella with open arms, but the outright hostility was pissing me off.

"Well, it will be your loss if you don't give yourself the chance to get to know her," I said. "You're going to lead a miserable, boring life if you only talk to people from Greece."

"I talk to people all the time. I'm only warning you to think twice about this relationship. She's an American and doesn't know our ways. She will want to go home soon. Will you follow her or give up on her?"

"I don't know, Dad."

"It's something to think about," he said. "Giving your heart to a woman you can't have is going to make you the miserable person."

"I haven't given her my heart," I argued.

He tilted his head to the side and studied me closely. "Haven't you?"

CHAPTER 30

BELLA

Amanda took me around, made some introductions, and then ditched me to go take care of her daughter. I found myself a little lost and not knowing what to do. I realized then that most of the older women were absent from the backyard. I suspected they were in the kitchen. I was used to helping out at the many potlucks and picnics back home and decided to make myself useful.

"Hi, can I help with anything, Mrs. Gabris?" I asked, walking into the kitchen and finding her and two other women slicing fruit.

"No thank you," she snapped, not at all friendly.

"You can slice that cheese," one of the women said, gesturing to a hunk of cheddar cheese resting on a cutting board.

"Perfect, I'd love to," I said, relieved to be of some help.

Mrs. Gabris said something in Greek. I realized she was purposely shutting me out. Adrian's warnings were not unfounded. The woman was extremely prickly and obviously hated me.

"Are you from America?" one of the women asked.

I nodded. "I am. I'm working at Adrian's company as an intern."

"Oh, you work with him?" the woman asked.

I tried to hide my grimace, realizing I may have said too much. "I do."

"So, you've only been together a short time?" Mrs. Gabris questioned.

"Yes."

"I see."

There was more conversation in Greek before the two women took the bowls of cut fruit and left the kitchen, leaving me alone with Adrian's mother. In my mind, I had just stepped into the ring with the woman, and I had better be prepared for a few blows.

"This is a big party," I said politely. "Do you do this kind of thing often?"

She dropped the knife she was holding and came around the center island. She moved one hand to her hip and made a big showing of looking me up and down. It was an intimidation factor, and if I were made of lesser stuff, it would have been effective. As it was, she didn't scare me in the slightest. I had dealt with women like her my entire life.

"I do," she snapped. "Why are you with my son?"

"Pardon me?"

"I asked, why are you with my son? Is it his money?"

I raised my eyebrows. "His money? That's why you think I'm with Adrian? Have you seen Adrian? Have you spoken with him? Do you know him?"

She glared at me. "I know my son very well, and I know Americans very well. I know you all want money. You sell your bodies and your dignity for money. You make those stupid television shows and take naked pictures of your bodies and put them all over the internet. Americans don't understand anything except money."

I smiled, taking a deep breath in the through my nose before slowly letting it out. "Adrian is a good, kind man, and his money means nothing to me."

"I don't believe that for a second," she snapped.

"And that's your prerogative," I said in a sweet voice, letting her know she wasn't going to get a rise out of me. "I think I'm going to take this cheese out to the table. Did you need me to take anything else?"

179

I wouldn't disrespect Adrian and go rounds with his mother. It took all of my willpower to keep my mouth shut. I promised myself if she kept going, I would say something, but words weren't going to be what broke me. I had heard and seen prejudice all my life. She was nothing new.

I put the plate of cheese on the table and looked around for Adrian. I needed a drink but had left mine in the kitchen. There was no way I was going back in to get it. I felt out of place and noticed the stares coming my way. My blonde hair and fair skin stuck out like a sore thumb in the backyard full of dark-haired people with beautiful olive complexions.

"You look lost," I heard a deep voice say.

I turned around and found Stavros coming toward me. I scanned the area for Adrian but still didn't see him.

"Not lost, just taking in the scenery," I said. "You have a beautiful home, and this backyard is amazing."

He smiled and nodded. "We have our son to thank for all of this."

"You must be very proud of him."

"We are," he said. "He's a good boy. His mother thinks of him as her baby still."

I could tell Adrian got his friendly side from his father. It certainly didn't come from the woman in the kitchen. She was hard, jaded, and prejudiced against poor people.

"There you are," Adrian said, walking up to us and putting his arm around my shoulders.

I leaned into him, relieved to have him back by my side. "You're back."

"Everything okay?" he asked, looking into my eyes.

"Yep, great," I said with a bright, fake smile.

"I'll leave you two alone. I need to find my brother." Stavros walked away.

"Is everything okay with you?" I asked in a quiet voice.

He nodded. "Yes, my dad just wanted to talk for a minute. Where did you get off to? I came back and didn't see you. I was worried you had tried to find the bathroom and ended up in the ocean," he teased.

"Ha. Ha. I was in the kitchen—with your mother."

He stiffened. "Oh?"

"It's fine. I cut up some cheese and brought it out."

"Okay, good," he said, sounding relieved.

I understood it all now. He knew his mother well. She could filet a person with her sharp tongue. I suspected his past girlfriends had been subjected to her warm welcome and he knew what to expect.

"We're ready to eat!" Mrs. Gabris hollered, clapping her hands together.

It was a bit like a tidal wave. The sea of people rushed toward the tables, lining up while chatting and laughing. They all looked like very happy people and very close-knit. I envied the big family thing, but I also appreciated the bond my father and I had. It was only the two of us, and we never had to worry about a lot of drama.

"Keep your hands in, and you'll be fine," Adrian joked as we got in line.

"They do seem hungry," I said with a laugh.

With our plates piled high with a variety of foods, some I had never heard of, we found seats at the table. Several tables had been pushed together to create a U. There was a happy hum of conversation as people ate and caught up on their lives.

"Has everyone met the American?" Mrs. Gabris asked loudly from her spot at the center of the U.

I closed my eyes and inwardly groaned. I looked at Adrian, who had a frown on his face. He turned to look at his mother from where we were seated on her left.

"Mom, stop, please," he begged in a low voice.

"My youngest son has brought home an American," she said, practically spitting out the word.

The conversations around the tables ceased. Everyone was looking at me. I could feel the eyes and wanted to shrink into my seat. I waited for Adrian to jump to my defense. He didn't.

A male voice called out from across the U. "Why an American, Adrian? Are Greeks not good enough for you?"

I looked around, trying to see who had said it.

"He refuses all the suitable young ladies I have introduced him to. Instead, he goes searching in the dark corners of the world." His mother scoffed.

I raised my eyebrows, knowing that would definitely be what set Adrian off.

"Mother!" he scolded.

I used my hand to cover my smile. Adrian was going to put her in her place.

"Yes, son?" she asked, her voice cool and the look on her face a little frightening.

"Please stop," Adrian said in a soft voice. "You haven't even gotten the chance to know her."

My mouth dropped open. I looked at him, wondering where in the hell my big, masculine hero had gone off to.

"I don't need to know her," she said with a smile and staring directly at me. "She works for you. I understand now. You're having a little fun. Americans are good for that. When you're ready to settle down with a real woman, I have a few I would like you to meet."

I cleared my throat, taking a drink from the bottle of water I had picked up.

"That's enough," Adrian growled.

It wasn't a forceful growl by any means. I had seen him be sterner with a client he was trying to woo.

"It isn't enough by any means," she said. "You've disrespected me and your family by bringing her here."

I turned to look at Adrian, waiting to see what he would say.

"I've done no such thing," he said. "You're being disrespectful. I told you I was seeing someone, and you insisted I bring her."

She curled her lip in disgust. "I wouldn't have extended the invitation had I known she was an American working for you."

There was a gasp from all around the tables, as if working for Adrian was akin to being a beggar. I didn't understand how she could be so haughty when Stavros had just told me it was Adrian who bought their home. I knew they were comfortable, but they weren't wealthy like their son was. They weren't any better than I was.

"What are you saying?" Adrian snapped.

"I'm saying your girlfriend, if that's what you want to call her, is not welcome at my table."

I smiled, put the cap back on my water bottle, and slowly pushed my chair back. "I'm sorry to have ruined your family gathering."

"You've ruined nothing," she said. "Adrian, you are not welcome at our table until you learn to show some respect."

"Mom, you're being ridiculous," he said. "I've never known you to be so hateful and rude. Dad, you need to get her in line."

"He will do no such thing," she shouted, slapping her hand on the table. "I am not a woman to be handled. He agrees with me. All of us agree on this. You disrespect your heritage by bringing that woman here. You know better. I will not sit here and eat a meal with you when you are so blatantly thumbing your nose at us."

"I'm not disrespecting anyone!" Adrian said. "I wasn't aware there were rules about who I could date."

"You know better!" his mother shouted back.

I looked to his father, who I thought had been nice and liked me, but I realized he was only being polite. He wasn't thrilled to have his son stepping out with an American either. He'd just been too polite to say it.

I searched the tables and found Amanda. She'd been kind. She looked embarrassed, but she wasn't willing to speak up for me either. I knew I wasn't wanted, and there was no reason for me to stay. Adrian didn't need a fake girlfriend. He needed a priest to perform an exorcism.

"I'm going to wait outside. It was nice to meet you all, or at least, I think it was. Have a good day." I excused myself from the table.

I walked across the patio with my head held high. I would not let the woman think she had broken me. She was a vile woman in desperate need of a serious attitude adjustment. I yanked open the front door, letting some of my anger out where no one could witness it.

I was hurt. Not by what she'd said, but by what Adrian hadn't said.

CHAPTER 31

ADRIAN

"Bella." I called out her name as she walked away. She didn't stop. "Let her go. You don't need her," my mother said, clearly very satisfied she'd chased Bella away.

I growled. "What is wrong with you? Why would you do that?"

She swatted away my words. "You can do better. Don't you dare bring a woman like that to my home."

"A woman like that? You didn't even give her a chance!"

My mother scowled at me. "Go. I will not have your tone here. You come back once you have your priorities straight."

I had no words that would mean a damn thing to my mother. She'd embarrassed me and pissed me off all at the same time. She didn't seem the least bit ashamed of herself. I tossed my napkin on my plate and shoved my chair back, shooting her a look of disgust before heading inside to look for Bella.

She wasn't in the house. I hadn't really expected her to be. I walked outside, slamming the door behind me.

She was leaning against my car, her arms crossed over her chest and her sunglasses on, hiding her expression. I wasn't sure what to expect from her. I hoped there weren't tears. I wasn't sure how I would deal with tears.

I felt horrible for what she'd endured. She'd put herself out there for me and been raked over the coals. I owed her an apology and so much more. She'd only come to my parents' home to try and help me. No good deed goes unpunished, I thought to myself.

I stopped in front of her, waiting for her to say something. I thought she was looking at me. I couldn't see her eyes behind the glasses. Her lips were pressed together. It wasn't a smile, but it wasn't a grimace. It was just there—lacking all emotion.

"Bella, are you okay?" I asked gently.

"I'm fine. Are you okay?"

I nodded. "I am. That's my mom for you."

"I'm sorry to have ruined your family day. I didn't realize my American status would be such a huge issue."

"You didn't ruin anything. This is not your fault. At all. We were ambushed."

"Ambushed is one word for it," she muttered.

I grimaced, feeling the anger coming off her. "I didn't think it would be that bad."

"Whatever. Can we go now?"

I pushed the button on the key fob and unlocked the doors. I moved to open the passenger door for her. She got in without saying a word. I had never seen her quite so cold and withdrawn. I got in the car and pulled away from my parents' home. Bella sat quietly, her head turned away from me. She was pretending to be interested in the scenery. I knew she wasn't. She was fuming. I could feel the anger radiating off her.

"Are you angry with me?" I asked after we'd been driving for fifteen minutes without a word from her.

"No."

I cringed. I didn't have a lot of experience with women, but I was pretty sure that "no" meant a "yes." I'd had girlfriends in the past, and I had inadvertently pissed them off at one time or another. It was the nothing and the no that sent up a red flag.

"Where are you going?" she asked when I pulled into the parking lot of a strip mall.

"I was thinking we could use a little ice cream," I said, hoping to charm her with sweet stuff.

"Oh," she whispered.

It wasn't exactly an enthusiastic yes, but I was hoping once she got a little ice cream in her, she'd loosen up a little. I'd discovered her love of the cold treat while we'd been in Athens. It was one of her weaknesses. She took a seat at one of the outdoor tables, leaving me to get the ice cream. I was going to have to do more than buy the woman ice cream.

"Here you go," I said, putting the bowl of chocolate chip ice cream in front of her.

"Thank you," she said, her tone flat and lacking the enthusiasm I was hoping for.

She finally took off the sunglasses and looked at me. I couldn't get a good read on what she was thinking. I was afraid to ask. It was pretty clear her mood had definitely soured since this morning, and I couldn't blame her.

"I'm sorry," I blurted out.

"It's fine."

"It isn't fine. I'm sorry for the way you were treated."

She took a bite of the ice cream. "I guess I should have heeded your warnings. I tried to tell myself it wasn't that bad, that it couldn't be that bad. You're a good guy, and I reasoned that you couldn't be who you were if it was as bad as you were making it out to be. I guess I was wrong."

"Bella, I'm sorry. I really am. I promise you, they are good people. They just... I don't know. My mom, she has this idea in her head about who I should be with, and she can't let it go. She isn't like that with my older brothers, just me."

"It was definitely not what I expected. Your warnings made me think your mom might be rough. That was—I don't have the right words to describe what that was. Your mother is like a tigress, a mama bear protecting her cub. You could have told me she had razor sharp claws."

186

I smirked, finding her assessment spot on. When she didn't smile in return, I quickly wiped the smile from my face. "She is protective."

She scoffed. "You think?"

I shook my head. "She isn't normally that brusque. I don't know if she was showing off or what was wrong with her."

"Your dad seemed nice, at least to my face. I suppose that little conversation he pulled you away for probably had something to do with you bringing an American to the party." Her tone was a little snide. "He certainly wasn't offering up any help."

"My dad is usually pretty laid back. I don't think he necessarily has a problem with you. It's just that my parents are very traditional. Greeks are proud people." I tried to explain. "They've been trying to marry me off since I was born. Then when I started making money, they worried I would be taken advantage of, and that's when my mom really got a little crazy."

She raised an eyebrow. "Wow, I hadn't noticed."

I could tell she was irritated with me. "Bella, please don't let what they said affect you."

She dropped her spoon and folded her arms, resting them on the table as she leaned toward me. "It isn't what *they* said that got to me. I can handle that kind of nonsense. I don't like it, but I can handle it."

"Okay, what is it?" I asked curiously. "What has you upset?"

"I guess I was a little surprised to see how terrified you are of your mother."

The way she said it was not meant to be a compliment. I immediately took umbrage to the comment.

"Terrified? I'm not terrified of my mother."

Both of her brows arched upward. "You sure about that?"

It was my turn to raise my eyebrows at the way she was talking. "I'm sure about that." I mimicked her tone.

"Why did you sit there and let your mother talk to me like that and you? You don't strike me as the kind of man who would take that kind of shit from anyone."

Now I knew she was pissed. She was speaking very bluntly, something I had never heard before. "I'm not going to start a fight with my mother over something that isn't real."

Her eyes narrowed. "Isn't real? I assure you, I'm very real, Adrian. What your mother said wasn't just an insult to me as your girlfriend. It was an insult in general. I didn't like it."

"She was pissed because she thought you were my girlfriend. If she knew there was nothing between us, I doubt she would have talked to you or about you the way she did."

I saw her take a deep breath before she reached for her sunglasses and slid them back on. It was the equivalent of her hanging up on me or slamming the door in my face.

"Nothing between us," she repeated the words in a dangerously low voice.

"You know what I mean," I said with exasperation.

"No, I don't think I do. I'm not sure what you mean. You said you didn't bother defending me because we are a fake thing anyway, or something like that."

"You agreed to come with me and act like my fake girlfriend, right?"

"Yes, I did, but that was before," she whispered. "Was any of this real?"

"Bella, we've been having a great time together. I love spending time with you. This last week has been amazing." I meant every word.

She smirked. "You mean you love having sex with me, but now that we're back, and your parents didn't approve of your fake girlfriend, you don't need me around."

"It isn't like that. Besides, you're going to be leaving soon. Why do you care what my parents think? You'll be back home soon, and you'll never think about me or any of this again. You'll go on with your life, and I'll go on with mine." I hoped she would argue with me.

She sighed and reached for her purse. I watched as she quietly opened it, pulled out her phone, and did something on it before putting it back in her purse.

"Thank you for the ice cream," she said, her eyes not meeting mine as she got up from the table.

She turned and walked inside. I assumed she was going to the bathroom. I took another bite of my own ice cream, letting the cold sit in my mouth before swallowing. I should have kept my cool. It was insulting to have her think of me as a man scared of his own mother. It might have been a little true, but I didn't want her to think of me like that.

"Shit," I groaned after I'd been sitting on the small patio alone for over five minutes.

She hadn't gone to the bathroom. She'd left. I knew it when she got up. She wasn't coming back. I didn't try to stop her or go after her because a part of me wanted her to go. I needed some time to figure out what was going on in my head. I had a lot of thoughts and feelings, and they were all jumbled up, leaving me a confused mess.

I got up from the table and headed for my car. There was a small sliver of hope she would be there waiting for me. She wasn't. I got in the car and sat behind the wheel with the AC running, the car still in park. I'd fucked up.

I had really, really fucked up, and I wasn't sure I could fix it. I wasn't sure I wanted to fix it. Maybe it was better this way. It would be easier and less messy if we left things as they were. We didn't need to hash out the feelings or talk about what had happened. It was time to walk away and put some distance between us before one of us ended up with a broken heart.

I put the car in drive and started the drive back home. The cab ride she must have taken was going to cost her a small fortune. I was going to reimburse her for it. She shouldn't have to use her own money to flee the disaster I had dragged her into.

CHAPTER 32

BELLA

I was mentally kicking myself for being so dumb and foolish. I got caught up in the idea of a romance with a gorgeous man. I got caught up in the ambiance of the foreign land and the whole living like a queen thing. It was easy to forget I was nobody from nowhere and had no chance of ever living the lifestyle Adrian had given me a glimpse of. That wasn't me. That wasn't my life. My life was back in the tiny mining town I'd lived all my life. I had been a complete fool to think I was good enough to get a job offer.

I shoved the last of my clean laundry into my suitcase. I was leaving Crete and the job. It wasn't worth my dignity and self-respect. I couldn't stand the thought of seeing Adrian and have him tell me again the few days in Athens had been nothing, meant nothing.

I walked into the bathroom, tossing the extra toiletries into the Ziploc bag. I had my change of clothes in my carry-on, along with the basics like a toothbrush and toothpaste. I tossed them into the open suitcase and started my look around the room to make sure I hadn't left anything behind. The drawers and closet were empty. I zipped up the suitcase and carried it out to leave by the door. As I was walking away, I heard a knock on the door.

It could only be Adrian. I didn't want to see him. He had made no attempt to call or text me since I'd walked out of the ice cream shop yesterday. His lack of an attempt to reach out made it pretty clear I was nothing more than a notch in his belt. I was not going to tell anyone back home about my dalliance with Adrian. I was mortified enough. I didn't need people looking at me with pity or disgust.

The person knocked again. "Fuck it. He's going to get a piece of my mind." I stomped to the door and yanked it open. "Cassia?"

"Were you in the shower?"

"No. What are you doing here?"

"I thought I'd see what you were up to today. Want to do a little shopping, check out the sites?"

She walked into the room and stared at my overstuffed suitcase and then back at me. I knew I had a guilty look on my face. I had thought I was going to escape without having to see anyone. I knew that was a coward's way out, but it was all I had the energy to do.

"I was going to call you," I blurted out.

She turned to look at me. "Were you?"

"Yes, from the airport," I mumbled.

"What the hell is going on? You're scheduled on Monday!"

I groaned. "It's a long story."

"Then you sit your skinny ass down and tell me. I want to hear this."

We moved to the sitting area, her sitting on the sofa and me taking one of the chairs. "Things are complicated. I can't work there anymore."

"Did your friend tell her boss how she felt about him?" she asked.

I chuckled. "No, but the boss told my friend she meant nothing. The time together was nothing."

"Ouch."

I nodded. "Exactly. It's worse than that. I'm going to tell you, but you have to swear you won't say anything. Please?"

"I'm a vault. You can tell me."

"Before my friend's boss and her hooked up, he had shown her a great deal of kindness. There was time spent together away from the office. He told her about a personal problem he was having, and she offered to help." It was easier to speak in the third person hypothetical. It allowed me to maintain a tiny bit of my dignity.

"What kind of personal problem—hypothetically?" she asked.

"His mother had set him up with a woman, or rather, she wanted to set him up. He didn't want to go out with another one of his mother's choices and told her he had a girlfriend. The mother asked to meet the girlfriend. My friend agreed to go with him and pretend to be his girlfriend."

"Ah, I see."

I shook my head. "No. It's so much worse than that. His mother apparently hates Americans."

"Oh no," she gasped.

"Oh yes. Not hate. She humiliated my friend. She was horrible and nasty, and my friend's boss did nothing. He didn't defend her, not like he could have or should have. He let his mother say horrible things to my friend in front of everyone." The fresh pain and embarrassment flooded my emotions.

"Oh no. I'm so sorry. For your friend," she quickly added.

"When my friend talked to her boss, he said there was no point in defending her because she wasn't really his girlfriend," I said, the words stinging and giving me a real pain in my heart.

Cassia's mouth dropped open. "Wow. That doesn't sound like him at all. I'm shocked and a little appalled."

"Me too."

"And that's why you're leaving?" she asked.

"Yes. I can't face him. No one wants to look at a mistake day in and day out."

She looked sad. "I'm really sorry."

"So, am I. I thought things were different. My friend feels like a complete fool."

"Can I tell you something?"

"Of course, anything," I said, thrilled to hear one of her secrets.

"In our culture, mothers are kind of the boss," she explained. "No one messes with a Greek mother. They are the ones who run the house. The fathers, they're important and do have a say, but it's the moms kids grow up afraid of."

I shrugged. "I understand that, but seriously, the things that were said were pretty rude. She told me to leave. Well, not directly to me because she refused to speak to me. She kicked out Adrian as well and he took it! He didn't try to defend himself or anything. I don't understand!"

Cassia let out a long sigh. "I'm really sorry. But a good Greek son would never stand up to his mother. They are taught from a very early age their mothers are to be respected and feared. Obviously, there are some that aren't good and treat their mothers like garbage, but the good ones know better."

I scoffed. "Well, some of those good boys need to grow a pair of balls."

She burst into laughter. "I agree, but it is going to be a hard habit to break. He loves his mom. He isn't going to want to do anything that might hurt his mother."

"I get that, and honestly, I don't want him to do that," I said. "I don't want to cause him any problems. I can see that he loves and respects his mother and his father. I would hate to be the person that gets in the middle of things. I don't belong here. It's time to go home."

"Are you sure? This internship is a good experience. You're doing so well. You have more to learn, and we could all benefit from what you have to offer."

I smiled. "Thank you. I appreciate that, but I don't think this is going to work out. It isn't good for me, and it won't be good for him. He's already got a lot of work to do to get back in his family's good graces."

She nodded. "I understand. I mean, I don't, but I do. When do you leave?"

I looked at the clock. "Two hours."

"Wow. You're not playing around."

I giggled. "No, I'm not. I take humiliation pretty seriously. I don't like it, and if I can avoid it, I will."

"I can't believe you're leaving," she pouted. "I feel like I just got to know you. I was really looking forward to hanging out with you more."

"I'm sorry," I said. "You've made my time here fun, and I am so glad I met you. I wish things would have worked out differently. This just isn't the place for me. Like my dad would say, it is like trying to fit a square peg into a round hole. I don't fit. A stronger person would push on. I'm not that strong."

"Stop. You're very strong. It's the circumstances that really suck. Not all of us hate Americans," she said with a small smile.

"Thanks."

"If you do ever come back, you better find me. I have your personal email. I'm going to flood your inbox with gossip and pictures of me at the beach, having a good time."

I giggled. "I'd like that. You know, planes fly to America as well. You're welcome to visit. We don't have the beautiful beaches like you do in my hometown, but we have some gorgeous mountain ranges and rivers that seem to go on forever," I said, feeling homesick.

"I might take you up on that. I've always wanted to travel."

"I hope you will," I said. "Thank you again for being kind and willing to give me a chance. I really did have fun hanging out with you. Tell everyone at the office goodbye for me. I feel kind of bad for running away without saying anything, but I think it's for the best."

She let out a long sigh. "Does he know?" she asked softly.

"No. Please don't say anything to him. He'll figure it out soon enough. I just need to make a clean break."

She nodded her head. "All right. This is your choice. If he asks, I have to tell him though."

"That's fine. Tell him tomorrow—if he asks. I think he'll be just as happy to know I'm gone as I am to leave. I know Rand will be happy. He warned Adrian about me from the very first day. He was convinced I would ruin the company. I'm getting out before this little thing can become a bigger thing and cause problems in the office. I don't need the entire world knowing I was a naïve, country bumpkin who fell for the big-city billionaire's tricks. I'll have to live with my humiliation, and that's plenty." The pain of it still burned in my soul.

She grimaced. "I'm so sorry you feel like that. For what it's worth, Adrian isn't like that. At least, I don't think he's like that. I can't say I know him personally all that well, but from what I do know of him, he is a good man."

"Lucky me. I brought out the rotten side in him."

"Do you need a ride to the airport?" she asked, changing the subject.

"No thank you. I have a car coming in about thirty minutes."

"All right. I'll let you finish packing. Again, I'm sorry things didn't work out. I'll miss you."

We both stood and hugged before I walked her to the door. Once she was gone, I closed my eyes, leaning against the door. I was a mess. Part of me was demanding I stay and talk to Adrian. I knew he wasn't nearly as bad as I was making him out to be. Then I started thinking about how he'd sat there while his mom said horrible things and his statement that we were nothing, and I was resolved in my decision to leave.

There was no easy answer to make the hurt go away. It was my fault for getting mixed up in a romance with my boss in a place I was only going to be temporarily. I knew better, and I had gone and done it anyway. That was my fault. I could have told Adrian no. I didn't have to offer to be his fake girlfriend. Hell, he'd rejected the idea several times, and I kept pushing it on him. This one was definitely on me.

I had made the mess, and now I got to deal with the consequences.

CHAPTER 33

ADRIAN

As the elevator took me up to the floor where my office was, I mulled over how I would approach her. I was going to start with an apology. That would disarm her and hopefully make her more willing to listen to what I had to say. I'd given her two days to cool off. Hell, I had needed the day to get my own head around everything.

I walked to my office, putting down my briefcase and phone and going over my approach again.

"Hi, can we talk?" I whispered, testing out the way the words sounded.

I'd get her to come into my office so we could have a little privacy. "I'm sorry I didn't stand up for you. I should have. I'd like to make it up to you."

The words didn't sound right. She was pissed because I'd said we were nothing. That required a little more finesse to handle.

"I didn't mean what I said," I muttered. "Fuck!"

Everything I said was going to come out all wrong.

Bella was a reasonable person. She would hear me out and understand that I hadn't meant she was nothing or what happened between us was nothing. I rubbed a hand over my jaw. I had been stewing on the matter since she'd walked out on me. I kept telling myself it was for the best and her leaving me was a good thing. I didn't want to have feelings for her. I didn't want to be the one who got hurt when she left me. It was my self-preservation that had me pulling away from her.

Standing in my office, stewing over it, wasn't going to solve the problem. I had to talk to her. If she told me to get lost, I would accept it—maybe. I walked out of the office, heading down the hallway to the open work area where her cubicle was situated. I didn't see her and looked around for the other interns. They were all at their desks. She was probably in Cassia's office.

I changed course, heading for the other office. The door was closed, which told me they were probably already hard at work and didn't want to be disturbed. Perk of being the boss—I could disturb and not get yelled at.

I knocked once. "Cassia?"

"Come in," she called.

I put my hand on the handle and mentally prepared myself to see the hurt and anger on Bella's face. I opened the door and saw Cassia at her desk. She was the only one in the office, which meant Bella must be roaming the halls. I smiled at the thought of her loss and frustrated.

"Hi," I said, feeling a little foolish for interrupting her.

"Did you need something?" she asked, her tone a little terse.

"I was looking for Bella," I answered.

She nodded. "I'm sure you were."

"Excuse me?" I snapped, not in the mood to have one of my employees talk to me in such a way.

"Bella isn't here."

"I can see that. Is she in the conference room? Break room?" I was not really interested in roaming the entire floor in search of her, knowing there was a chance I would miss her in passing. The downside to having such a large office and too many damn walls.

Cassia looked down at her hands on her keyboard. "She isn't *here*," she said again.

I scowled with frustration. "I get it. Where—"

Then it hit me. I felt like I'd been bowled over. In an instant, I felt a sense of emptiness, like a part of me had been ripped out.

"I'm sorry, Adrian," Cassia said in a soft voice.

I knew she and Bella had become friends and had spent time together. That meant Bella had likely confided in her. I trusted Cassia to keep what she knew to herself. "She's gone?" I asked.

She nodded her head. "She left yesterday."

I closed my eyes, praying for self-control before opening them and finding her watching me. "She left yesterday," I repeated.

Cassia nodded again. "I'm sorry."

"Thanks for letting me know," I mumbled and walked out.

I walked back to my office, barely seeing anything or anyone. My sole focus was getting to the privacy of my office. Then, and only then, would I allow myself to feel. I slammed the door behind me, put my hands on my hips, and sucked in a deep breath, blowing it out and repeating the action. It wasn't helping. I was pissed! Furious with myself, the situation, and her for leaving me without so much as a "fuck off."

I stared at my tidy desk and grew even angrier. I stomped across the plush carpeting and picked up the pen holder, throwing it against the wall. Pens flew in every direction. I grabbed the stapler and threw it where the pen holder had landed. It was one thing after another. Throwing hard and watching the objects shatter, just like my life.

"Woah, Adrian, slow down," Rand said.

I stopped, mid-reach for the laptop that was sitting on my desk. I turned to face him. "Go away."

He walked toward me and quickly picked up the laptop, moving it out of my reach. "What the hell is going on?" he asked.

"Get out. I want to be alone."

"Obviously, you're in no condition to be alone," he said. "Sit. Tell me what happened."

Rand was a big guy, and I knew if he had to, he would bodily force me into a chair. I exhaled and flopped into the chair on the wrong side of my desk. I didn't feel like being the guy that sat on the other side.

"She's gone," I muttered.

"Who's gone?" he asked calmly, taking the seat next to mine.

"Bella. She left."

"Left the company?" he pressed.

"Left Crete. The company. Me."

He groaned, leaning back in the chair and rubbing his hand over his face before looking at me and shaking his head. "I warned you."

"Stop. I don't want to hear that bullshit."

"Why did she leave?"

"We had an argument," I said, glossing over what really happened.

"An argument? About work, I hope?" He grimaced.

I slowly shook my head. "No. I took her to my parents' house on Saturday. She was supposed to be pretending to be my girlfriend. It didn't go well. My mother refused to talk to her, and then when she did, she kicked her out of the house because she wasn't welcome."

Rand was nodding his head. "And Bella is mad at you?"

"Yes."

"You're leaving out some really big chunks of information. What did you do to piss her off so badly that she ran away from a damn good job?"

"As you know, we spent some time together last week," I said, without giving him all the dirty details.

"Against my very good, sound advice? Yes, I know. You slept with her. You wined and dined her."

I glared at him. "It wasn't like that."

"Get to the part where she jumped on a plane and fled the island," he said, clearly frustrated.

"My mother said some things, and Bella didn't feel I said enough to defend her. After we left my mother's house, I told Bella I didn't say anything because she wasn't really my girlfriend. I wasn't going to get into a big thing with my mom and the rest of my family defending a woman who wasn't my girlfriend. I said we were nothing."

He sucked in air through his teeth. "Ouch. That's not good. What the hell were you thinking?"

"I know, I know, but I didn't mean it to sound as callous as it did. I only meant we weren't really together and getting into a big fight with my family didn't seem worth it. She was going to be going home. She wasn't going to stick around and be my real girlfriend. Do you get it?

199

Do you see why I didn't want to start a war for a woman who would be out of my life in a few weeks?" I hoped he would tell me I had done nothing wrong.

"She isn't like that," he said in a low voice.

"What? Who?"

"Your girl, Bella. I didn't even know her that well, and I could tell she wasn't the kind of woman you spent a few days locked up in a hotel room with and walked away unscathed. I saw the way you looked at her. You were drawn to her because she was different. She was innocent and wide-eyed, and she was into you. You led her on," he said bluntly.

My mouth dropped open. I wanted to argue with him, but it would have been futile. "I didn't lead her on. Not intentionally. It wasn't supposed to be that way. It just happened."

"I told you to keep your distance."

"Yeah, yeah, yeah, you told me. You were right. Fuck that. Tell me what to do! How do I make this right?"

"It's over. Let it go."

I shook my head. "I can't! I don't want to let her go. That's the thing. When I said there was nothing between us, I lied. There is, or there was. I didn't want her to leave, but I don't want to ask her to stay and give up her world."

"Let it go, Adrian. You'll move on. No good can come from this."

I stared at him. His words rang true, but I couldn't believe them. I wasn't the kind of man who sat back and let life happen. I wasn't the kind of man who found a beautiful woman who checked all the boxes and then let her go. "I can't."

"She's gone. Let her stay gone. Let her move on."

I shook my head. "No. I'm going after her. I have to make things right at least. If we can't be together, I'll have to accept that, but I want her to know it wasn't nothing to me."

"This is a mistake," he warned.

"Maybe, but the real mistake is letting her go and allowing her to believe she meant nothing to me. Even if she rejects me, I have to tell her the truth."

"For her or for you?" he asked.

"Both of us. I need her file with her address in the states." I jumped to my feet.

"I'm sure HR has it," he said, making no move to get up.

"Get it for me. I need to get my jet ready. You'll be in charge while I'm gone." I was already pulling up the number for my pilot.

"Adrian, stop and think about this. You're not thinking about the consequences to all this. She left you. She left the company without so much as a thank you for the job. This girl is not one you want to get mixed up with. Let her go. I know it might be hard to do, but in a week, you will have forgotten all about her. You can get back to doing what you do, and you can work things out with your family. You said your family doesn't like her. Do you really want to invite that kind of drama into your life? Do you want to be with someone your mother will never approve of? Do you want to be with someone who lives on another continent? She doesn't want to live here. You need to think about this all the way through before you make a rash decision."

"I have. Get her file."

"What a fucking disaster," he protested in Greek before stomping out of my destroyed office.

As I listened to the phone ringing on the other end, I looked around at the mess I had made. Housekeeping was not going to be happy with me. I was a little embarrassed by my behavior, but it had made me feel a little better.

CHAPTER 34

BELLA

I was exhausted and couldn't wait to take a nap in my own bed. I was relieved to find my dad was still at work when I got home. He would have a lot of questions, and I had no answers. Facing him was going to be rough. I knew he would support me no matter what, but it was still going to be hard to admit I had failed.

I dragged my luggage into the tiny bedroom, already missing the spacious hotel room, and left it in the corner. I would unpack later. I kicked off my shoes and walked into the kitchen, happy to see it was neat and tidy. I opened the fridge, looking for a snack and scowled when I saw the leftover pizza, a box from one of the local restaurants and a myriad of other junk food.

"Dad, Dad, Dad," I griped, grabbing a slice of the pizza and taking a bite.

I'd lecture him later about his eating habits. I quickly stuffed the pizza in my mouth and walked back into my room, closing the door and crawling into my small bed. It wasn't quite as luxurious as the one at the hotel, but it was mine, and it was what I was used to. The familiar smell of the sheets and the weight of my blanket felt good, even on the warm day. Another thing I was going to have to get used to was the lack of central air. The house was old and didn't have central air. I threw off the blanket, turned on the fan in the corner, and got back into bed, pulling just the sheet over me.

I closed my eyes, trying to push out all thoughts of Adrian and Greece and all that I had left behind. I felt like I was running away. I *was* running away. I had dug a big hole for myself, and instead of dealing with the mess I had created, I'd bolted. I ran back home to my daddy. I let the exhaustion brought on from being up almost a full twenty-four hours take me away into oblivion, where I didn't have to think.

"Bella?" I heard my father's voice from far away.

I moaned and rolled to my side.

"Bella, wake up!" my father demanded.

I opened my eyes and found my father standing in the doorway of my room. "What time is it?" I asked.

"It's five," he said. "What the hell are you doing here?"

I yawned and sat up, smoothing down my hair. "I came home."

He gave me a dry look. "No kidding. Get up. We're going to have a conversation."

I sighed, knowing there was no avoiding the talk. "I'll be out in a minute. I need to change."

He left, closing the door behind him. I pulled open my dresser drawer and pulled out a pair of shorts and a loose tee. I grabbed the scrunchie off my dresser and put my hair up on my head before rubbing my face, trying to wake up.

When I walked into the kitchen, there was a hot pizza sitting on the table. "Dad," I said.

He shrugged. "I didn't know you would be here."

"I can see that. Enjoy that pizza, mister. It will be your last for a while."

"Sit down and tell me why you are home," he ordered.

"It wasn't working out," I said nonchalantly.

He raised his eyebrows, his forehead wrinkling. "It wasn't working out? When I talked to you a few days ago, you sounded happy. You said you helped secure a big account, and the boss was talking about having you work with him. To me, it sounded like it was working out very well."

"Things changed."

"Bella, I know you, and I think you're leaving out a big part of your story."

He wasn't going to accept anything but the truth. I knew my father was an understanding man and wouldn't hold my mistakes against me. Telling him might even make me feel a little better.

"I got involved with the owner," I confessed, letting the hurt out. "Things were going great between us until I met his family. They hated me. Not that they actually spoke to me or gave me a chance at all, but they hated me. His mother most of all. She asked me to leave her house. She doesn't want her son with a money-grabbing American, or something along those lines. She was so insulting, Dad. What she said was bad, but it was his lack of defending me that really hurt. He let her talk to me that way and didn't try to defend me or us at all. He told me he didn't bother because I would be going home soon anyway. He made me feel like I was insignificant and didn't matter."

"You matter," he said. "Don't ever let anyone make you feel anything other than that. You matter to the people that count."

"Thanks, Dad. It looks like I'll be sticking around for a while. I can't very well put that job on my resume. They'll see I quit without notice after a measly two weeks. I shouldn't have run away, but I couldn't stand the thought of busting my ass for a man who saw me as insignificant."

He nodded. "I don't blame you. However, the way you felt may not be the way he feels. His words could have been poorly chosen."

I scoffed. "I don't think so. He could have tried to explain. He didn't. I think he's going to be relieved to have me gone."

"You know, a very long time ago, your mother and I had some serious problems at the beginning of our relationship. I knew I loved her, but I knew she deserved so much better than what I could give her. She always told me she didn't care about any of that. My own insecurities made me question her statements. One night, we got into an argument. I stormed out, determined to never see her again. I went home feeling completely miserable. After thinking about it all night, I decided I wanted her in my life."

I smiled, obviously knowing how the story turned out but interested to hear him tell what happened before they got together. "And she took you back, and you had me."

He chuckled, shaking his head. "It wasn't quite that simple. She told her mom about our fight. When I went to see her, your grandmother refused to let me talk to her. She told me I wasn't good enough for her daughter. She said I was a loser and would always be a loser. I told the woman I loved your mother and would walk through fire to make sure she was taken care of."

"Wow! I didn't know you and grandma hated each other!"

"I didn't hate her. We had a rocky start, but I was persistent. I came back day after day, and finally, your mother agreed to talk to me. We worked things out. Shortly after we got back together, she got sick. I stuck by her side, nursing her back to health with your grandma's help. It was a slow process, but she finally saw I wasn't going anywhere and that we were truly in love." He smiled, and his eyes stared into space as he relived those fond memories.

"She came around because you made her see the truth. You made her see that you loved Mom for who she was. That is very sweet and admirable. I'm glad Grandma finally came around."

"So am I. Sometimes, we have to just do what we do and prove who we are inside through our actions. You can't butt heads with someone who already has their mind made up about you. It isn't going to get you anywhere. You do you, and let them fall into place. If they don't, you don't need them in your life. You are beautiful inside and out, and the people that really know you, they know you are pure and honest and caring. They know you don't give a damn about money or anything else. If that woman can't see that about you, it's her loss. Don't waste another minute of your life worrying about her."

"She isn't the problem," I grumbled.

He smiled. "You left because you didn't like what the mother said, right?"

"Partly."

"I can't tell you what to do, but I think it would be wise to give the man a chance to explain."

I shook my head. "That's just it, Dad! He didn't! He let me walk away."

"Ah, I see. You wanted him to chase you."

I was immediately embarrassed. "Maybe."

He grinned, his eyes lighting up. "We all want to be chased. Maybe *he* wants to be chased."

"Dad, he's a billionaire with hundreds of women chasing him. He doesn't need me to chase him."

"What if he doesn't want them? What if he wants you? What if he needs to know if you want him for him and not for who he is?"

I groaned, putting my hands over my face. "Oh god. Did I just make a huge mistake?"

"Nothing worth having is easy," he said, something he'd told me a million times.

"But this is different. I think I really screwed this up."

He shrugged a shoulder. "I don't know about that. It isn't like you can't go back to Greece or pick up the phone and call the man."

"He might not want to see me, and then I will have wasted all that money flying back there to have him laugh in my face and turn me away."

"If you really want something, you have to be willing to be laughed at a little. You have to be willing to make sacrifices. That tells you how bad you want it. If you give up because it's too hard, you don't truly want it. If that's the case, then my advice to you is to leave it alone."

"I can't! I don't want to leave it alone."

He chuckled. "I didn't think you did, but do you see how you are reacting? Do you feel that?"

"Feel what?"

"That burning in your gut. That fire that can't be extinguished until you get what your heart desires. That's what has to motivate you. That's what tells you when you are on the right path. If there is no fire, there's no reason to try," he said easily, as if it were that simple.

"I don't know what to do," I whispered, mulling over my options and playing out the possible outcomes.

I couldn't handle being rejected by him a second time. I didn't think my heart would survive him telling me he was serious when he'd said our time together had meant nothing. I wanted to believe he was only saying it to protect himself, but what if I was wrong?

The truth was, I didn't know Adrian all that well. I knew him, but I had to wonder if it was part of who he was. I thought about the cost of my mistake in a monetary value. With no job and no immediate prospects, I could be putting a huge financial burden on myself for nothing.

I quickly dismissed the financial aspect and focused on the way he had looked at me at the ice cream shop that day. I replayed the words and thought about our last night together. It had all felt very real. I didn't think anyone could fake that kind of passion.

I had to believe I meant a little something to him.

Now I just needed to know if I had ruined any chance I had with him.

CHAPTER 35

ADRIAN

The plane touched down in a small town I didn't even know existed. My pilot had done some research and managed to get me as close to Bella's home as he could. I had slept on the plane—or attempted to sleep. I kept replaying the last conversation I had with Bella.

I had analyzed it to the point where I could find every missed opportunity to tell her how I felt. I had been kicking myself for the past twenty-four hours. I was hoping she would hear me out and give me a chance to apologize.

The car I had hired from a nearby city was waiting for me at the tiny landing strip. The driver had a GPS unit to guide him to Bella's house. I watched out the window, finding the area to be remarkably beautiful. I wondered where all the people lived. It was farms and houses here and there and lots of trees.

"This is it, sir," the driver said, pulling to a stop in front of a small, white house that looked very old. The paint had faded and was chipped away in places. Despite the rundown appearance of the house, the yard was immaculate. I smiled as I walked up the broken red-brick path with flowers on both sides. I knew that was Bella's work. She admired the flower gardens in Athens, proclaiming she wanted them for her yard.

I knocked on the front door, having no idea if Bella would even agree to see me. An older man, maybe early fifties, opened the door. He looked me up and down and grinned. It wasn't exactly the response I had expected.

"Good afternoon," I said, not entirely sure it was afternoon.

"You must be Adrian," he said.

I raised an eyebrow, wondering how he could have guessed. No one besides Rand knew I was coming. I knew Rand wouldn't have called ahead to warn her.

"I am. You're Peter?"

He smiled, nodding his head before extending his hand. "Peter Kamp, Bella's father."

"And, as you guessed, I'm Adrian Gabris."

"Why don't you come on in?" he asked, his voice stern. "I think you and I need to talk."

"Yes, sir."

I followed him inside the neat, small home. There was an old couch with a crocheted blanket over the back. Peter gestured for me to sit down. "Can I get you a drink?"

"Um, sure, please. Anything will be fine."

He walked through an archway and returned a couple of minutes later with an off-brand can of cola. I popped it open, took a long drink, and let the sugar hit my system, which livened me up a little.

"So, you came all the way over here," he started, taking a seat in an old, dirty, orange-colored recliner.

I nodded. "I did. I would have been here sooner, but I…" I cleared my throat, not entirely sure how much the man knew.

"But you?" he pressed.

"I didn't know she had left," I admitted, feeling a little foolish.

He smiled. "I don't imagine you did."

"Is she here?" I asked.

He shook his head. "Nope."

I got the idea he wasn't going to tell me anything more. He wanted to have a conversation. I owed him that much. I knew Bella and her father were close. She would have told him what happened with my mother, but I wasn't sure how much she would have told him about what happened between us.

"I'm going to assume you know there is—or was—something going on between us," I said, just getting right to the heart of the matter.

"I do."

"Sir, if you could please tell me what I should do here, I'd appreciate it," I said, not above begging.

He smiled. "I can't tell you what to do. I do have some questions for you, though."

I nodded. "I imagine you do. I'll do my best to answer them."

"What are your intentions with my daughter?" he asked, his eyes holding mine.

I blinked. The question was direct and took me off guard. "Uh," I started, not really sure how to answer it.

He burst into laughter. "I'm only kidding. Kind of. I *do* want to know what it is you think you're doing with her. My little girl is nobody's fool. I don't know the details about what went on over there, but I do know she was hurt. I don't like to see my little girl hurt."

"I understand that. I didn't mean to hurt her. I'm not great with relationships. I've never really been in a serious, adult relationship before. I've dated, but none of the women I've been with have been like Bella. She's different."

"She's special. My daughter is a very special woman, and for her to have even let herself get involved with you tells me she sees something in you. And it has nothing to do with your bank account," he added, his voice stern.

I winced, knowing he was referring to what my mother had said. "I am really sorry for how my family treated her. I know she isn't interested in me for my money. I sensed that from the very beginning. Did she tell you about our first meeting?"

Peter shrugged a shoulder. "She said she'd gotten lost, and you went to pick her up."

I smiled, thinking back to the day. "Yes, but I didn't tell her who I was. She thought I was just another one of the guys at the office. It gave me a chance to be anonymous and allowed me to get to know her without her holding back or trying to impress me. Our breakfast was short, but it was enough for me to know she was different."

The man looked proud, and he was right to be proud. He'd raised a good daughter. "Bella isn't world wise. She's been through some hard times, and life has not been easy for her. She's tough, but she hasn't really been exposed to the kind of negativity she experienced over there."

"I'm so sorry."

"I think you are. Here's the thing. I want my daughter to be with a real man."

I took offense to that. "I *am* a real man."

"A real man knows how to protect his woman. A real man will do whatever he must to keep his woman safe. Maybe I'm a little old fashioned and some of my expectations have rubbed off on her. Regardless, Bella is a woman to be revered and treasured—not insulted and disrespected."

I nodded, taking his lecture. I wasn't going to try and make an excuse for my behavior. I'd gone over it and realized I had let her down. I didn't like that feeling, like I was inadequate or less of a man.

"I understand, and it will be my one big regret," I said. "I plan on making it right."

He studied me for several long seconds. "I believe you."

"Thank you." I groaned and shook my head. "Now I just need to convince Bella."

He chuckled again. "Bella is stubborn but not overly so. I think you could persuade her to give you another chance."

"Great, got any tips for me?" I asked, knowing I was probably pushing it a bit.

"I do have one tip."

"Really? What?"

"When you see her, be honest," he said. "There is nothing Bella hates more than a liar. She doesn't like bullshit or empty platitudes. She's a cut and dry kind of girl."

That part, I had already surmised from our time together. "I understand. Thank you."

"You're welcome," he said, nodding. "No matter how this all plays out, I want what's best for Bella. I don't know what that is, but I will support her in whatever she decides. You seem like a good guy, but if she tells you to get lost, I'm going to ask you to do that. I'm not saying you don't press her a little bit if you think that's what she needs, but if she means it, then you go. You don't drag this thing out and make it any worse than it needs to be. Bella is her own woman. She can think for herself, but when she's made up her mind about something, it's pretty much a done deal."

"I give you my word, I will not do anything that will hurt her. If she tells me she never wants to see me again, I'll respect that. I'll leave her alone."

He grinned. "Great, then you better hurry."

"Hurry?"

"Bella headed over to the airport this morning to try and get a flight back to Greece," he said with a smile.

My mouth fell open. "She what? Right now?" I nearly shouted the words.

"Yep, right now. Hell, she might already be in the air."

"No. She'd tell you. Did she tell you?" I pulled out my phone and searched for the number of the car service I had used to bring me out to the middle of nowhere. I was hoping the guy wasn't too far.

"I suggest you get a move on, son," he said, still laughing as I rushed out the front door.

I paced in front of the house, waiting for the driver. It only took him about ten minutes to make it back. Thankfully, he'd just been getting gas.

"Airport, now," I shouted and jumped into the backseat.

The man clearly understood my rush. "It's about an hour away."

I slapped the back of the headrest. "Hurry."

"Yes, sir."

By the time the car pulled up to the drop-off area, I was damn near in a panic. I kept telling myself it was okay. If she was already on the plane and in the air, I'd hire a pilot to get me and my jet back to Greece. I knew we'd make better time than the commercial flight. I'd still have a chance to talk to her. I knew I had a chance—a really good chance if she was trying to get back to Greece.

I rushed inside the airport and checked the flights. There was one flight heading out. I looked at the line for the ticket desk, knowing the only way I was going to get past security was with a ticket. I got in line, anxious and barely able to suppress my frustration with how slow the line was moving. When it was my turn, I bought the first ticket the woman offered on the flight I was sure Bella was on and handed her my black AMEX card.

"Do you have any luggage, sir?"

"No. Can I have my ticket please?"

I grabbed the ticket and rushed to the security line, shifting from one foot to another. It'd been a long time since I had to do the whole airport thing. I forgot how irritating it could be. Once I finally made it through, I raced through the terminal, looking for the gate I had seen on the reader board. Of course, it was the gate the farthest away.

I rushed up to the desk where they were announcing it was the final boarding call. I was out of breath when I handed the woman my boarding pass.

"You almost missed your flight," she said with a smile.

"I almost missed a lot more than that," I muttered.

"Do you have any bags?" she asked.

"No, can I go?" I asked impatiently.

Her frown told me I had offended her. I didn't care. If Bella wasn't on the plane, I needed time to get off and look for her in the airport. I was hoping like hell she was on the plane.

I wasn't sure what I was going to say, but I had to try.

CHAPTER 36

BELLA

After maxing out my credit card, nearly forgetting my suitcase in the taxi I took to the airport, and losing my sunglasses at some point along the way, I could finally relax. Relax wasn't the right word. I was still nervous about actually seeing Adrian after I had run away. I wasn't sure if I should apologize, or demand an apology, or both. I sighed, just happy to be on my way back. If things didn't work out, I would come back home and start my new life. I would find a job and, eventually, a man.

I looked to my right, smiling at the older couple holding hands in the seats next to mine. "Are you on vacation?" I asked them.

The elderly man with thick white hair smiled and nodded. "We are. We'll be going to Athens. It's where we took our honeymoon fifty years ago."

"Wow! That is amazing! Congratulations!"

"Are you going to Athens?" the woman asked.

I shook my head. "Crete. I was there last week. I had an internship, and then I kind of got involved with the boss. Things got a little weird, and I ended up running home."

Both the man and woman nodded, small smiles playing on their lips. "And now you're going back?"

"Yes. I have to tell him I'm sorry and see if we can work things out. He—"

The old man held up a wrinkled hand. "If you don't mind, my wife and I are tired and would like to try and get a little rest before we land in Athens."

I felt my face staining red. "Oh, I'm sorry. Yes, I understand," I murmured and turned away.

It was going to be a long flight. They'd seemed liked nice, caring people. Apparently, they weren't. I let out a long sigh, staring down the aisle. I noticed the flight attendants gathered near the front of the plane, talking.

"Good afternoon, sir," I heard one of them say. "Glad to have you aboard. We'll be taking off in a few minutes. Take your seat please."

I hated when there was that one straggler holding everyone else up. As if they were so important, the world would wait for them. When I saw the tall figure with black hair, his back to me, I froze. There was no possible way it could be him. I watched as he said something to the flight attendant before turning around and looking down the aisle.

I couldn't move or breathe. It was him. Adrian was on my plane. In the United States.

What. The. Hell?

His eyes scanned the rows as he made his way down the aisle. He hadn't seen me yet. I knew I should raise my hand and grab his attention, but I was shell shocked. Then his eyes met mine. He stopped moving.

We both stared at each other for several long seconds.

"Adrian?" I whispered.

He started moving again. His long legs brought him toward me, stopping next to my seat. "Come with me?"

"You want me to get off the plane?" I asked with confusion.

He nodded. "Please."

"I—"

I turned to look at the older couple beside me. Instead of looking happy for me, they were scowling as if I was interrupting their nap. I realized they were anxious to get on their way, and I was holding them up.

"Bella, please," he said in a low voice. "I want to talk, and I'd rather not do it here in front of everyone."

I nodded. "Okay," I said, feeling completely crazy. I grabbed my purse and laptop. I had forgone the carryon with my essentials in my rush to get back to Greece.

"Sir, you need to take your seat," a flight attendant barked.

"We'll be getting off," Adrian said, taking my hand in his and facing off against the petite woman blocking his exit down the aisle.

"Sir," she scolded, her head moving to the side to look at me. "Are you getting off, too?"

"Um, yes. I'm sorry."

Adrian didn't wait for the woman to accept my apology. He plowed ahead, and she had no choice but to move out of our way. I could feel everyone watching us. Several women stared at Adrian and then looked at me, huge grins on their faces. We'd just made it to the front of the plane when I heard a hoot, followed by cheering.

I grinned, feeling pretty damn fortunate to have a man like Adrian pulling me off a plane. We moved through the airport, Adrian practically dragging me behind him. I could feel his determination vibrating where he was holding my hand.

We made it to a relatively small, private corner of a gate that wasn't being used. "Sit," he ordered.

I sat down in one of the chairs. He sat next to me, taking my hand in his and looking into my eyes. My heart was dancing, jumping for joy, and praying he had made the trip to tell me he was madly in love with me.

"You're here," I said with disbelief.

"I'm here."

I was still a little befuddled. "Why? How? I don't understand."

"I'm here because you're here."

I grinned. "I almost wasn't here."

He chuckled. "I noticed. Your dad waited until the very last minute."

"My dad?"

"I'll explain that later. I had to come. I had to talk to you and make things right between us. When I went to work yesterday, I had hoped to talk to you. When Cassia told me you left, I knew I'd screwed up." His voice was low and full of regret.

I put my hand on his knee. "I shouldn't have run away. That was childish, and I'm so sorry for doing that. It was a knee-jerk reaction to what had happened Saturday. I should have stayed and faced things head on, but I ran."

He shook his head. "I don't blame you for running. I gave you no reason to stay. What I said at the ice cream shop, I want to explain."

I nodded, swallowing my nervousness. This was the moment of truth. He could tell me I wasn't the woman for him, or he could tell me he was madly in love with me. I was still hoping for the latter, but I knew we came from different worlds, and despite what we had shared for a very short time, there was a chance things would never work out between us.

"I'm listening," I whispered, ignoring the din of the busy airport around us.

Just then, it was only him and me in the dark corner of the closed gate. His hand closed over mine, resting on his knee.

"It wasn't nothing," he said, those striking blue eyes boring into my very soul. "Those few days together were something very special to me. I'm sorry I said what I did. It wasn't meant to hurt you. I was trying to protect myself from being hurt, and I ended up hurting you. That was never my intention. When we're together, I feel like a different person. I feel free and happy and whole. I was wrong for not standing up to my mother. I was wrong for letting her talk to you like that, but most of all, I was wrong for letting you walk away that day without trying to stop you. Will you forgive me?"

"Adrian, of course I forgive you. I know things were weird. Neither of us talked about what was happening between us. I think we were both so caught up in the moment and afraid of ruining what we shared by talking about where things were going, so we avoided it. I was afraid if I talked about how I felt, it would burst the little bubble we were living in."

He smiled at me, and his eyes held mine. "I didn't know how to navigate the conversation or any of it. I knew the moment I saw you, I wanted to spend time with you. I started to worry it was just an infatuation and, after a day or two together, it would wear off. It didn't. Please tell me you'll give me another chance to show you I can be a good man, a man worthy of your affection."

I bobbed my head up and down. "Yes. Absolutely. I really am sorry for leaving like that. I swear I won't do that again. I'll stick around, and talk to you, and work things out instead of running away."

He visibly relaxed, his shoulders slumping forward before he leaned in and gave me a quick kiss. "I'm so glad to hear that. I've not stopped thinking about how that day went."

"Me either."

I reached up and put my hand on his jaw, feeling the dark stubble under my hand. I could see the dark circles under his eyes and knew he hadn't been sleeping well either.

"Want to get out of here?" he asked.

"I do. Did you fly commercial?"

He smirked. "No. My jet is on a small airstrip outside your town."

"Oh, wow," I said, shaking my head again. "I can't believe you're here."

"Honestly, me either. I can't explain how I felt when I found out you were gone. I knew I had to chase you."

I smiled, thinking of what my father had said. "I was ready to chase you. I gave up too easily, and that was stupid."

He smirked. "I felt the same way. I'm fighting now, though. I want you in my life. I don't know how that works, but I know what I want."

"Let's worry about logistics later," I said. "Right now, I think we could both use a hot meal and a good night's rest. We can stay in the city tonight. Unless you're in a rush to get home?"

He shook his head. "I want to stay here."

"Good. It's my turn to show you around. I know a great restaurant. It serves all the American comfort foods I love."

"That sounds great. I'm starving. I'll book us a room." He pulled out his phone.

I didn't even think about stopping him. I knew him well enough to know he liked comfort and style, and I couldn't afford that. This was a little vacation for him, and I wanted him to be able to truly enjoy it, and it looked like he could use the rest.

We walked out of the airport, our hands clasped together, my head leaning against his shoulder. The car he had apparently hired was waiting for us.

"I'm so glad you're here," I whispered, snuggling against him in the backseat.

"I'm so happy to be here. I didn't like that feeling at all." He made a cute pouty face.

I had to giggle. "What feeling would that be?"

"The feeling that I had lost you for good. I felt like I had lost a piece of myself. It was very uncomfortable."

"Uncomfortable?" I teased.

"You know what I mean."

"I do. How did you find me?"

"Rand found you. He pulled your file and gave me the information."

I groaned. "Oh god. I'm sure he really hates me now."

"He doesn't hate you," Adrian said. "He sensed the connection between us from the very beginning as well. He was worried I would lose my focus and devote all my time and energy to you and somehow bankrupt the company."

"I wouldn't let you do that," I assured him.

He nodded. "Rand is my best friend, and he was looking out for me. I hope the two of you can talk and get to know one another. You're both very important to me, and I want you to be friends. He's a good guy."

"I will. I don't have anything against him." I paused. "To be honest, he kind of intimidates me."

Adrian chuckled. "Most people say *I'm* the intimidating one."

I turned my face to look up at him. "From the moment I saw you, I knew you were a good guy. I wasn't intimidated in the slightest."

He grinned. "Because I was your rescuer."

"You're my hero," I said in a high-pitched voice, and we laughed.

It felt good to laugh together again. Like finding a missing piece of myself.

Like I was whole again.

CHAPTER 37

ADRIAN

The hotel reservation had been last minute, and I had no idea what I was going to be getting, but I was pleasantly surprised to find the place was quite luxurious. I didn't think of myself as a snob, but I did know what was good and what was substandard. Strolling across the gleaming black and white marble floors of the hotel lobby told me I was in a good place.

"I've never been here," Bella whispered from beside me. "I've seen it on those tourist brochures, and I know when the few celebrities that come this way stay in town, this is where they stay, but this is gorgeous!"

I smiled, wrapping my arm around her shoulders and pulling her in close. "I'm glad I get to be here with you."

"Did you bring luggage?" she asked.

I chuckled. "I did, but in my rush to get here, I left it on my jet. I didn't think I would need it. I'm not worried. I'll talk with the concierge and have something delivered—for both of us."

"You don't have to do that," she quickly assured me.

"Bella, your luggage is on its way to Greece."

She groaned. "And this is why my dad says I should always have a carry-on."

I shrugged. "It's not a big deal. We can go shopping for ourselves if you prefer."

"No, I don't think either of us is up for that," she mumbled.

We checked out the suite, which was much finer than the room we'd had in Athens. I was thoroughly impressed and made a mental note to use the hotel when I came back for visits, which I was already planning to do as often as I could.

It was still early when we left the hotel, after talking to the concierge to get myself a change of clothes delivered to the room, along with something for Bella, despite her insisting she was fine. I liked being able to spoil her.

The restaurant she had picked for us was very casual. I felt a little overdressed in my slacks and dress shirt, but she assured me it was fine. Our roles were reversed, and I had a much better understanding of how she'd felt in my hometown.

"I'm going to let you order for me," I told her. "I don't recognize what a lot of these dishes are"

She giggled. "They use silly names. I think you'll like the country fried steak."

I grimaced. "I'm going to take your word on that."

I watched as she ordered for us, along with two bottles of Bud Light beer. I was on her turf and willing to let her lead the way. I trusted her and knew she wouldn't lead me astray.

"So, my dad texted and asked if you made it to the airport on time," she said with a grin. "I didn't realize you went to the house."

"Yes, I did. Your father and I got to talk for a bit. He's a good man."

"He's the best man," she said proudly. "What did you talk about?"

"You, me, us, the future," I said nonchalantly.

"I see."

"He gave me the typical warning a father would dole out to his daughter's suitor, but I got the feeling he liked me," I ventured.

"I'm sure he did. He wouldn't have told you where I was if he didn't." She laughed.

"Why hasn't he remarried?" I asked. I knew it was a blunt question, but I found it odd a man would stay single and alone for over twenty years. He seemed very nice, and I supposed he was a good-looking man. Everything Bella had told me about him was positive.

"I've asked him that same question a few times. He always says he was married to the one true love of his life and no other woman could ever compare to her. I hate that he is alone now, but honestly, when I was younger, I was kind of glad he didn't remarry. Several of my friends had stepmoms or stepdads, and they all had really rocky relationships with them. I was worried he would remarry, and the woman wouldn't like me and steal him away. I realize that was selfish now. I want him to find someone he can spend the rest of his life with."

"Do you feel like you have to stay here to take care of him?" I asked in a quiet voice, almost afraid to hear the answer.

She took a drink from the beer bottle. "In a way, yes, I do. He always tells me I don't have to, but how can I leave him all alone? I'm all he has."

"Do you think your dad would like to travel?" I asked.

"Like the country or the world?"

I shrugged a shoulder. "I don't know. Both, either."

"He's talked about buying an RV and traveling across the country after I leave home, but I'm pretty sure that's just him talking. He and I both know I won't leave home, and I really don't like the idea of him out there all alone."

I smiled, wanting to kiss her. "You're a very thoughtful daughter. I don't know if a lot of parents have the luxury of having a kid like you, who is willing to sacrifice their own futures for the sake of their parents."

"I'm not sacrificing anything. I have to look out for him. He's the kind of man who will work for four days straight and not take a break. He needs someone there to make sure he eats and rests."

I nodded. "I understand that. Would he move to Greece?"

Her mouth dropped open. "What? Really?"

"Yes, really. I want you working in the company. You're an asset to anywhere you go, but I want you with *me*."

She looked thoughtful for a second. "I don't know. I don't imagine they do a lot of mining there."

"Why not ask him to retire?" I suggested.

She scoffed. "I may as well ask him to move to the moon."

I grinned. "Bella, I know this is fast, and I understand if you say no, but I'm offering your father an early retirement."

"No way. I can't accept that from you, and he will certainly never accept charity."

"If we offer you a full-time position at the company, you could afford to support him and live a comfortable life," I told her.

"You're tempting me, but would I be in Crete just to work for you?" she asked in a quiet voice.

I shook my head. "No. I want you with me. I don't want to be apart from you again. I'm not really in a position to move here, but if that's what it takes to be with you, I'll make it happen. The last twenty-four hours has shown me I don't want to be without you. I know it's fast. It's crazy, and I know people think we're rushing this, but have you ever just known when something is right?"

"Yes," she breathed out the word.

"You'll come home with me?"

She nodded. "I will. I don't know what the future holds, and I don't know if my father will ever consider early retirement, but I will ask. I want to be there—with you."

"Good."

"But Adrian, if you're serious about hiring me to work at the company, I don't want special treatment. I want the standard job offer and pay. I have to do this on my own."

I nodded. "Absolutely. You'll be treated just like one of the employees."

She grinned. "We might not have to go *that* far."

Our dinners were served before I could answer her. I stared at the pile of food on my plate and was hesitant. It was certainly not quite as appealing as the food I usually received when I ordered a meal at a restaurant, but I was willing to give it a try. I wanted to show her I was open to trying new things and learning more about her world.

I took a bite and was pleasantly surprised to discover it was actually quite good. She was watching me, waiting for me to say something.

"I like it."

"Good. I had a feeling you would, even with your refined tastes."

"What did you call this?" I asked.

"Country fried steak."

I took another bite, bobbing my head up and down as I ate. I was interested to see what other things she could show me here in America. I had been to New York a few times but had never made it to the west side of the country.

"Are you ready to head back to the room?" I asked her after we'd finished our dinners and consumed a few beers.

She nodded. "Definitely."

There had been a heated energy between us as we talked more about the future and her coming to live in Greece. The more I thought about a future with her, the more excited I became. I was anxious to spend my days and nights with her. I didn't know what that was going to look like yet, but I felt like we needed to celebrate our reunion, even if we'd only been apart a few short days.

There were three bags sitting just inside the door of our hotel room with the clothes I had asked to be delivered. There was a bottle of champagne chilling on the table, along with several varieties of wine.

"What's all this?" she asked.

"I was hoping we could celebrate," I replied.

"With champagne?"

"Yes."

"What exactly are we celebrating?" she asked coyly.

I put my arms around her waist and pulled her closer to me. "I was hoping we could celebrate us being together again."

She leaned back a little. "*Together* together, or just together?"

I shook my head. "I have no idea what you're asking me," I said with complete confusion.

She giggled. "Are we together as in, we're going to be on the same continent and working together, or are we together like an actual relationship?"

I smiled, giving her a kiss on the tip of her perfect nose. "I want to be with you. I want to be your man. I want you to be my woman."

She giggled again. "I'm waiting for you to start pounding your chest."

"I will do anything you ask me to do."

"Anything?" she asked, her voice husky, her eyes dropping to my mouth.

"Anything."

"I think I'd like to start here, now," she said, pressing her body against mine.

I inhaled the scent of her and closed my eyes. My mind, body, and soul had missed her. When I had thought I'd lost her, my world had been turned upside down. I wanted to take a minute and simply cherish the moment. Holding her close to me was worth dropping everything and getting on the long-distance flight to track her down.

"I'm ready to start over, start fresh," I told her. "This is real. There is nothing fake about the way I feel about you. I'm going to show you just how real this is to me."

I used my hand to push her face up so I could stare into her eyes. I needed her to see I was serious and I meant every word.

"What I feel for you is very real," she said. "I'm taking a huge leap of faith and following my heart. My dad told me to do whatever I had to, and I'm ready to do whatever it takes. I'll chase you to the ends of the earth, if that's what you need to believe I want you for *you*. Nothing you have makes a difference. It's you I want."

Her words resonated deep within me. I couldn't begin to understand how my soul knew she was the one, but it did, and I was not about to fight it another second. I dropped my mouth to hers, my lips brushing over hers before I gave in to the passion and the heat I felt for her.

CHAPTER 38

BELLA

He tasted so good, I wanted to devour him alive. I was heady with the excitement of being reunited with him and knowing he wanted to be with me. I was with the sexiest man in the world. He was mine. I could call him mine.

I moaned into his mouth. "I want you."

"I want to take our time. I want to treasure every inch of your body. You are mine." He growled, his hands reaching down and squeezing my ass.

"You're mine, mister. All of you. I think I want to check out just what it is I'm buying here," I joked.

He chuckled. "Is this the, 'I'll show you mine if you show me yours' game?"

I nodded. "You bet your fine ass it is."

I squealed when he swatted my ass. I dashed into the bedroom of the suite, stopping when I saw the rose petals strewn over the bed.

"Surprise," he whispered.

"You are good," I told him.

"I want to make love to you on a bed of roses. This was the best I could do on short notice."

"This is beautiful."

"It is, but it's you I want to see," he said in a low voice.

I nodded my head, eager to comply. "Have a seat."

His gaze roamed my body before he stepped back and sat down in one of the plush chairs in the room. I slowly pulled off my shirt before pushing down the jeans I had put on, wanting to be comfortable for the long flight.

"Turn around," he ordered.

I slowly turned, stopping with my back to him, and looked over my shoulder at him. His gorgeous blue eyes were focused on my ass. Feeling emboldened by the heated look, I reached behind me, unhooked my bra, and let it fall forward to the ground.

I covered my breasts with my hands before turning around again, standing before him in my purple thong. I cupped my breasts and lifted them, my eyes on him as he stared with rapt attention. I slowly walked toward him. I saw the clenched jaw, the eyes that were heavy-lidded, and could practically feel the heat radiating off him.

"Adrian, I want to feel you inside me. I want you." I stood in front of him, his face in line with my chest.

He looked up at me, reaching up and pushing my hands away from my breasts and squeezing them, gently at first before increasing the intensity. I gasped, dropping my head back and looking up at the ceiling. His other hand slid up my back, pulling me forward. His mouth closed over my nipple, sucking it between his teeth.

One hand on my back held me against his mouth, and his other hand slid between my legs. He yanked at my panties, tugging hard until I felt them tear. I cried out, the very act nearly bringing me to orgasm. It was him revealing that passionate side that he kept contained, except for moments like these. I felt the fabric fall away, leaving me bare. His fingers played over my nether lips before he parted my folds, pushing in one finger.

I cried out. My hands reached for his head and pulled him against my breast, demanding he suckle me. His teeth were working over my hard nipples, and his finger worked inside me. It was too much. My self-control was no match for the ecstasy zipping through my body. My hands fisted in his hair as my body began a slow spiral that left me

228

gasping and crying out his name. I held him close to me as the release took me higher and higher. He didn't let up for a second.

My body went slack once the orgasm released me from its grip. I collapsed against him. It was his arm around my waist that kept me from slumping to the floor in a pile of heated lava. He stood up and walked me backward to the bed. I slid onto the mattress, sitting and waiting for him to join me. His eyes roamed over my naked body. I wanted to feast my eyes upon his naked glory as well.

"Off," I ordered. "All of it."

He smirked. "You're demanding."

"I want you."

"You have me. Never doubt that for a second. You have me. All of me." His eyes burned with passion.

I watched as he slowly unbuttoned his shirt, taking his sweet time, heightening the pleasure for me. When he opened the shirt, revealing a wide swath of tanned skin and those tattoos along with the smattering of chest hair, I bit my lip. His chest was beautiful.

It took all my self-control to stay on the bed. I wanted to jump him —literally. The shirt hit the floor, quickly followed by his pants and then his underwear. He stood before me, naked and glorious. I stared at the man that was mine—all of him.

He walked toward me, his erection jutting out. I scooted off the bed, landing on my feet. I reached for him, running my open hand across his chest. He reached for me, his hands holding my face as he kissed me.

I leaned against him, and our naked bodies pressed together. The kiss intensified, his mouth working over mine before dropping to my jaw. I rubbed my body against his, feeling the hard curves and the erection pressing against my stomach. He lifted me up, placing me on the bed before crawling over me. His knee nudged my legs apart as he held himself up on his elbows, staring down at me. I spread my legs wide, making plenty of room for him to nestle in between my thighs.

"You're so beautiful and so mine," he whispered, his hand brushing over my cheek before moving into my hair.

"I'm yours," I replied, staring into the blue eyes I was so familiar with.

His heavy cock found my opening, pushing inside a little at a time. Our eyes were locked as our bodies joined together, connecting us body and soul. I moaned, letting the passion and ecstasy flood my body. I leaned up and kissed him while he pushed deeper, stretching me and filling me completely. I opened my eyes, lying back on the bed, watching him watch me. I felt like we were permanently bonded, our souls imprinted on each other forever.

I sighed with supreme contentment. "I never want to move from this place," I whispered.

He groaned. "You feel so good. This. This is what I've waited my whole life for. You are my everything."

"I've dreamed about you for years, not knowing you were real. I never thought a man as good and as kind and as handsome as you existed. You're my dream come true."

I felt his cock jerk inside me, and his eyes dropped closed for a second before opening again. "I'm real. I'm yours."

I nearly wept with ecstasy. "Please," I whispered.

He dropped a kiss on my lips and began to move. It was a slow burn, sliding in and out. There was no rush. It was him and me, and the world didn't matter. I closed my eyes, giving myself completely to him. My hands moved to his hips, pulling him in and pushing him out. The rhythm was slow and steady, each scrape over my raw nerves inciting new electric shocks with each stroke.

"This is what I want," he rasped.

"Me too," I moaned, the sensations shooting through me, over me, inside me.

I could feel the tension in his body. It was like a rattler coiled and ready to strike. I could feel rapture hovering just out of reach. I appreciated the slow lovemaking, and it was absolutely decadent, but my body craved more.

"God, Bella, I'm so into you," he grunted, his words sounding strained and almost pained. "I don't want you to ever leave me again. Promise you'll stay with me."

"I promise," I vowed. "I promise I'll be here."

It was like a switch flipped. He kicked up the pace, his body moving faster, his strokes deeper and longer. I lifted my hips, taking him deeper. He rode me with the greatest care but with a fierce intensity and dedication that moved me more than words could explain. I felt myself climbing that ladder to sweet release. I let him take me higher and higher until I could feel myself cresting.

He groaned. "I have to let go. I'm going to explode. I can't hold back."

"Don't. I want it all."

"You've got it all. You have all of me." His mouth closed over mine, and his tongue plunged between my lips.

I closed my eyes and shut down my brain, only letting myself feel. It was only him and me and the melding of our bodies and souls. I let out a long keening sound as my body fell over the edge. He'd taken me to heaven, and now I felt like I was floating.

"Oh fuck," he groaned before I felt him lose himself inside me.

Our bodies came together, erupting and spasming, each of us gasping and groaning as our orgasms mingled together. He gently laid his body next to mine. His chest pressed against my breasts. I could feel his heart pounding. The rhythm was soothing and gave me a sense of complete calm.

"So good," I murmured.

"Yes, good," he said.

I giggled softly. "Are you okay?"

"Good God in heaven. If I was any more okay, I would be dead."

"What are we going to do?" I asked, knowing I was killing the afterglow of a beautiful moment.

"About?" he asked, rolling away from me and pulling me against him.

"About *us*. I mean, I know you love your mom, and I don't want to be the thing that comes between the two of you."

He sighed. "You won't."

"Adrian, I heard what she said. I saw how serious she was. She doesn't like me. She isn't going to change her mind. I can't subject myself to that. I'm strong, but that is asking for torture, and I'm not about to do that."

"It's going to be fine," he said. "I'll take care of it. And you. I will never let anyone disrespect or mistreat you again. You can count on me to be your fierce protector."

I smiled, believing his words. "Okay then."

"I'm sorry, but I'm so tired," he murmured, his voice already sounding very sleepy. "I'm going to pass out fast. I want to stay awake, but my body is demanding sleep."

"Me too. Sleep. We'll talk more tomorrow."

"Thank you," he whispered.

"For?"

"For giving me another chance," he said softly. "I won't screw it up this time. I might make you mad, but I will never let you walk away from me without fighting like hell to keep you."

"And I won't run away again," I replied. "This is something worth fighting for, and you better believe when I fight for something, I fight to the very end."

I sighed against him, my hand on his chest, my legs tangled with his, our flesh pressed together. It felt right to be in his arms. I had no idea what the future held for us or even if we had a real future, but I took comfort knowing we were both going to fight like hell to be together.

That had to count for something.

CHAPTER 39

ADRIAN

"We don't have to do this," Bella said as I held her hand, practically dragging her over the stone pathway that led to my parents' front door. It had been a month since we returned to Crete.

"Yes, we do."

"You don't have to do this for *me*," she said. "I know where we stand, and that's all that matters to me. I don't want to come between you and your family."

I stopped walking and dropped her hand. With both hands on either side of her face, I looked into her eyes, forcing her to look back at me. "This is something I need to do. I want you there with me. Please?"

She sighed, her eyes softening. "Okay. I'm here for you only. I don't need this closure."

"Thank you."

I rang the bell, nerves flitting low in my belly as I thought about the conversation that was about to happen. I had barely spoken to my mother since the day I had left. My mother was the type that could hold a grudge until her last, dying breath. I knew there was a very good chance she would disown me.

I knew it, but my heart was with Bella. I couldn't give her up for my mother. My mother's foolish reasons for me staying away from Bella would only make me miserable. I refused to be miserable and lonely because my family couldn't see past their own prejudices.

The door opened, my mother on the other side. She looked from me to Bella, her lip curling with disgust. "What are you doing here? With *her?*"

"I've come to talk to you and Dad. Is he here?"

"He's here, but he doesn't want to talk to you either, not until you choose better people to spend your time with."

"Move, Mom. I'm coming in, and you will listen to what I have to say." My tone left no room for arguing.

I grabbed Bella's hand again, pushing past my mother and heading into the house in search of my father. He was sitting in the living room reading a newspaper. "Adrian, were we expecting you?" he asked, getting to his feet.

"No. This won't take long. Have a seat. Mom, sit or stand if you choose, but you will listen to me."

Her mouth fell open, and I saw the anger flash in her eyes. Twenty years ago, that look would have terrified me. Hell, two weeks ago it would have scared me, but not today. Not anymore. I would always love and respect her, but she would not get to keep treating Bella like shit.

"I'll sit," she snapped.

Bella and I stood in front of them. They both were sizing her up. Bella stood at her full height. We were in control of the room.

"What's going on?" my father asked.

"I came to tell you both that Bella will be in my life. If the two of you want to be in my life, you'll have to accept that. You will treat her with the respect she deserves. You've judged her without knowing her. You've made assumptions about her because of preconceived ideas that have nothing to do with her. You don't know her. I think if you did, you'd like her. I won't be back here until you've figured out how to accept her as part of my life, and I won't accept any half-ass attempts. It's all or nothing." I looked from my mom to my dad and tried to judge their reactions.

My mother looked downright murderous. I had expected as much but had hoped she'd apologize and welcome us both into her life with open arms. That wasn't going to happen. My dad was a blank slate. I couldn't get a good read on him. Then he winked.

There was a hint of a smile and a nod of his head. It was a small relief, but it was my mom's approval I was most interested in.

"I see that you've made your decision then," my mother said in a cold voice.

I looked at Bella. Her eyes were full of sadness. I took a deep breath before turning to look at my mother. "I have. Goodbye."

I turned and walked out of the room, pulling Bella along with me. I couldn't stop to think about what had just happened. I had to keep moving, or I would feel that sense of regret and sadness. I didn't want to feel any of that. I knew I was doing the right thing. I knew Bella was the woman for me, and I was just going to have to learn to live with that feeling of being alone in the world—besides Bella and Peter.

I drove back to the city, parking my car in the driveway of the small house I had been spending a lot of time at lately. We hadn't spoken the whole ride back. She was giving me time to process my thoughts, which I greatly appreciated. I wasn't ready to talk about how I felt.

"I'm sorry," Bella said when I shut off the car.

"It's not your fault. You know that, right?"

She offered a small smile. "I know you say that, but there is a tiny bit of this that is my fault."

"You can't change who you are," I said. "I don't want you to change who you are. I like you just the way you are. It's them that have the problem."

"Let's go see what my dad is up to," she said with a smile.

"Probably has that new barbecue he bought fired up. I don't know if I can eat another hamburger." I groaned.

She burst into laughter as we walked up to the front of the beach house. The smell of the water and the sound of the waves comforted me. It was a sound I loved, but the last two weeks had made them even more special. It was a sound that reminded me of Bella and her father and the many hours we had sat on the beach together, talking about everything and soaking it all in. Life was good, but I didn't realize how good until I had someone like them to share it with.

"He loves this house," she said. "I can't thank you enough for buying it for him. He's always loved the beach, but this is way beyond anything he could have ever dreamed of. Me as well."

"Hey, I wanted to do this for him. I will always think of him running into the water the first day we got the keys. He acted like a kid. It was good to see him so happy."

"I swear he's regressed," she said. "He's like a twenty-year-old starting over. It makes my heart happy to see him really happy. I honestly can't believe he agreed to move here and retire. I was prepared with some really good arguments to convince him it was for the best." She laughed. "He really stole the wind from my sails."

"I was prepared to buy him his own jet to fly back and forth if he refused to move here," I said with a laugh. "But I'm happy it was an easy sell."

Bella knocked on the door before turning the knob. "Dad! We're here!"

There wasn't an answer. We headed inside, moving to the back deck that overlooked the beach. The deck was empty.

"Down there," I said, pointing to a man sitting in a folding chair on the beach.

She grinned. "He better have put on his sunscreen. Let's grab a beer and head down."

That was something that had been a new addition to my life—beer. Peter enjoyed beer, as did Bella. I had developed a taste for it, preferring the craft beers. Each of us carried a cold beer as we took the stairs down to the beach.

"Peter!" I shouted.

He looked up from the book in his hand and waved at us. "I didn't know you were coming by," he said, getting to his feet to give Bella a hug.

"I see you're working hard at this retirement thing," Bella teased.

He held up the book. "I've always wanted to read a book on the beach. I can't believe I'm actually doing it. There's a blanket in that bag if you two want to pull up a seat."

"I'm happy for you, Dad," Bella said, leaning down to kiss the top of his head after he settled into his chair once again.

I grabbed the blanket and spread it out for Bella and me to sit on. Out of habit, I took off my socks and shoes and rolled up my pant legs, sinking my toes into the warm sand.

"How did the conversation go?" he asked.

Bella grimaced, turning to look at me. "Not great," she muttered.

"It's fine. We knew it was probably going to go that way." I shrugged.

Peter nodded sadly. "I'm sorry to hear that. Maybe I can talk to them."

I shook my head. "That's okay. They've made their choice."

Bella's hand moved to my back, rubbing up and down to comfort me. She was always doing things like that. A subtle touch on my shoulder or a swipe as she passed me in the hall at work. It was an unspoken language between two lovers. It was a relatively new language to me, but I liked it. A simple touch or a look was all that was needed to communicate.

Bella laid down on her back, stretching out her gloriously long legs, clad in shorts. She'd kicked off her sandals and looked completely relaxed. I moved to lie down next to her when my phone began to vibrate in my pocket. I pulled it out and looked at the screen.

"It's my mom," I muttered.

Bella sat up. "You should answer."

"What if she's going to yell and scream about how bad a son I am?"

Bella shrugged. "Then you end the call. Give her a chance first, though."

I took a deep breath. "Hello?"

"Adrian, I'm sorry," she said.

I turned to look at Bella, my eyes wide. She questioned me with her eyes.

"You're sorry?" I repeated, not sure I had heard correctly.

"Yes, I'm sorry. I want you to be happy. You know that's all I've ever wanted for you. I worry about you being taken advantage of. You're a good boy, and girls will prey on you."

"Mom," I said, ready to shut it down.

"No, no," she said quickly. "I don't think Bella is like that. She seems like the real thing. You've never spoken to me in such a way."

"I needed you to understand this is serious."

"I understand. Your father and I would like to have dinner with you and Bella. We'd like to get to know her."

I blinked. "You do?"

"Yes, Adrian," she said, and I could hear the emotion in her voice. "I see the change in you. It's a good change. If she is the cause of this change, I want to know her. I want to be a part of your life."

"Thank you, Mom. I look forward to the two of you getting to know each other. I promise you'll like her."

"I'll call you and set up dinner," she said before ending the call.

I slid the phone back in my pocket, smiling as I looked at Bella and her dad. They were both grinning. "I take it that went well?" Bella asked.

"It did. She'd like to have us over for dinner. She wants to get to know you."

She threw her arms around me, hugging me. "I'm happy for you. I'm so happy you can have a relationship with your mother."

"Thank you for being so patient and willing to give her another chance," I told her.

"Congratulations, you two. It looks like everything is looking up." Peter smiled down at the two of us from his chair.

"It certainly is," I agreed.

EPILOGUE

BELLA

Six months later

I turned sideways in the full-length mirror, checking to make sure my dress wasn't too horribly wrinkled. It was a sleeveless wrap-style dress that cost way too much, but Adrian had insisted he buy it for me. The deep-green color made my eyes look even greener.

I turned to face the mirror, the noise of the party beyond the door beckoning me. I'd excused myself a few minutes ago, needing a little break from the exuberant members of Adrian's extended family. His family was huge.

I took a deep breath and opened the door. There was music and the laughter of people having a good time drawing me back outside.

"How ya' doing, kid?" my dad asked, handing me a bottle of water as he approached.

"Good. How about you?"

"Very good," he said, turning to look out at the crowd. "They're good people."

"I saw you had a bit of an admirer," I teased.

He chuckled. "She's a nice lady."

"Is she a distant cousin to the Gabris family?"

He shook his head. "No. Yes. I don't know. She's the widow of the brother of a cousin or something like that. I don't know. Things get a little confusing."

"I see."

"We're going to grab dinner next week," he said without looking at me.

"Good. I think that's great! Can I meet her?"

"Sure, I'll introduce you, but right now—" He stopped talking and gestured with his head. "Incoming."

I looked up to find Mrs. Gabris headed our way. I smiled and waved.

"Bella." She greeted me with a hug.

"Hi, Helen," I said. "How are you?"

"I'm very good. Are you having a good time?" She took my hand in hers.

"Yes, you sure know how to put on a great party," I said.

"Thank you."

"Can I give you a hand with anything?" I offered.

"No, no. You are my guest. Where is Adrian?"

I shook my head. "I'm not sure. He went to talk to Stavros about fifteen minutes ago."

"Have you met everyone?" she asked.

My eyes widened. "Oh gosh, I don't know. I've met a lot of people. My dad has been making the rounds as well."

Helen chuckled. "Oh, yes. Peter is quite the hot topic among the single ladies."

I burst into laughter as my father blushed three different shades of red. "Oh, now," he mumbled. "I don't know about that."

"I think he just told me he has a date," I revealed.

"Bella," he growled.

"Congratulations," Mrs. Gabris said. "My family tree is quite expansive. If that one doesn't work out, you let me know and I will find you a good woman."

My dad groaned. "Thank you, but I think one will be plenty."

"You must have been talking to Adrian," she said with a smirk.

"Oh, you mean the bearded woman you set him up with?" I teased.

She cackled, slapping her thigh. "She was a nice girl."

"A bearded woman?" my dad asked, a look of horror on his face.

"Yes, her facial hair was thicker than mine," Adrian said from behind me.

"Hey, there you are," I said, turning to face him.

He wrapped an arm around my waist, taking a sip from the glass of wine he was carrying. "Sorry, I was waylaid on my way back here."

"Adrian, introduce Bella to the rest of the family. I'm going to grab a couple more bottles of wine. Oh, Peter, come with me. I'd like to introduce you to a couple of people." Helen grinned in a way that said she had something up her sleeve.

My dad looked at me for help. I shrugged a shoulder. "Have fun."

He scowled at me, following Helen across the yard.

Adrian pulled me a little closer. "I think this place has three bedrooms," he said in a husky voice. "Do you want to go check one of them out? Test the mattress?"

"Stop. We can't do that."

"That dress is killing me," he whispered close to my ear. "I want to unwrap you and devour you."

"Adrian Gabris, if you make me wet and horny at your mother's party, I will make you pay dearly," I hissed.

"I like the sound of that," he said with a cheeky grin.

"You're incorrigible."

"I'm horny."

"Stop," I said, giggling. "We're at your parents' house."

He sighed and popped out his lower lip. "Fine."

"Your mom has certainly done a one-eighty since the first party I attended here," I said, turning to watch her lead my dad around the group.

"She likes you. She raves about you to all of our family and her friends. You've impressed her, just like I knew you would. Thank you for giving her another chance. She really is a good woman, and when she's in your corner, you know you have a prizefighter behind you."

"Thank god. She's a little scary." I was only half-joking.

I watched as Stavros emerged from the house, pulling Helen aside. I assumed they were running low on wine or the little cheese crackers they were serving.

"Come with me," Adrian said, taking my hand and pulling me toward the center of the backyard.

"What are you doing?" I asked, watching as he climbed onto a chair.

He towered over me. I looked up at him, wondering what the hell was going on. He held up his hand and whistled. I turned to look around the backyard. Everyone formed a circle around Adrian. Stavros and Helen were standing nearby, staring at their son with a great deal of pride.

"Can I have everyone's attention please?" he called in a booming voice.

The backyard quieted.

"Go ahead, son," Stavros said authoritatively.

"Thanks, Dad. Everyone, I want to thank you all for coming out today. Most of all, I want to thank Bella and her father. As you know, they've come here from the United States. For those of you that don't know—that's a long way."

The crowd burst into laughter. "We can't all be as smart as you, little brother."

I turned to look and saw a slightly older, shorter version of Adrian coming through the crowd. He was followed by two more men that all resembled Adrian. I assumed they must be the brothers I had never met.

"Hey, you made it!" Adrian exclaimed from his makeshift pedestal.

"We wouldn't miss this for the world," one of the brothers shouted.

I thought it was sweet that they all cared enough to show up for family events.

"Bella, these people are all a part of my family. Some of them are a little crazier than the others, but they're family. You and your father have become like a second family to me. I thought it was important for all of you to meet and get to know one another. A couple of weeks ago, I called my mom and asked if she'd be willing to host this little gathering. You all know my mom." He smiled.

There was a round of cheers and sounds of agreement, along with some muffled comments. I was surprised to hear it had been Adrian's idea to have the party. He'd told me we'd been invited, but not that it was his idea.

"My mom jumped at the chance to entertain. She loves to pour wine and cook, and that's just one of the many reasons I love her. Bella, I wanted you here tonight to meet every single one of these people. I love you more than I can put into words. That first day I met you, I knew you were someone I wanted to know. Then you got lost, and I found you—repeatedly," he added in a dry tone.

I scowled at him while everyone else laughed.

"You have made me laugh and given me a fresh, new look on life. I can't imagine my life without you in it. You are truly beautiful inside and out, and I thank my lucky stars every damn day that you came into my life. My life feels complete now that I have you in it."

I raised my eyebrows, unsure what to say. "Thank you," I murmured.

"Now that you've met my family, I need to ask you something very important," he said, jumping off the chair and taking the few steps toward me.

"What is it?" I asked, a little embarrassed to have all the attention on me.

He smiled and reached into his pocket, pulling out a small black box. I stared at him and then the box, slowly shaking my head.

He dropped to one knee, opening the box and holding it up for me to see the massive rock inside. I could feel tears welling in my eyes as I stared at the ring.

"Now that you've met them, I have to ask you. Will you marry me and become a part of this crazy family?"

"I—oh my god—I can't believe this is happening," I whispered.

He raised his brows, questioning me with his eyes. He wiggled the ring in front of me as if to remind me of what he was doing down there.

"Of course, I'll marry you!" I exclaimed.

The crowd erupted into shouts and cheers. Adrian got to his feet and yanked me close, hugging me before kissing my cheek and then my lips.

"Let's see if this fits," he said, grabbing my left hand.

My hand was shaking as he slid the ring on my finger. There were more shouts and congratulatory statements from everyone around us.

"It's beautiful," I whispered.

My dad was by my side when I looked up. He wrapped his arms around me and gave me a warm hug. "Congratulations, sweetie."

"Dad, look," I said, the tears of joy flooding down my face.

He smiled and held up my hand to study the ring. "It's beautiful. You did well, Adrian."

"I couldn't have done it without you," Adrian said.

"You knew?" I asked with shock.

My dad nodded. "This man is a real gentleman. He asked for your hand."

I looked at Adrian. "You did?"

"Of course. I'm a traditional man. You've met my family. Tell her," Adrian said to my dad.

I looked at my dad. "Tell her what?" I asked.

He held up my hand, pointing to the ring on my finger. "Those two stones on either side are from your mother's wedding ring."

I gasped, the tears likely smudging my makeup as they poured down my face. "Thank you, Dad. This means so much to me. I will treasure this forever."

Helen and Stavros came over to hug each of us. Helen actually had tears in her eyes.

"You two were meant to be together," she said. "You're a good woman, and I'm happy you have made my son a happy man. Thank you for forgiving me and giving me another chance." She hugged me again.

"Helen, thank you for giving me the chance to prove I love your son for *him* and not because of who he was," I told her. "You've raised a good man, and I am very happy to join your family."

Stavros raised his hands high. "Let's have a toast! The champagne is ready to pour!"

I realized then that they all had known what was going to happen. The whole party was for this very moment. I grabbed Adrian's shirt-front and pulled him close, giving him a sultry kiss and earning more hoots from our rapt audience. "I love you. That's it. I love you so much. You are my world, and I cannot wait to start the rest of our lives together."

"Why don't we drink a little champagne and then get home?" he asked. "I think I'd like to celebrate our engagement in private."

"Home. Our home. Our home in Greece." I spoke the words aloud, reminding myself that I was living a dream.

Except it wasn't a dream. It was my life. Reality was better than any dream.

The End

ABOUT THE AUTHOR

Hey there. I'm Weston.

I'm a former firefighter/EMS guy who's picked up the proverbial pen and started writing bad boy romance stories. I co-write with my sister, Ali Parker as we travel the United States for the next two years.

You're going to find Billionaires, Bad Boys, Mafia and loads of sexiness. Something for everyone, hopefully. I'd love to connect with you. Check out the links below and come find me.

OTHER BOOKS BY WESTON PARKER

Toxic

Untapped

Stealing First

Hot Stuff

Doctor Feelgood

Captain Hotness

Mister Big Stuff

Debt Collector

Worth the Risk

Worth the Distraction

Worth the Effort

Deepest Desire

Ryder

Axel

Jax

Sabian

Aiden

Rhys

My Last First Kiss

My First Love

My One and Only

Made for Me

Air Force Hero

Light Up the Night

Love Me Last

Take A Chance On Me

Brand New Man

We Belong Together

Good Luck Charm

Made in the USA
San Bernardino, CA
10 July 2019